# Point of Departure

Carol Ohmart Behan

MeadowMuse Productions in
cooperation with Trafford Publishing

*For you, Debbie,*
*So very glad our paths*
*crossed at Mystery*
*School —*
*Blessings of Love*
*and Light,*
*Carol*
*Ohmart Behan*
*Dec. 3, 2004*

Grateful acknowledgement is made to Jan Phillips for the use of
her photograph, *Tree and Swing* on the cover.
She may be contacted at www.janphillips.com

This is a work of fiction. Names, characters, places, and incidents
are the products of the author's imagination or are used fictitiously.
Any resemblance to actual events or persons, living or dead, is purely
coincidental.

**National Library of Canada Cataloguing in Publication**

Behan, Carol Ohmart
    Point of departure / Carol Ohmart Behan.

ISBN 1-55369-276-4
    I.°Title.
PS3602.E38P64 2002      813'.6   C2002-901155-8

# TRAFFORD    *PRINTED IN CANADA*

**This book was published *on-demand* in cooperation with Trafford Publishing.**
On-demand publishing is a unique process and service of making a book available
for retail sale to the public taking advantage of on-demand manufacturing and
Internet marketing.**On-demand publishing** includes promotions, retail sales,
manufacturing, order fulfilment, accounting and collecting royalties on behalf of
the author.

Suite 6E, 2333 Government St., Victoria, B.C. V8T 4P4, CANADA
Phone      250-383-6864      Toll-free   1-888-232-4444 (Canada & US)
Fax         250-383-6804      E-mail      sales@trafford.com
Website   www.trafford.com
TRAFFORD PUBLISHING IS A DIVISION OF TRAFFORD HOLDINGS LTD.
Trafford Catalogue #02-0089     www.trafford.com/robots/02-0089.html

10     9     8     7     6     5     4     3

# ~ Acknowledgements ~

Looking back along the path I've traveled as a writer, I find it peopled with an amazing number of individuals and kindred spirits who deserve my heartfelt thanks.

I hold an immeasurable sense of gratitude for two writers, Robert Cormier and Lary Crews, who, though they never met, together persuaded me, an uncertain amateur, to take myself seriously as a writer.

And as that energy was beginning to take hold, a lively group of my high school students cheered me further along, the ASPS of Edmeston Central. Their own creative writing efforts inspired me to stay true to my own writer's voice. And a thank you to the students of my Writer's Fire classes of this past year. Your willingness to be risk takers helped me to take these final steps.

Thank you to the women I've been privileged to meet through the International Women's Writing Guild and the inspiration gained at our Skidmore College conferences. Thanks in particular to Jan Phillips for passing the stardust and inspiring me to pass it on, to Emily Hanlon and Susan Omilian who convinced me I could do this, and to Basia Conroy who said I would.

Without the support of family and friends I doubt *Point of Departure* would have ever become a reality. Thank you to Ken, Justin, and Sarah who (mostly) left me alone all those years when they saw me at work on this and other projects, and whose love and faith sustains me. Thank you to Keith and Cliff, and our parents who have gone on, but who taught the three of us to believe in ourselves, no matter what.

Members of my larger family, thank you for your love and support over the years, especially those who have reminded me of how this was my mother's dream for me too and how happy she would be to see this book.

And where would I be without the fabulous women I'm privileged to call my friends, old and new? Heartfelt thanks to my lifelong friends, Judy, Lorraine, Peg, and to nearly lifelong ones, Pat, Bernadette, Marna, and Carol. To Mary Kay, Elaine, Laraine, Susan, Linda, Sandy, all of you wise women. To Laura at Spellbound Books who helped me visualize it all. And to the amazing nineteen Turtleweavers who shared in my Glastonbury pilgrimage and beyond.

Finally, a special thank you to Michelle Gallant for never doubting this day would come, even if I lost faith, and for helping me fashion Joanna's story into one that honors the journeys we all make.

Carol Ohmart Behan
February, 2002

This is for Nedra, for the Ednas,
all of you, and for Robert—
for how you pointed the way
and, flashing your bright smiles,
told me, "but of course you can!"

# ~ One ~

Things just wouldn't add up. She'd been at it a solid hour. Joanna leaned on her elbows over the yellow legal pad and frowned at the last figure she had circled, nearly lost among the uneven columns of numbers, cross outs, cryptic notations and pointing arrows. If she could just get to next week's paycheck.

The refrigerator wheezed and lapsed into silence. She leaned back in the chair, massaging her tired hand and eyeing the small pile of unwashed supper dishes. The food hadn't even put away yet. Good thing Gwen actually enjoyed having boxed mac and cheese with hotdogs twice a week.

Then she stood and stretched, weighing the benefits of reheating what was left of her tea. The odds of actually getting a full night's sleep already seemed remote. Maybe it was time to give Kim's offer serious thought.

While the microwave hummed, she stood with arms folded and studied the calendar taped to the cupboard door of the trailer's cramped kitchen. Then she took the pen kept on the window sill and drew a neat blue slash across the day's date. Sixty-two days. The microwave bell dinged. "Damn Larry," she said to the calendar, and punched the door latch to retrieve her tea.

Leaning against the counter she took sips of the tepid liquid. The aging microwave had done its best. After all, they'd gotten it secondhand when her cousin Marie remodeled her kitchen. She thought sometimes how it was lucky the trailer had a steel frame since it kept the deteriorating, secondhand contents of her home from collapsing around her in a sorry heap.

The phone's sudden ring jarred her. "Hello?"

"Jo? It's Lou," came the unmistakable rasp of her mother-in-law's voice. "I was thinking about all of you this evening and thought I'd call. How are things? That damn snow gone finally?"

"No, it hasn't gone completely. There's still a snow bank by the road." Louise Quinn had moved to Florida three years ago citing her long-held aversion to temperatures below fifty degrees. That and the sight of snow.

"Ugh. You poor souls. You've got my sympathy. Hang on..." There was the click of a cigarette lighter and then the puff of her first drag. "Okay. So how's that great kid of yours?"

"Gwen's doing fine, Lou. She's already asleep or I'd have her say hello herself." Joanna twisted the phone cord wondering how to field Lou's inevitable questions.

"Uh huh. Great. Got an Easter card to get in the mail to her pretty soon." There was another pause. Joanna pictured her in her flowered bathrobe, pink terry-cloth turban on her head, sitting at her kitchen table with a cup of cold coffee and an overflowing ashtray close at hand. "And what have you heard from that son of mine since he took off for P.A.? It's been what, two months? I hope he's finally started earning his keep like he should."

Louise's pointed question was not casually put. Joanna knew that not much escaped her notice even with the distance between Upstate New York and Florida. She'd had enough experiences with unreliable men and didn't spare Larry any of her disapproval. Just before he'd gone to Pennsylvania she'd called and given him an earful.

"Hello? You still there, Joanna?" A sharp cough followed and Joanna had to hold the phone away from her ear for a moment.

"Yes, I'm still with you, Lou. Sorry, I was just thinking of what to say." She sighed into the phone. "To be truthful, no, he's not earning his keep." She glanced at the pile of bills on the table next to the yellow pad. "The second check he finally sent us bounced this last week which has made for a bit of a mess, I'm afraid."

"Oh, God." Lou gave her own sigh. "And I thought this new

job was going to get him turned around. So what's he have to say for himself?"

"Not much. Actually..." Maybe it was time she told the truth to someone, "actually, I haven't heard from him in almost two months and I don't have a number anymore to call him to find out what's going on."

"You mean he's walked out on you two?" Lou's voice rose sharply. There was a sudden metallic clang. "Hold on. I knocked the damn ashtray over."

Joanna listened to the sounds of things being cleaned up. There wasn't much point in mincing words. When Lou came back on the phone she said, "To answer your question, Lou, I'm starting to think that, yes, he has walked out this time."

"Why that lousy bastard." Even for Lou these were strong words. "I thought I'd talked some sense into him in January."

"You may have at the time. To tell you the truth, I'm not all that shocked anymore. I'm sitting here tonight sorting through my options. It's not like I can't manage on my own. Plenty of women do. After all, Lou, look at you."

"Well, Hon', God knows that's a fact." Louise paused, sucking out another long drag of her cigarette. "I just hate the thought of you having to be put into something like this. It's a tough row to hoe. You've got some options, you said?"

"A few. For one thing, the landlord said he understood and would give me a little extra time this month." She massaged the knot in her shoulder with her free hand. "And then a friend of mine I work with needs a roommate and says she has space for Gwen and me. So I am giving that a thought. And just now I've been trying to get all the bills straight. It looks like I can get to the end of this month anyway."

"Uh huh. I'm hearing some good news in all that. Maybe moving in with your friend would be a smart idea, at least for a while. Nothing like friends when the going gets rough. Listen, here's what I'll do. I'm going to give my sister, Betty, a call and see if anyone over there in Auburn's heard from him. If I can get hold of him, he's sure going to get a piece of my mind."

"Be my guest, Louise. Who knows, maybe he'll turn up soon with money and a logical explanation."

"Hah!" Louise snorted a laugh and was waylaid by another cough. "And the Pope's Polish too, so's you know. Let's hope he's somewhere getting himself clear on his responsibilities. But for now, you call me if you and Gwen decide to move anywhere. Okay?"

"I will. Thanks for calling, Lou."

"All right, Hon'. My love to Gwen."

There was a click as she hung up.

She went to check on Gwen, feeling her way along the narrow, unlit hall. Noiselessly she pushed open the bedroom door. The soft pink glow of the Little Mermaid nightlight cast deep shadows on Gwen's sleeping form curled beneath the covers. One bare foot stuck out from under the pale blue spread, some of its worn fringe tangled around her toes. With practiced stealth Joanna gently disentangled Gwen's foot and pulled the spread gently down over the bed's edge. She stirred but remained in sleep. Baxter the bear had fallen to the floor. Joanna tucked him back in alongside Gwen and made her way back to the kitchen light.

She picked up her tea once more from the table and stared again at the yellow pad, noticing she'd written "Dad" in two places, a line drawn through it both times. Tapping her wedding ring on the cup handle, she wondered why she hadn't remembered doing that twice. Footfalls scuffed suddenly on the outside steps followed by a hesitant rap on the door. On the clock it was just past nine. "Who on earth...?" Through the door's frosted panes she recognized her landlord, Tony Cataldo. She sighed. Hadn't she gotten things straightened out with him yesterday?

"Hey there, Joanna," he nodded to her when she opened the door. "I saw your lights still on so I thought it was maybe okay to knock." The light over the door picked up the sheen of his black Brylcreamed hair slicked back behind his ears. For a guy in his mid-thirties he'd always reminded her of a fugitive from the Fifties, tight black jeans and all. "Got a minute to talk?" He leaned towards the half-open door.

She thought for a moment and then let go of the handle. "I guess." What more could she possibly say about the fact that Larry's check had bounced?

Inside he stood looking around for a moment, hands in his pockets. A wave of his Aqua Velva after shave reached her, a scent he seemed to douse himself with daily. Though they only rented the trailer from him, she resented the proprietary way his eyes took things in. "Your little girl in bed?"

"Yes. It's a school night." Joanna faced him, cup in hand, her back to the dining table with its stack of bills and the pad with its leering numbers.

"Uh huh. Well, I promise not to bother you too long. But I've been giving some thought to your..." he paused and wet his lips, eyes resting with an odd weight on her face, "your situation."

Sweat prickled under her arms, her grip on the cup handle tightened. "Listen, Tony, all I asked for was a week, maybe ten days to straighten things out. If you could just have a little patience. Like I said, I'm sure that..."

He raised a hand, gesturing her to stop. "Hey, not a problem. We talked about that yesterday." His voice had an apologetic, soothing edge to it. "Really, I know things have got you a bit in the corner here. Believe me, I understand that, Joanna." One side of his mouth turned up in a crooked smile meant, she was sure, to be pleasing. "I'll bet you're thinking I stopped by to hassle you some about it." The black eyes held her in a long stare.

"Well, I..."

He interrupted her again and stepped closer. Speaking softly, like he was talking to a skittery child, he said, "Let me get right to the point and we might both feel better. I think I've come up with a way to help you out. Especially if that man of yours isn't likely to turn up anytime soon, like you said." Again his eyes darted around the trailer and then back to her with look that swept her up and down. Its chill pinned her to the table like some squirming lab specimen. A curl of black hair had fallen onto his forehead. "Money isn't the only way to pay for your rent here, you know. A night or two a week I could, you know, drop in late for a visit with you. Say twenty minutes or so and then I'd be on my way." He spread his hands towards her and it felt like he'd opened her shirt. The tip of his tongue flicked snakelike across his lips and he smiled again at her frozen face. "So what do you say to that?"

He stood waiting. The cup started to slip from her grasp. Almost without thinking she flung the tea at him. He threw up his arm and it splattered on the sleeve of his leather jacket.

"Jesus!" he spat out, leaning towards her, eyes daggers, but then seemed to change his mind and backed towards the door.

Mindful of Gwen asleep down the short hall, she hissed the words that finally came loose. "That's what I say to you, you creep. Now get the hell out of here and don't ever suggest something like that to me again." Without another word he closed the door with a slam sending a last cloying drift of Aqua Velva swirling around her. His shadow slid away from the window and she heard the crunch of his steps retreating down the park's drive. Bile rose in her throat. She ran for the bathroom, making it just in time to throw up in the toilet.

"Too bad it wasn't scalding hot," Kim's blue eyes snapped. "What a bastard."

Joanna felt relieved to have shared last night's ugliness with her. Once she got to work she'd been counting the minutes until their morning coffee break. A cold March rain fingered the windows of the second floor snack bar making blurred images of students hurrying to their ten o'clock classes at Seneca County Community College."If it had been he'd probably be suing me, not that he wouldn't have deserved a good scalding."

"And then you could have collected on sexual harassment."

"Yeah, right."

"Hey, I'm serious, Jo. He was more than out of line with what he said to you. God, what an awful thing for you to have gone through. And on top of everything else."

"Well, I survived, at least. Or shall I say, I'm surviving." Stirring what was left of her coffee, she contemplated the question she'd been rehearsing since last night. She glanced around to see how close they were to others. "I'll tell you what I do wish I'd done, and that's said to him 'Get the *fuck* out of here' rather than just 'Get the hell out'."

"Too bad you didn't," Kim said. "So do you think he's changed his mind about giving you that extra time to pay the rent like he'd told you on Saturday?"

Maybe this was the sign to ask. Was she about to bring it up? "I don't know. He seemed totally okay with it when we talked then, but maybe it was that he was hatching this optional payment plan idea on the spot. Anyway, I could always threaten to tell his wife, poor woman, stuck with such a creep." She paused, gathering her words, but Kim spoke again.

"Too many ways for men to screw us, aren't there? No pun intended. Men will be men. Even Gary can be pretty annoying at times. Hope you don't mind, but I told him how the check Larry sent you bounced and that you didn't know how to get hold of him. He was sorry to hear about the mess."

"That's nice of him." The conversation had veered in another direction. "And, no, I don't mind you telling him. Just be sure you hang on to that good guy of yours. All of us should be so lucky in boyfriends. He'd never walk out on you and his child, I'm sure." She swallowed the rest of her coffee, and decided to plunge in. "Kim, about what you suggested last week..." Her words seemed to stall.

"About my needing a roommate?" Kim's face brightened. "Are you considering volunteering, I hope?"

"Well, yes, I guess I am."

"Great! I was sitting here trying to figure how to bring it up because last time I suggested it, it went over like a lead balloon. But you did say something about maybe talking to your Dad first."

"Yes, I know I did. I thought better of it. There's still my mother's hospital bill and all." *And I'm not totally desperate yet*, she thought silently.

"So how soon can you come?"

"Remember, you'd be getting a seven-year-old in the bargain."

Kim waved that away. "Not at all a problem. I think Gwen's a pretty neat kid."

"Well, are you sure you can fit us in?"

"As long as you don't mind sharing a bedroom. But it is a pretty big room. You know the one downstairs."

"I do. That should be fine. But what if..."

"Joanna Quinn," Kim interrupted, and leaned towards her. "This is not something I'm going to let you talk yourself out of."

Was she doing that? "Okay. I won't. But one more thing, it won't have to be a long-time arrangement. Hopefully just until the fall."

"We'll just take things a little at a time. And that's the last 'but' out of you for today. It's all going to work out just fine, you'll see."

Joanna studied her friend's face, nearly overwhelmed by the caring she saw there. A lump rose in her throat. "Well, then, let's try it out and see where it gets us."

Joanna slowed the car to peer through the rapidly fading dusk. She hadn't been to Kim's in months and wanted to be certain of the right driveway. Once she'd locked the trailer's door the drive into Rockford Mills hadn't taken long, leaving hardly enough time to figure out if the heaviness that pressed on her shoulders like a dank cloak was due to weariness or despair. A yellow cat dashed out of the shadows and Joanna stepped hard on the brakes.

"Jesus! Blasted cat!" Anger mixed with quick relief as she

saw it leap safely away across a yard.

"Did we run over a cat, Mommy?" Gwen straightened up to look out the window, her voice anxious.

"No, Gwen, fortunately it was a fast cat. I'm sorry I swore. Darn thing surprised me." She held her breath and stepped carefully on the gas, glad to find the sudden stop hadn't stalled the aging Chevy Nova. It coughed a protest but went another half block where she pulled up at the curb before a tan-shingled duplex. Lights glowing through the front windows cast a welcoming beam out onto the sodden remnants late winter snow.

"Is this Kim's house, Mommy?"

Joanna looked over at her daughter who had sat silent most of the way, Baxter on her lap. Her outgrown ski jacket was frayed at the cuffs, a wisp of its lining trailed out at the hem. A lock of brown hair has escaped from her red barrette. The child's dark eyes were as much trusting now as they had been when Joanna had made the day's packing seem like an adventurous game. The Nova gave another warning spasm.

"Yes, Hon, it is. We're here." The backdoor light beckoned. There was nowhere else to go. She shifted the car into gear and drove into the driveway.

Kim had the door open as they came up the steps. "Hey, here you guys are at last. I was beginning to wonder if I'd have to send out a search party. Who's that cute furry creature with you, Gwen?" She reached for one of the suitcases Joanna carried.

Suddenly shy, Gwen regarded her with a cautious smile. She looked up at Joanna who was helping her out of her jacket and then back at Kim. "He's Baxter."

"Well, so glad to meet you, Baxter." Joanna smiled gratefully at Kim over the child's head. Kim winked. "Let's the three of us take these suitcases down the hall and I'll show you where you're going to stay."

Gwen silently checked this with her mother again. Joanna nodded. "Go ahead, Gwenny. I've got some more things to bring in from the car."

Safely back outside in the dark, she at last allowed the tightness in her throat to spill over into quick hot tears. *Things aren't supposed to be this way.* She leaned back against the car, welcoming the bite of the chill breeze on her hot face. The dull cold of the car's frame at her back gave an odd sense of comfort.

"Need some help carrying anything?" Light spilled out the door Kim opened.

"Thanks, no. I'll be right in." She found a tissue in her pocket and blew her nose, then wiped her cheeks with her coat sleeve. Choosing a box from the pile of the back seat, she returned to the house.

Gwen greeted her with a beaming smile. "Mommy, wait till you see our room. It's got shelves and everything! Oh, and Kim asked me if I wanted some milk and cookies. Is it okay?" She pointed to a glass and plate on the kitchen table.

"Sounds wonderful. Here's the box with your books and things. Let's get you busy putting them away. We'll just take your milk and cookies along too if you can carry them carefully. And be sure to say thank you to Kim."

"She already did," Kim said. "How about some coffee, Jo? It's decaf. I put some on just before you got here."

"Mmm...it smells terrific too. I'll be right back for a cup." Their eyes connected for a moment before Joanna could turn away towards the hall. She mustered up a brave smile hoping Kim wouldn't see she'd been crying.

A steaming mug was waiting for her on the metal kitchen table. Kim sat stirring hers and simply smiled at Joanna. Wordlessly she passed the cream across and then went back to stirring. Joanna was grateful for the generous silence that settled around them, allowing at least a brief space to clear her thoughts. Down the hall Gwen was humming a contented tune.

At the second sip of the hot coffee, she closed her eyes, welcoming the warmth spreading out inside her, soaking up the chill. She opened her eyes to find Kim regarding her, sympathy registering in her gaze. "Been a long day, I'll bet," she said.

"And then some," said Joanna, watching the steam wavering up from the mug. "Gwen was really a big help with the packing. It was so nice of you to fix up that side of the room for her. Just listen to her in there."

Kim waved this off. "Oh, it wasn't so much. I never really had much use for those shelves and I knew Gwen would need her own little place to keep things. What seven-year-old doesn't? Did you want to bring in anything else from your car tonight?"

"No. It can wait till the morning. I'm pretty beat anyway. Are you sure there's room to store some of my furniture here?"

Kim nodded. "Lots of room. I showed you the space down in the basement. It's a big place even with two people renting it." She referred to her cousin who had moved out to get married in January. "As I've told you ten times already, Jo, you and Gwen moving in here really works out great for both of us. I'm sure it's not easy for you to be going through this, but I hope you and Gwen will settle in and make yourselves at home."

Joanna looked around the kitchen, taking in the pine-paneled cabinets, the tidy counter with its set of blue pottery canisters and mug rack, the gas stove with a pair of red-checked towels folded neatly on the handle. Kim's kitchen. How long would it be until she had one to herself again? Tears pricked at the corners of her eyes. She blinked them quickly away. "We'll certainly try," she said in a voice she hoped sounded upbeat. "Gwen's already excited about all the space there is here. Just the fact there's an upstairs is a thrill for her." The trailer's narrow confines appeared in her mind's eye. She flashed a heartfelt smile. "Kim, you know you're a life saver, don't you?"

Kim grinned, the dimple on her right cheek flashing. "Now I've been called a lot of things in my twenty-six years, but 'life saver' is certainly a first. Hey, you'd do the same for me if things were the other way around. Warm up your coffee?" She got up and took the carafe from the counter.

"Thanks, yes." She slid her mug over, searching for something else to talk about. "Are you sure you don't mind spending your Sunday helping me move the rest of our stuff?" "Not a bit. And it seems to me I've told you that a few times too." She waggled a scolding finger towards Joanna. "Cataldo hasn't given you any more grief, I hope."

"No. Actually I think he's tried to avoid me. I had to laugh, when I went to the office to say I was moving out, his wife was there. I think he may even have been praying I didn't spill the beans or something. He certainly was very accommodating about giving me back the security deposit as soon as possible."

It was true he couldn't do enough for her that day. Joanna had found herself almost giggling at his exaggerated efforts to please.

"Too bad you couldn't have put his feet to the fire somehow, at least a little."

"Believe me, I thought about it, but I've had enough to do trying to figure out how to explain to Gwen why we were moving." She sighed, recalling Gwen's tentative reaction to their Tuesday night conversation.

"Could I ask what you told her? That is if it's not being too nosy."

Joanna shook her head. "It's not. Probably you should know in case it comes up while we're here." She looked towards the hall to be sure Gwen wasn't within earshot. "I've told her that her father's job has gone on longer than we thought it would and that while we're waiting for him to come back, I thought it might be fun to live in town with you. Thank goodness it doesn't mean her changing schools or anything."

"Well, it's certainly true I'm looking forward to having Gwen here. So she's under the impression her father's coming home? I wouldn't ask that, Jo, but ..." Kim looked uncomfortable.

"I think that's what she's expecting, though the God's honest truth is I've avoided talking about it and she doesn't bring it up much. Even when we talked this week all she had to say was would he know where we were going to be now." She massaged her forehead, trying to will away the start of a headache. "I mean, in some ways I'm almost happy Larry's gone, but that's just for myself. There've been signs for so long, years practically, that things were ending. You know that. This whole past year I was just getting my feet under me after losing Mom and was too tired to do anything or even care. With Gwen though, it's a whole different thing. I think this was just the easy way out for him as far as the two of us go, but, after all, he does have a daughter. And the more time that passes the angrier I am that he's doing nothing to make this easier for her. One lousy postcard, that's the only thing she's had from him."

"Really? That's all?"

"One lousy postcard. Every time I see it, it makes me sadder. No, it makes me madder." She heaved a sigh and rubbed her forehead again.

"Oh Jo, I didn't mean to say something that would bring all this up tonight."

"That's all right. I need to start figuring some of it out, at least for Gwen's sake."

"Mommy?" As if on cue, Gwen appeared at the kitchen door. The happy look on her face reassured Joanna she hadn't overheard anything. "Can you come and see what I've done?"

"You bet, kiddo," she said, putting on a smile and getting up at once.

Gwen beckoned shyly to Kim. "And you can come too, if you want, Kim."

"I was hoping for an invitation, young lady," she said. "Lead the way."

Gwen's breathing was a soft whisper in the still room. Her dress-up dolls kept watch from the shelves beside the bed. Joanna could just make out their frilled skirts in the half-light. It had been an immense relief how she had settled into her new bed without hesitation, almost as if nothing out of the ordinary was going on in her life. When she'd checked on her ten minutes later she had already drifted off to sleep, Baxter held close under her arm.

Joanna shifted around, cocooning herself deeper under the covers. The street light out front angled a narrow finger across the ceiling. She studied its path, listening to the night sounds of the apartment, the faint ticking of the radiator cooling, the soft fall of Kim's slippered footsteps overhead as she returned from the bathroom to her bedroom. How long would it be until these became just background noises?

She closed her eyes. Odd to think that she'd never pass another restless night listening to the trailer's old refrigerator kick on and off. At that moment she missed the comfort of its familiar complaints and half-wished herself back there.

Gwen murmured in her sleep and turned on her side. Joanna raised herself up on one elbow and looked across at her. She waited while Gwen's breathing smoothed out once more. Light reflected from something behind the dolls at the back of the shelf. She leaned forward peering at it, then lay back against the pillow, fighting tears, and stared again at the ceiling.

It was Larry's postcard.

# ~ Two ~

The next morning she drove on ahead to the trailer. Gwen was riding over with Kim a little later. Expanding Kim's household by two people, and one a child, still seemed an awful lot to ask. But the animated conversation between them at breakfast seemed to Joanna a hopeful sign. Perhaps the worst that would happen was that now Gwen was talking Kim's ear off.

The muted sunrise had come up on low gray skies, the sort that promised at best only a uniform dullness to the day. A bit of sun would have been nice, Joanna thought, picking up speed as she headed the Nova towards Green Glade Court. The Court was two miles outside of Rockford Mills. It was a collection of twenty-odd trailers, homes to a shifting population of mostly young families just starting out but with plans to end up elsewhere soon. Except for a few older people and retired couples, most were gone after a few years. Somehow she and Larry had gotten mired down there, and the dream of moving out and on had slowly receded like some desert wanderer's mirage.

After sleeping fitfully, Joanna had woken thinking about her mother. If she were still alive, no doubt she'd be viewing this day with a sort of grim satisfaction. She'd always disliked the trailer and Green Glade, visiting only if it was something important for Gwen. Joanna had grown used to her boycott because she understood; understood that it was just another disappointment added to the string of them that began when she dropped out of college and married Larry. When your only child falls short of the dreams you have for her, how else could you feel? A run-down trailer in a run-down trailer park was definitely a sign of falling short. She would have known that anyway, but heard it in just those words from Phyllis, her mother's sister. And she had meant it kindly when she said it to Joanna. While she was growing up, it was her Aunt Phyl she most often brought her problems to. Beyond the patient, nonjudgmental hearing she always had ready, her advice was couched in fair and quiet words. Heaven knew her counseling skills were put to their greatest test when Joanna had gone against her parents' advice and married Larry Quinn.

The Court showed few signs of life on this Sunday morning, except for her neighbor two lots down, Arlie Spencer. He was just returning from town with his Sunday paper and gave her a jaunty wave with it as she drove past. He was alone now. Edith, his wife of forty-two years, had died just after Christmas. Edith and Arlie had always been neighborly and Gwen especially was a welcome guest anytime. On occasion she stayed with them after school if her regular sitter wasn't available. The past Wednesday evening Joanna had gone over to tell him they were leaving and he'd teared up a little while they stood talking on his porch. "Well, that little gal of yours will certainly be missed," he'd said with a slow shake of his head. Then he'd given her a wise and knowing smile. "People come and people go. That's a fact of life. But it's like I say, if life's been good to you, and mine has, you've got happy memories to take out and enjoy anytime you need 'em." She reassured him they'd keep in touch and walked back to the trailer in the deepening dusk, his words replaying themselves. His and Edith's long-enduring marriage made her eight years with Larry seem all the more hollow and sad.

She swung the Nova into the narrow driveway and sat for a moment looking at the faded bronze trailer they'd called home for five years. Yellow curtains still hung at the kitchen window with its view of the scraggly wood lot that edged one side of the Court. She'd never known for sure but guessed it was this bit of swampy woods that had inspired the trailer park's name. Gwen would miss the adventures she pursued there, though this spring at least she'd have fewer red blotches from scratching all those mosquito bites she came home with.

Part way up the steps she stopped and looked down at the remains of her small flower garden. A few bent stalks still held up ragged seed heads. She'd miss it and the simple pleasure its summer colors had always given her. Probably it would be the only thing she'd miss. She wanted to believe the next people to live here would tend the little bed of calendulas and Johnny-jump-ups which always re-seeded themselves, and even now were just waiting for the dirt to warm up.

Inserting the worn down key in the lock a last time, she finagled it back and forth until the locking mechanism decided to let loose. At least this aggravating daily ritual would no longer plague her. If she had a nickel for every time Cataldo had promised to fix it, she often said, she could retire.

The trailer's dim confines greeted her. Boxes and large green bags were scattered about looking like someone had trashed the place. She tried to feel something but couldn't get past the numbness that she'd woken with. There was nothing else to do but try to get through the day.

The calendar was still in its place on the cupboard door. Hesitantly she made a final slash, looked at it, and then traced it more firmly a second time, darkening the blue line. "Sixty-nine days," she said aloud, tapping the date with the pen. Then she raised her voice. "Sixty-nine days, and eight and a half years. I guess that's just about enough." Unexpectedly, a slow smile spread across her face, and she took the calendar down, folded it shut, and set it in the half-packed box on the counter, tucking the pen in beside it.

That was done.

She'd forgotten to bring a hair tie. A short search turned up one in the bathroom. Pulling her hair back into a ponytail, she made a face at the reflection in the dingy mirror. It wasn't the style she liked, but haircuts had become a luxury she couldn't afford. The gray hairs that had begun appearing among the dark auburn ones were easier to ignore when her hair was short. A lot more than haircuts were low on her list of priorities now.

She stood in the kitchen surveying the work remaining.

Dishes were stacked on the counter waiting to be packed. "Damn Larry." She set the newspaper-wrapped platter in the box with the calendar.

This day's business might not be happening at all if Larry had lived up to his end of the marriage better the past few years. It all seemed well past rescuing now.

When he'd left in early January for the construction job in Pennsylvania, she wasn't all that surprised when the promised checks had only amounted to two, with the second one long in coming. At first she'd thought they could manage on just her income, she and Gwen. But the rent, the food, and then an unplanned car repair bill had begun squeezing her paycheck more than she'd feared.

The truth was their finances had begun to erode over two years ago. Larry was fired from his job with one of Berlin's busiest contractors, something she'd seen coming but had been unable to prevent. Her mother fell ill that year. At times she had wondered if it hadn't been for the stress and distraction of those months, that she might have been able to head this trouble off. Larry's adolescent partying habits, subdued for the first few years of their marriage, began to creep back in. Too many hangovers made it hard getting to work on time, and his boss finally ran out of patience.

Losing his job seemed to stun him enough to straighten up some and he found work as a custodian at Tall Pines Nursing Home out at the edge of Rockford Mills. It was less money than his construction work, but their income had evened out for a spell. First his hours were cut, and then his pickup needed a major overhaul, that cost adding its weight to the rest of the bills. Thanksgiving and the start of the Christmas season found them more and more often at swords' points. Most of it was about money, but with the advent of football season, Larry's Friday nights "with the boys" were extended into Sunday afternoons. His best buddy, Hank, had one of the new wide screen televisions and it drew in Larry and the rest like a beacon every Sunday.

It angered her that he saw less of Gwen and she quietly resented how nearly all of the parenting work fell to her. She knew in her heart of hearts that their marriage had more weaknesses than strengths. The passing months saw an ever greater imbalance. The tension had never been worse or so constant. It would begin as soon as soon as both were home at the end of the day, the last one in the door seemed to set off some invisible trip-wire releasing a cloud of seething animosity. For Gwen's sake, Joanna would stifle her feelings while they ate supper. She'd busy herself helping Gwen with her schoolwork or reading books with her. Then there'd be Gwen's bedtime routine and a last few minutes of forced tranquility while Joanna returned to the kitchen to straighten things up, wanting Gwen to be safely asleep before anything started.

Things seemed to empty out between them day by day. Then he came home with news there was good-paying construction work down in Pennsylvania. In that smiling persuasive way he had when he wanted to talk her into something, he convinced her he'd be able to send fat checks home soon and get them on their feet.

He was gone the day after New Year's, waking Gwen to give her a goodbye kiss and pausing in the kitchen long enough to fill his travel mug with the coffee Joanna had gotten up to make. She'd stood at the living room window streaked with winter grime and watched him drive out of sight, his parting kiss evaporating on her cheek.

There was one last cupboard to go. Gwen had packed all the plastic glasses and mugs the day before leaving the breakable ones for her mother. Joanna wrapped each well for what could be months of storage. A few odd ones she added to the give-away box. Pushed to the back of the cupboard was the black mug that had been Larry's favorite, a souvenir of the one Buffalo Bills game he'd gone to see years ago. Their red and blue banner waved itself at her as she lifted it down. Keep it or toss it? Maybe Gwen would like it? She ran a finger around the edge finding a thin crack running down one side. "It probably leaks anyway," she said aloud, and then laughed at the truth behind the words. She put it in the give-away box.

A car horn tooted outside signaling Gwen and Kim's arrival. The door swung open and they came in, Gwen leading Kim by the hand. Gwen greeted her with a wide smile. "Hi, Mommy! I'm going to show Kim my room first, okay?"

Joanna exchanged grins with Kim. "Fine. And then you can finish putting your clothes from the dresser in that box on your bed." The two disappeared down the hall.

When Kim returned Joanna said to her, "Hope that child of mine hasn't talked your ear off yet."

"Not at all. I just wish I had some of the energy kids have. She's busy packing her clothes like you wanted her to." Kim took off her jacket and pushed up her sleeves. "Now, please tell me where I can pitch in."

"How about the pots and pans over on the shelf? There's a box right there to use. And when you finish with that, the cookbooks over by the phone I hope will fit in too."

With two of them working, things began to move fast. Soon everything in the kitchen was packed. Gwen was sent outside to play and she announced she was going across to the woods and then down to see Arlie.

"Jo, do you want this list of phone numbers taken down?" Kim asked.

Joanna looked up from emptying the refrigerator. "Yes, I'll need them if you can manage to get the tape off the wall."

"I'll do my best," she said. "Got some sort of knife I can work up the edges first?"

Joanna found one. She looked over Kim's shoulder at the yellowed sheet of paper. "Maybe I should just copy the ones I need and have you rip it off rather than fuss with it."

"It's coming, I think." One side was already free. "Did you say your Dad knows you're moving to the Mills?"

Joanna turned back to the refrigerator. "No, I haven't told him yet. I sort of mentioned we might be moving last time I talked to him. That must have been two or so weeks ago. Things have happened so fast, I haven't had any chance to spread the word to anyone." That was true enough. Something she hadn't shared with anyone, not even Kim, was that she had been avoiding her family since Larry left. At their Christmas gathering he'd been full of talk about going down to Pennsylvania. Joanna preferred everyone still think this was going well and no one had need to be concerned, or to disapprove.

She set the last jars into the picnic cooler and straightened up. The empty refrigerator yawned at her. She shut the door. "There. That's done." Kim handed her the list of numbers. "Thanks. I was thinking I'd check in with my father tonight, and maybe my Aunt Phyllis and Uncle George. Then there's my mother-in-law. She's the only person who actually knows anything. I told her I'd give her a call when we got moved in with you." She surveyed the living room area even more cluttered now with boxes and plastic bags, swollen and lumpy. "Guess it's time we started moving things out to the cars."

By four o'clock they'd made two trips back to Kim's and now the last things had been taken out. Everything that she had an interest in and enough energy to move would soon be stored away in Kim's basement. She'd told Cataldo she was leaving the key on the kitchen counter. Not having to look him in the eye again suited her just fine.

The day's gray light was fading when she came out and shut the door behind her. There'd been no urge to look around the trailer one more time as she thought there might be. Kim had gone on already and Gwen was waiting in the car. In the little woods across the drive a robin hesitantly struck up his spring song. Pausing at the bottom of the steps to listen, her eyes once more rested on her flower bed. She reached down and snapped off two seed heads from the calendulas and wrapped them in a tissue she found in her jacket. Tucking them gently into her pocket, she walked to the car without looking back.

"Hey, partner, you ready to roll?" Joanna asked Gwen,

starting up the car.

Gwen mumbled an answer that Joanna didn't catch. She gave a toot on the horn as they drove slowly by Arlie's trailer. A light was on in his living room. She couldn't tell if he came to look out his window to watch them drive by. "We'll have to come and visit Mr. Spencer now and then, don't you think?"

Gwen had taken off her seatbelt and knelt on the seat looking out the back window. She didn't answer her mother. They reached the bend in the drive and Joanna stopped to check traffic before pulling out onto the highway.

"You were a terrific helper today, Gwenny. Now sit back down please and put on your seat belt so we can get going." Gwen slid down and silently pulled her seat belt across her lap. They drove out of the Court.

"How about picking out a radio station for us to listen to on the way to Kim's?"

Gwen didn't answer. Joanna glanced over and caught sight of tears brimming above the tight line of her mouth. "I miss my room, Mommy," she said, her voice quavery and small.

Joanna's heart missed a beat. *Poor Gwen.* She reached a hand across the seat. "I'm sure you do, sweetie. Come on over and sit by me, and let's hug." Gwen scooted over in an instant, fastened the middle seat belt, and nestled into the curve of her mother's arm. *Damn that Larry.* Joanna reached to turn on the radio. "Oh my goodness," she said to herself softly. Linda Ronstadt's sweet voice was saying it all. "You're no good, you're no good, you're no good. Baby, you're no good." Joanna smiled and tapped her fingers on the steering wheel along with the beat.

Halfway back to Kim's, Gwen stirred against her side. "Mommy, am I going to be able to get to school okay like you said?" Her voice still sounded uncertain.

"Absolutely, you are! Mrs. Timian wouldn't be too happy with us if we let you miss a day. And you said your library book was due tomorrow too, right?"

Gwen nodded her head. "But I'm going to have to miss my

bus like you said. Right?"

"Yes. Like I said, I'll be driving you to school this week and picking you up until I can talk to your principal and find out about what buses stop near Kim's house. Won't it be fun to ride with me for a few days?" She worked to inject jollyness into her words, tired as she was.

"I guess so. I've gotta tell Julie I'm not going to be able to sit with her anymore. And Mr. Holmes." She named her bus driver and her closest friend who lived in the housing development a short way from the trailer park. "Did you mean it when you said I can invite her over to where we're staying? I mean, at Kim's?"

"Sure you'll be able to. As long as it's okay with Kim, of course. But I don't think she'll mind." That would take some getting used to, having to make even the smallest decisions around wondering if Kim would mind. All the more reason to work towards getting their own place again as soon as possible.

Preoccupied with that thought, she was startled by Gwen's next question. "Mommy?"

"Hmm?"

"Does Grandpa know about our new home yet? Or Daddy?"

"Grandpa doesn't know exactly. Daddy either. You remember that we don't have a phone number for him right now. I'll try to call Grandpa tonight. You remind me after supper when we get everything put away, okay?" Joanna's father would at least want to know where they were. The same probably wasn't true for Larry. For the moment she hoped Gwen wouldn't pursue that question.

She didn't.

When the last things had been unloaded and moved down to the basement, Joanna insisted on ordering a pizza for their supper, her treat, and a small thank you to Kim for all her help. Driving over to pick it up gave her a few minutes of welcome quiet. She took a right turn at the end of Lombardy instead of a left, deciding to explore the streets on the way downtown.

Other than doing her shopping in Rockford Mills, she wasn't familiar with all of it. She found herself in a neighborhood of large, well-kept homes, many of them dignified Victorians. It was past dark so lights were on, giving glimpses into people's living rooms where blinds had not yet been drawn.  Joanna drove slowly, trying to picture what it must be like to own such spacious, well-furnished homes. It might as well be wishing to own the Taj Mahal.

Near the end of Elm Street she crossed a bridge which spanned Eight Mile Creek. The car headlights caught a sign that read Rockford Mills Park. She knew the place. As a child she had come here for picnics with her family and one summer as a teenager had had a job assisting with a recreation program for kids. Perhaps it would be close enough for her and Gwen to walk to once the weather got warm. That is, if they hadn't gotten another place by summer.

Her father. She still had the phone call to make.

She took a left and drove the two blocks to Main Street. The marquee of the Capitol Theater was lit up advertising the current Mel Gibson movie. Despite the competition from the new multiplex at the edge of town, it managed to do enough business to stay open. Sal's Pizzeria, a few doors down, benefited from its proximity to the Capitol. Several booths were full with teenagers probably waiting for the seven o'clock show.

The slight young man behind the counter told her it would be a few more minutes until her pizza would be ready. She took a seat on a stool at the end of the counter, somewhat self-conscious of her old jeans and denim jacket that she'd worn all day to do the moving. She hadn't touched her hair since morning and now reached up to smooth some loose strands back into her ponytail. But no one seemed to pay her any attention.

In the nearest booth, a boy who looked to be in his late teens and a much younger girl sat with arms entwined. Joanna decided she couldn't be more than fourteen. He was smoking a cigarette, talking to the couple that sat across the table, practically ignoring his girlfriend nuzzling him. An oval, purplish mark showed clearly on his neck, the sign of a recent passionate evening. Shades of the days of her Eric Miller madness. She swung her stool seat around wanting to avoid any further reminders.

She focused her thoughts on what she'd say to her father, an only slightly less discomfiting topic. Frowning, she tapped her toe on the footrest, mentally rehearsing opening lines she could use. 'Hi, Dad. Just wanted you to know we've moved out of the trailer.' 'Hi, Dad. Larry really screwed me over good this time.' She pictured him standing there in the shadowed kitchen, hearing her words through the phone receiver. There'd be silence. He'd clear his throat. Maybe she'd have to speak again. 'Well, Dad, guess you were right. Or maybe I should say Mom was right.' But if she said that, then she'd want to scream, '...but she's not here to tell me, only you are.' But she wouldn't utter any such thing, make any such accusation. It wouldn't be fair, she'd told herself time and time again. He had tried, hadn't he?

"M'am...your pizza's ready." She looked up. The young man gestured to the pizza he'd placed on the counter.

"Oh. Thanks." She got out her wallet, paid the bill, and took the box he held out to her.

*Since when did I start looking more like a 'Ma'm' than a 'Miss'?*

The question both amused and annoyed her. Kim laughed when she told the story over their supper of pizza and the salad Kim had made.

"The kid must have been all of sixteen, Jo. Anyone over twenty looks old to someone that age!" She winked at Gwen. "Am I right, Gwen?"

"Yup." Gwen took another big bite of her pizza slice.

"You're probably both right, but it was annoying. And it's 'yes' not 'yup'. And one more thing, don't take such huge bites at a time, Gwen." She noticed by the kitchen clock that it was nearly seven. "Hey, we've got to get your bath started pretty soon, young lady. You've had a busy day and you're going to need a good night's rest for school tomorrow. Did you find our towels while I was gone for the pizza?"

Gwen nodded. "Uh huh. And guess what? Kim's letting me use some special bath stuff that she says smells real nice." She gave Kim an adoring look, and then turned back to her mother. "And I already told her thank you, Mommy, without you even telling me to."

Joanna smiled, first at Gwen and then Kim. "Well, that I'm glad to hear. First thing you know Kim's going to spoil you. But that's really nice, I've got to say." Soaking in a tub of hot, fragrant water sounded inviting to her too. Maybe after she got the call to her father out of the way.

But the call never got made. After supervising Gwen's bath and getting her settled down, she heard Kim on the kitchen phone talking with Gary. Joanna had come across her journal as they unpacked. It seemed a good time to make use of it while she waited for the phone. In the living room she settled on Kim's blue corduroy coach and turned on the television for company. A sitcom's laugh track seemed suitable background. She found an empty page in her notebook and stared at its blank space. At a loss for how to begin, she leaned her head back and closed her eyes. The next thing she knew Kim was shaking her arm gently.

"Hey there, sleeping beauty, why don't you get yourself to bed?"

She straightened and grimaced at the cramp that had settled in her back. "What time is it?"

"Going for eleven. Want to jump in the shower first?"

Joanna smiled sleepily and stretched her stiff back. "Hey, that would be great. You're going to spoil me about as fast as you're spoiling my daughter."

Kim grinned, her dimple flashed. "Maybe. But then we can all use a little of that now and then." She crossed the room and switched off the television. Joanna started for the stairs. "Oh,

Jo! You wanted to call your Dad, didn't you. Sorry I didn't say something sooner. Is it too late now?"

Joanna paused in the hallway and looked back at her. "That's okay. It can wait."

Gwen got slowly out of the car the next morning when they pulled up to the rambling, one-story brick school. She hesitated before closing the door and leaned back inside to look at her mother. The damp mark left from Joanna's kiss shone on her cheek. "So after school I'm supposed to wait for you by the front door? Will Mrs. Timian know?" Worry creased a small dent along her forehead.

Joanna gave her an encouraging smile. "Yes, that's right. I'm getting out of work early today so I can come and talk to Mrs. Murray. So you can meet me at her office or I'll be waiting right outside your classroom. Either way, don't worry. And don't forget to return your library book." She blew her another kiss. "Now I've got to get to work. Have fun today."

"Okay. I will." She smiled at last and the worry line disappeared. She closed the car door, waved, and started up the sidewalk.

Joanna watched her go, a lump rising in her throat. "Well, Joanna, old girl. There's work to be done and bills to pay." She eased the Nova gently into gear and drove out to the street.

Ten minutes later she pulled into the college parking lot. For four years she'd been the secretary for the director of the Continuing Education program. It had been a fortunate day when Alita Belden had hired her. She was a student at Seneca Community first, dropping out after a year and a half to marry Larry. Working as a cashier at K-Mart was not what she'd dreamed of doing, but at least it helped pay the bills.

When the opportunity came along to return to SCCC as an employee, it was a welcome step up from her K-Mart job and helped mend things with her mother. She was glad to put to use the skills learned in her college business courses.

She quickly earned Alita Belden's praise. What began as a good working relationship deepened when Joanna's mother developed colon cancer. Throughout her mother's illness Alita had insisted Joanna take all the time she needed to handle everything. If it hadn't been for her quiet, steadying support, Joanna doubted she would have come through the ordeal as well as she did.

The day promised to be a busy one. Joanna was glad to have her mind taken off the past weekend's business by the final whirl of work needed to get out the summer program material. She took the last of the brochures to the mailroom and stopped at the snack bar on her way back, glad to find Kim there.

"Phew! What a morning it's been," she said, sitting down with her coffee and the doughnut she'd decided to treat herself to. "The best news is that Alita was fine with my needing to go and pick up Gwen for a few days until we get things straightened out."

"That's good to hear. I knew she wouldn't have any objection," Kim said. "Gwen got off to school all right?"

She nodded. "Yes, and I made it here in good time too. Even though she said she liked riding in with me, I could tell she was nervous about my showing up after school to pick her up. I sure hope we weren't in your way getting ready this morning." Joanna could already see that three people with only one bathroom was going to require cooperation on weekday mornings. The last thing she wanted was for them to become an inconvenience for Kim.

"Not at all. I think we managed just fine."

"Well, good. But Gwen has to learn to hustle a little more." She fidgeted with the coffee stirrer. "Well, in a few days we'll have a definite schedule worked out. I'm going over to the school this afternoon and find out about the bus routes for your part of town. We saw a bus go by the corner about the time we left today. I wish now I'd taken time to do that last week."

Kim placed her hand on Joanna's arm. "Jo, there are only so many hours in a day, not to mention a week. Things are going to working out great with you, Gwen, and me. Just take things one day at a time."

"Thanks for the encouragement." Joanna returned her smile. "Speaking of one thing at a time, I'm thinking about driving over to my father's after I pick Gwen up. I never did call him." She swirled the remaining coffee in her cup. " If we do go, we might be late getting back and I wouldn't want you to be concerned."

"No problem. I said I'd make us my mouth-watering tuna casserole supreme for supper and that keeps just fine if it has to. Take whatever time you need at your dad's. And you can assure Gwen she's got that dishwashing job I offered her."

## ~ *Three* ~

Arranging for Gwen to be picked up for school in Rockford Mills proved to be easy. In a matter of a few minutes she had explained their change of address to the school secretary and filled out the appropriate form. The only loose end left was arranging for an after-school sitter. Kim had the name of teenage girl who lived down the street and thought she might be interested in babysitting.

A more immediate concern was the conversation she would have shortly with her father. Their occasional phone calls were usually only brief exchanges, how Gwen was doing in school, what everyone's health was at the moment. After Larry left she found herself avoiding calling people in Berlin. It spared her from having to find ways to paper over the hard truth of his continuing absence.

School was letting out at about the time she finished in the principal's office and Gwen appeared, all smiles when she spotted her mother. Berlin was a fifteen-mile drive from Rockford Mills. Much of the way there on County Route 80 wound along the banks of the Seneca Creek. It was high with spring run-off. In places the water had spilled over the banks stranding gigantic lumps of gray-streaked ice in muddy cornfields. With a few miles to go they drove past an orderly farmstead where two blue Harvestore silos loomed above a collection of sturdy red barns. A mailbox bearing the name 'Lupinski' stood at the road's edge.

"That's where your friend lived, huh, Mommy?" Gwen had paused in a story she'd been telling to ask the question. In truth, Joanna had been only half-listening.

"Mmhmm. Rachel Lupinski." Joanna added silently, *my former friend.*

"And you and she used to go swimming in the creek?"

Joanna found a genuine smile for that. "Lots of times. You remember how I'd tell you we'd swing out over the creek on this big rope tied to a willow tree and splash into the water?"

"Uh huh. And sometimes you'd come out of the water with a big bloodsucker on your leg. Yuck! But it must've been lots of fun! I wish I had a friend with a farm and a swimming place."

"Not that many kids live on farms any more. But you have some pretty nice friends."

"Like Julie."

"Yes. Like Julie. So tell me again what happened with you and her at recess."

Gwen returned to her story with fresh enthusiasm. The Lupinski farm disappeared from the review mirror. She sighed. Funny how when you were Gwen's age, not even ten, you think of your friendships as never-ending. Certainly she and Rachel had.

People always said what a good pair they made, she and Rachel. Rachel with her coal black hair neatly divided into two long braids, eyes ever-alight with mischief; she with her auburn hair usually pulled into a pair of swinging pigtails, somewhat more reserved in personality but ready for whatever fun that might come along. They complimented each other, her edge of caution tempering Rachel's love of adventure, and Rachel's enthusiasm coaxing Joanna out of her quiet corner. Though Rachel lived outside of town which meant she had to ride a bus to and from school while Joanna walked, each of them begged often enough to get one or the other mother to drive them back and forth nearly every Saturday. Or else after Sunday school they'd wangle permission to spend the afternoon together. Joanna was an only child, and Rachel had three brothers who tended to pick on her, so their mothers agreed the steady companionship was good for them both.

There was always more for them to do at Rachel's country home. Other than swimming in the creek when the weather was hot, there were woods to explore, trees to climb, and the barn's cavernous haymow that would be filled nearly to the rafters with June's sweet-smelling hay. One of their favorite pastimes was creating stories to act out, usually high-adventure tales where one would take on the imaginary trappings of a knight on a quest while the other would play the loyal, but bumbling companion, or be a fair maiden in distress. Oddly enough, Joanna preferred the knight's dash and verve and she could usually talk Rachel into the role of the princess.

How such a long and close friendship could come unraveled remained in some ways a mystery to her. The events still of that spring lingered in clear detail but Joanna did what she could to avoid remembering them.

The blue-metal facade of the new Ames store at the edge of Berlin came into sight. She checked her watch. Likely her father would be home by now from work. He was head mechanic at Ferguson Auto Sales and Service.

Gwen's voice brought her back to the moment. "I hope Grandpa's got some of his candy today. I'm hungry."

"We'll see. Most likely he will, but I don't want you to go barging in there and ask him that the first thing like you sometimes do." She slowed the car to a stop as Berlin's solitary traffic light changed to red. "Actually, my tummy's growling a little, too."

"Are we eating supper there, Mommy?"

"Not this time." They drove on down Main towards Madison Street. "Kim's getting supper for us. That reminds me. She wanted me tell you she's got you signed up for dishwashing after we eat. What do you say to that?"

"I say 'fine'. Look, there's where Grandma used to work." She pointed out the car window towards the building where a gilt-lettered sign announced *Thelma's Beauty Nook.* "Can we stop and say 'hi' to Mrs. G?"

Joanna glanced towards the shop's window as they drove slowly past, catching a glimpse of Thelma Gigliotti's large form in her customary place standing behind a seated patron. She pictured her pausing in mid-snip to waggle her scissors at the mirrored reflections, emphasizing some point of the conversation. What countless hours after school had she sat waiting for her mother, pretending to be engrossed in the pages of a fashion magazine, but really eavesdropping on the adult talk that swirled around the beauty shop. On their walks home together through the late afternoon streets, Joanna had her mother all to herself. The four blocks allowed ample time to share the day's adventures, her mother listening with unfailing attentiveness, a confidant for childish secrets. By the time they reached Madison Street the gay, animated woman who worked in the beauty shop often had fallen quiet, the sparkle in her eyes veiled. When Joanna was old enough to notice such things, she'd once asked if her mother was all right. "Yes, dear. I'm just tired from my busy day." An answer meant to satisfy, but even at eleven Joanna sensed it was only partly the truth.

"We'll visit Mrs. G. next time we come to Berlin, Gwen."

"Promise we will?"

"Promise."

Gwen barely waited until Joanna stopped the car in the driveway of 42 Madison before pushing open the door and dashing up the front walk of the two-story ranch. Her father must have heard them pull in since he met Gwen at the door and scooped her up for a hug. "Well, look who we have here! What brings you and your mom to town after all these months, little lady? I was beginning to think you'd forgotten where your old grandpa lived." Gwen giggled. Over her shoulder he fixed Joanna with a questioning look.

"Guilty as charged, Dad. Gwen and I came by for just a quick visit to tell you we have a new address."

"So you did move." If the news surprised him, his face didn't show it. "Well, I just put on some coffee. Come on in, you two, and we'll have ourselves a visit and find out about this new address." He set Gwen back down, winked at her, and led the way inside.

Gwen began chattering at once. "We're staying at Kim's

until Daddy comes back. She's a nice, pretty lady who works at the college with Mommy. You should see my room, Grandpa. It's not in a trailer. It's in a house."

"A house, you say? Now that's something. Oh, Jo, there's some mail for you on the buffet."

"Yes! In Rockford Mills. And I'm going to have to ride a different bus to school starting tomorrow morning."

Joanna trailed after them through the shadowy dining room towards the kitchen letting Gwen share what she wanted. It gave her more time to decide on a way to explain things. She paused by the buffet where the pile of letters and magazines occupied one end, trying not to notice how thick the dust was on her mother's antique silver candlesticks and the glass bowl with its faded plastic fruit. Parts of the house were exactly as they'd always been prior to her mother's death. Joanna wondered if it was because her father couldn't bear disturbing these small reminders of her. Every so often he'd try out a housekeeper but it had been months since he'd had anyone in. Regardless, conversation about Sylvia Smales was invariably too painful for either of them to pursue.

Sifting through the pile of letters, she found the one he'd mentioned. An unfamiliar woman's name was typed in the corner. She paused in the kitchen doorway to read it over, her lips pursing. It was an announcement of her high school class's tenth reunion.

Gwen was now telling her grandfather the highlights of her school day between sips of hot cocoa. An open package of Mallow Cups lay between them.

Her father passed her a cup of coffee as she sat down and pushed over the carton of milk. She nodded her thanks. He turned his attention back to Gwen. Edward Smales, nearly fifty-six, still had a full head of sandy brown hair that showed only traces of gray. His hands, large and scarred from his work, engulfed his cup. They were immaculately clean despite the grime of the garage. Growing up, Joanna had often observed his cleansing ritual each afternoon when he'd come home from work. He stood silent at the kitchen sink, sudsing his hands slowly and methodically with Lava soap until all traces of the day's labor were gone. After toweling them dry, he'd take out a small, folded file from his pocket and carefully clean his nails, completing the process. As a child he'd played piano, quite well she'd been told, but could never touch the keys unless his hands were spotlessly clean. She could remember the large, dark upright that had stood in the front room of her grandparents' house, could remember how much she wanted to open its hinged lid and touch the gleaming keys, but her stern grandmother seldom allowed it. Joanna had never heard her father play a single note, a mystery which was never explained, but the meticulous handwashing of his adult years she'd long ago decided was part of that story.

Gwen had paused finally and he looked across at Joanna. "From what I hear, it sounds like you two have found a comfortable place for yourselves. If you'd have said something, I could have at least helped you move your things." His mild expression didn't reveal much of his reaction.

"It all came up sort of fast, Dad. There really wasn't any time to have let you know." The fact of Larry's bounced check and her landlord's crude advances were not details she wanted to share.

"Seems the last I knew, things were a little tight but you were managing. Especially with Larry going off to that job in, where was it, Pennsylvania?" There was a pause while he seemed to reflect on this, but then he went on. "Has the Nova needed more work? You know you can always have my help with that."

"Yes, I know. Thanks. Basically it's running okay." She shrugged, looking for more to say which would satisfy him and bring the explanation to a conclusion. "I'm not exactly sure where I want to be say in another six months and I couldn't see paying the rent at the park with Larry still away when I could, well, I could save us money by moving in with Kim for a while."

It was close enough to the truth.

Her father had been looking at her steadily. He glanced at Gwen and then back at Joanna. He raised his thick eyebrows. "So...things are pretty well set then, are they? I mean, with Larry and all?"

She caught his unspoken question and resisted shifting nervously in her chair. "Yes. At least until the summer. Once Gwen's out of school we'll see where things are." She turned her attention to Gwen. "If you're about through with your cocoa, why don't you go use the bathroom before we head back to the Mills. Kim will be looking for us pretty soon." Gwen left the kitchen. "Say, Dad, what do you hear from Aunt Phyllis and Uncle George?" she asked him, wanting to steer the conversation in a safer direction.

"They're both fine, as far as I know. Actually, now that you mention it, I saw your Aunt Phyllis the other day in the supermarket. She said it had been a month or so since you last called and she was getting a little worried. I told her I'd see to it you gave her a call soon or stopped in. She'd probably appreciate knowing where you'd moved to."

Joanna had torn off the flap from the envelope and was writing down Kim's address and telephone number. "You're right. I've just been so busy trying to manage without Larry around. I'll call her in a day or two." She handed him the paper. "There's where we are now. Guess what this is?" She held up the letter, glad to have something else to talk about, even if wasn't a pleasant topic. "It's an invitation to my tenth high school reunion. They're planning a dinner and dance at White Acres in July."

"I thought I should know the name on the envelope. Wasn't her name Rebecca Simmons when she was in school with you?"

"Yes. That's who it was." *And I can still see her standing there at Rachel's party with that smirk on her face*, she thought to herself.

"White Acres is a nice place if you can afford it."

"Which explains why I'll probably not go." With luck she'd succeeded in talking around this matter like they did around most others in this house. She watched her father's face and when he nodded without comment and looked towards the door, she knew she was safe.

"Before Gwen gets back downstairs, let me ask you a quick question, Jo. What *have* you heard from Larry? He's sending you money like he said he would?"

Joanna pretended to be carefully folding the reunion invitation and fitting it into her purse. To her relief, Gwen came back in the kitchen at that moment. There was another half-truth to use. "He's sent two checks. Oh, good, there you are Gwen. I'll just run in there myself and we'll be on our way. Rinse out your cup for Grandpa and you two meet me out by the car." Then she escaped from the kitchen.

He had Gwen giggling about something when she got out to the driveway. "Let's get you buckled into your seatbelt, young lady." He settled her into her place while Joanna got in on her side. "Now you be good and do well in school this week."

"I will, Grandpa. Oh! Thank you for the candy." She looked at her mother who nodded her approval.

He held Gwen's car door open another minute, looking now at Joanna. "I'm glad you drove over to let me know the news, Jo. I wish I was in a better position financially to help. You know that, I hope. With any luck, the damn hospital bill will be paid by October." Then he shifted his eyes away from hers.

"I know that, Dad. But things aren't so bad for us." She started the engine. "Listen, I don't want you to worry, okay?"

"Well, all right then. I'll give you a call soon and find out how you're both doing. Bye, sweet pea." He stooped for Gwen's last hug and kiss and waved a hand at Joanna.

"Bye, Dad."

The sun had long since set. She turned up the car's heat to drive off the night's chill.

Well, that's done with, she thought to herself as they left New Berlin behind. Gwen was fiddling with the radio dial.

Snatches of music and loud commercials filled the Nova. What her father might have been thinking as they drove off was impossible for her to guess. Likely he wasn't pleased with what he'd heard, that was safe to say. But beyond that, who knew. Penetrating the thickets of his private thoughts was something she had never succeeded in doing.

She started the bath water and headed back downstairs, hearing Gwen chattering away to Kim in the kitchen. "Your bath's almost ready, Gwenny," she said coming into the room, smiling at the sight of her daughter energetically wiping off the place mats on the table. "You about done with your job out here?"

"Uh huh.  Kim says this is the last thing for me to do." She beamed her pleasure at what she'd done.

"I told Gwen what a great worker she is," said Kim who was putting away the clean dishes.  "It looks like she's got a permanent job. Coffee's hot...want some?"

"Absolutely. On your way now, young lady." Gwen waltzed from the room. "Give me a yell when you're through," Joanna called after and sank onto a chair, smiling her thanks as Kim handed her a mug.

"Gosh, what a great kid she is, Joanna. Milk in yours?" She held out the carton and poured some in when Joanna nodded.

"Thanks. Yes, she's a trooper, especially with all that's gone on lately. Boy, am I glad today's over. Thank goodness it was so easy to change her bus pickup for school. Hopefully I can talk soon with the girl you told me about and have that part fixed up too."

"You said you had a good visit with your father?" Kim's tone was conversational.

"As good as it could be."  She realized that sounded odd. "Oh, he means well. He's a great grandpa for Gwen. He and I, well, we just don't communicate with one another that easily. Since Mom died it almost seems worse."

"Did he have much to say about your moving here?"

"No. Of course I didn't give him much of a chance to, probably. He didn't seem too surprised, just sort of concerned." She frowned into her coffee. "Sometimes I think he's still trying to figure out how to be a single parent to me now that Mom's gone." She shook her head, then grinned wryly at Kim. "Too bad his only daughter's a problem child now and then, you know?"

"Oh, I know. I guess parents can't help being parents. My folks, I mean they're good people and all, but they can be annoying at times." She gave a short laugh. "Whenever I go home I'm never in the house twenty minutes before my mother has some subtle comment about my not being married yet. God!" Kim rolled her eyes and took a sip of her coffee. "Twenty-six years old and she's sure I'm doomed to become a dried-up old maid."

Joanna nodded sympathetically. "I wonder if we'll ever escape their expectations? For me it was that I didn't finish college like they wanted me to, especially my mother. She worked on me from the time I was ten. I think a lot of it was because she never got the chance to go. I know now she was right, but I went through that phase 'Who does she think she is to tell me what to do?' and before you knew it, I was a married twenty-year old convinced I'd gotten what I wanted. On top of that, they didn't much like Larry. He wasn't exactly who they'd pictured as their son-in-law. Oh, I knew how much I'd disappointed her when I dropped out to marry him. I even gave some thought to going back to finish, but then I got pregnant for Gwen and that was the end of that." She fell silent, stroking the warm surface of the mug she held. "Thank goodness it turned out she loved being a grandmother. It gave me a chance to redeem myself."

"Have you ever considered going back to school and finishing your degree? After all, you said you liked that Adult Ed. course you took last fall. What was it? A writing course?"

"Creative writing. Yes, you're right. I really liked taking it even if Larry made it hard to do."

"He made it hard? How so?"

"Oh, he'd complain about having to watch Gwen every Wednesday. Or sometimes he'd ridicule what I was doing saying things like, 'What the hell are you wasting time on that stuff for?' My husband, the supportive spouse. If it hadn't of been for Alita practically signing me up for it, I probably wouldn't have done it at all. Thank goodness I had her to push me."

"But if he's mostly out of the picture, what would stop you from going back now?"

"Well, the price tag, for one thing," Joanna said. "I'd have to figure out a way to afford it even with loans."

"I'll bet your Dad would love seeing you go back to school. Didn't he want you to go to college, too?"

"Oh yes, I'm pretty sure he did. But then, while I was growing up he was always sort of a mystery to me. He was one of those dads who went off to work every morning, brought home his paycheck every week and turned it over to his wife, puttered around the house after supper, and then sat in his easy chair watching television until bedtime." Memories stirred. "There wasn't much talking at our house. Maybe if there had been..." The unfinished sentence slipped out, an unpleasant echo of things she tried to leave alone now. The day was threatening to let some of them loose again. Her pocketbook hanging on the door knob caught her eye. "Hey, let me show you what came in the mail for me over at my father's." She retrieved the invitation and handed it to Kim.

"Hey, your tenth year reunion. Think you'll go?"

"Maybe, though at this point I don't much care if I ever see anyone from my old school. There's no one I've kept in touch with really. Do you still have friends back home in Rochester?"

"Not really. Once in a while I bump into some of my old girlfriends when I'm home. It's the people I met when I went to Genesee Community College that I keep in touch with. High school was a pretty forgettable experience for me. I've always thought a small school like the one you went to would have been nicer than my big city school."

"At times it was fun. Sports was always a big deal. The whole town would come out to the games. We'd have pep rallies and get really psyched up. Another nice thing was the musical every spring. Just about everybody got involved in that. When I was a junior I had a small part in 'Camelot'. It was great."

Kim smiled. "Sounds nice. The only thing I did was sing in the glee club. To be in sports you had to be a real hot shot. Now I know I envy you and your little school."

"Well, like everything, it has its positives and negatives. What wasn't so good was how everybody knew everybody else's business. You know, like who was going out with who or what boy a girl might be interested in. And when a rumor got going it could practically destroy someone's reputation, even when that's all it was, just a stupid rumor."

Again things were drifting towards treacherous depths. She got up from the table, swallowing the rest of her lukewarm coffee. "I think I'd better go up and see how Gwen's doing with her bath."

Once Gwen was in bed, she decided to make the call to her mother-in-law. Though it was past nine, she knew Louise was not one to retire early. Her husky voice came on the line at the fourth ring. "Hello? Who's this?"

"Hi, Lou. It's Joanna."

"Jo! I've been wondering about you and..." Louise lapsed into a hacking cough. "Oh, God. Sorry. Tell me the latest. You two have been on my mind the last couple of days."

Joanna described their move to Rockford Mills.

"Well, I'm sorry to hear you had to give up your place, but where you are with your friend doesn't sound bad at all," Louise said.

Joanna looked around the kitchen. "No, it's not bad. We're pretty much settled in for a while."

"And I don't suppose you heard one way or another from that son of mine?" She coughed again and then added,

"Worthless bum."

Joanna had to smile at this. "No, Lou, nothing. And with each day that goes by, I'm getting more convinced it might stay that way."

She heard the metallic click of Louise's cigarette lighter and then a puff as she blew out the smoke. "Well, Jo, I wish there was more I could do from my end. I tried calling Betty but she hasn't heard anything from him either. She'll let me know if he does turn up over there and I'll pass anything I find out along to you. I don't think we've heard the last from him. But let me tell you something, Joanna," Louise paused, sucking in another drag of her cigarette. "I've always thought you were a pretty resourceful person. It's not going to be easy, but you'll find a way to manage. Take it from someone who knows the territory."

When Joanna hung up she didn't know whether talking with Louise had encouraged her or only put things in a harsher light. Louise did indeed 'know the territory'. Larry's father had not been much of a parent while he was growing up. Joanna had known him only briefly before he'd succumbed to emphysema a year after they were married. It was long enough to figure out that Larry's less attractive habits had been learned at home. Louise's tough exterior was a survival tactic Joanna was beginning to understand.

## ~ Four ~

She dreamed of her mother that night, not as she had been those last few months when her illness and the chemotherapy treatments had made her a frail, hollow-eyed ghost, but as the sturdy, smiling woman who greeted her each morning. Joanna was a child in the dream, happily swinging on her backyard swing. It was early morning, long shadows holding the dew. She pulled hard on the ropes and rose into each arch, her bare legs flashed in and out of the golden light just reaching the yard. Over the rush of air flowing past her came the sounds of her mother singing. She got off the swing and tiptoed through the damp grass to stand on the porch looking in at the window. Her mother seemed unaware of her. She moved gracefully about the kitchen getting dishes from the cupboard, lifting hot muffins from the oven, stirring oatmeal bubbling on the stove, all the while singing a sweet song. Joanna strained to catch the words but only the tune was clear. Her mother's contented expression mirrored the tune's happiness. A chill air swept the porch. It was coming, but she did not turn to see its shadowy advance towards the house. And as she stood watching, she knew without a doubt that her mother was out of reach, caught in this happy scene, innocent of a looming darkness that the child-Joanna could sense reaching into the yard. How she wanted to pound on the window with her small fists, shout and warn her mother of the danger. Powerless to lift a warning hand, her arms hung helpless, caught between the tide of death and the vision of innocent happiness. When her mother finally paused and looked over the table set for breakfast, Joanna knew what would come next. She nodded, pleased with the preparations, and then stepped lightly through the door towards the stairs. The dream's last image was her mother's voice calling, "Joanna? Joanna, come down now! It's time for breakfast."

Joanna rolled over with a groan and blinked her eyes, needing a minute to realize she was in Kim's apartment. Gwen stirred but didn't waken. Joanna took a deep breath to calm herself. It had been months since she'd been troubled by the nightmare. Knowing she wouldn't fall back to sleep for a while, she got up quietly and went to the living room where she turned on the television low, flipping through the channels until she found an old movie.

The dream was accurate in only some of its details. The happy contentment that radiated from the dream-mother was seldom seen in real life. At times her mother's smile barely hid a sadness all too clear to Joanna, even when she was quite young. There were spells when a somber quiet settled in the house, its wraithlike presence insinuating itself between her and her mother. And, when she was old enough to see it, between her mother and her father.

The passing years hadn't provided all the answers. She was still finding clues to this mystery. One lay in the fact that Sylvia Everson had been an only child and had always longed for a sister or brother. Joanna enjoyed her mother's telling the story about how one of Edward Smales' attractions was his large family with his three sisters and one brother. His mother's sometimes chilly personality was outweighed by his jovial, good-hearted father who had welcomed his son's bride with real affection. Plans were for several children of their own and Joanna's arrival within eighteen months of their wedding was a joyous event. Three years followed with no new baby and no answer as to why. Finally there was a second pregnancy, the nine months passing uneventfully.

It was Phyllis who confided the details of her brother's birth when Joanna was fourteen. She could no longer bear not knowing what had gone on. Phyllis described the happy preparations getting the baby's room ready, setting up the crib Joanna had outgrown, presents from the family baby shower gaily displayed. Sylvia's labor had gone easily but when the little boy emerged, he was blue and struggling for breath. All efforts to save him failed; his short life lasting but two days' time. Even though years had passed, Phyllis wiped away tears the day she told all of this to Joanna while she sat motionless in her aunt's kitchen, hearing the full story at last.

Paul Edward Smales was buried in Maple Grove Cemetery. Joanna wasn't allowed to visit her brother's grave until she was ten. Perhaps her mother thought she should be shielded from the loss that had never let go of her. His name was rarely spoken but his small presence lingered at the edge of her growing up.

Joanna would sometimes sneak into the room that was to have been Paul's and carefully open the bottom dresser drawer. In it was the never-used layette wrapped in crinkly tissue, and the folded white paper with his tiny footprint made in the hours he had lived. She would place her hand beside it, measuring it, and tried to imagine what it would have been like to hold her little brother. Only once had her mother found her there, holding the green-knitted booties against her cheek. She hadn't spoken, hadn't scolded her as Joanna feared she would. Her eyes had held the deepest sadness but no reproach as she rewrapped the baby clothes, tucked them away, and then gently, ever so gently, slid the drawer closed. Then she'd slowly straightened and led Joanna out of the room. That was the last time Joanna had opened that drawer. That was when she had finally been taken to see his grave.

Joanna felt her eyelids drooping. She clicked off the television and sat for a moment in the silence before getting up and returning to the bedroom.

The two inches of snow that had fallen overnight edged the brick walkways of the campus quad and sparkled in the bright midday light. Her lunch finished, Joanna was sitting alone near a window in the snack bar thinking how the fresh whiteness had vastly improved the past weeks' dinginess.

One more day to the weekend. She was pleased and relieved

with how things were going after only four days of their new routine. Alita had readily agreed to her request to pick Gwen up at school and had set up a small table and chair for her to do her homework while she waited for Joanna. Yesterday, to Gwen's delight, she'd even given her a job dusting and straightening book shelves. At the apartment Gwen took great pride in washing the dishes and was planning to do the vacuuming when the weekend arrived. Kim and she were becoming thick as thieves, as her mother would have said. Last night it had been Kim who read her her nightly story, the two of them giggling over the antics of Amelia Bedelia. Not even a week since they'd left Green Glade and Joanna was starting to feel that she could draw a deep breath.

"Joanna?"

Startled, she looked up into the blue eyes of Scott McFadden, her instructor from the writing course. He was holding a tray with a salad plate and a can of soda. "Mr. McFadden...hi! How are you?"

"Just fine, thanks. I noticed you sitting over here and wondered if you wanted some company for a few minutes." His warm smile was the same one he'd used so well to put them all at ease as a roomful of novice writers back in the fall. It hadn't taken long to learn that his personal interest was genuine and that he seemed to enjoy nothing more than helping them discover their talents as writers.

"Why sure. I was just sort of daydreaming over my coffee before I have to get back to work. Please sit down if you like."

"Thanks," he said and settled himself at the table. "But one thing, as I tried to impress on you guys in class, I much prefer 'Scott' to Mr. McFadden. It always makes me look around to see if my father's come up behind me."

She laughed and a blush rose to her cheeks. It didn't help matters that he was also a nice-looking man, thirty-something, and someone who would draw any woman's eye if he passed on the street. "I'll certainly try to remember that...Scott."

This wasn't the first time they'd talked since the course

ended. Telling them all he had become their lifetime 'Writing Cheerleader', he'd explained that whenever their paths crossed he'd always want to know where they were with their 'writing lives'. True to his word, the four or five times he'd seen her on campus, he'd greeted her with his cheery hello and then inquired about her writing efforts. Once he'd even stopped in at the Continuing Ed office and had chatted with her for fifteen minutes.

Now here he was sitting across from her looking pleased at her getting out his first name. "So, you know my routine, how've you been doing on your writing? Last time we talked you said you were working in your journal. That's great writing practice."

"Oh, I keep it where I can get to it. Then things got a little hectic with work and all. And then just last week my daughter and I had to move." A blush threatened again.

He held up a hand. "Please, Joanna. I don't mean to put you on the spot. We 'Writing Cheerleaders' don't want to become just plain old pests." She smiled at his gentle joke. "You know, I'm offering a course in short story writing during summer session. You'd started a dandy one last fall. Think you'd be able to join the class?"

"Well, I'd love to consider it. At the moment things are sort of up in the air for my summer. Thanks, though, for telling me about it." She glanced at her watch. "Listen, I don't mean to be rude, but my lunch break's about over." She took one more swallow of her coffee.

There was an unmistakable twinkle in his eyes as he leaned forward. "Hey, I've got an idea. See what you think. Why don't you get some more work done on your story and then we'll make a date to get together and I'll look it over."

"Really? I mean, I haven't done much more with it. I...I'm not even sure I would know what more could be done to it. But it is so nice of you to..."

"Would you find it at all interesting to try?"

She'd slid to the edge of her chair, her hands poised on

either side of the tray. A small voice told her not to pass up this wonderful offer. "Yes, I guess I would want to try it but only if it's not asking too much. I know how busy you are and all..."

Her answer seemed to please him. He leaned back and smiled reassuringly. "Let's do this.  Is this your lunch time every day?" She nodded. "Okay then. Next Thursday, bring your story to work with you, whatever you've got done, and we'll meet right about here in the snack bar. Twelve-thirty?"

She nodded again and stood up to go. "Okay. At twelve-thirty. Thanks so much, Mister...I mean, Scott. Have...have a good week."

"And you too, Joanna. See you then."

On her way to pick up Gwen from school, Joanna wondered what had possessed her to agree to the idea.

She frowned and squinted against the slanting rays of the late afternoon sun. Some unexpected free time had presented itself when Alita had chased her home early for the weekend a little after three. Gwen was staying overnight at Julie's house and Kim wouldn't be home until five. Thursday's clear weather had held over beckoning her out for a walk when she'd reached the apartment. She'd changed into comfortable clothes and sneakers and set out, turning in the direction of the park at the end of the block.

She breathed deeply as she strode along, a hint of spring in the mild March air. The weekend lay ahead with nothing dire to have to handle. And tomorrow she and Gwen were to visit her aunt and uncle in Berlin.

At the park entrance she leaned against the bridge railing for a while watching the water as it foamed and tumbled nosily over the rocks. When water splashed high enough a rainbow flashed in the spray. The damp air rising held a wet, clean smell, the promise of spring with its new beginnings. Perhaps at Green Glade Court tender shoots were stirring in the cold ground by the trailer steps.

The only other person in sight was a woman walking her

dog. A car passed behind her on the street. Otherwise she had the place to herself. The picnic tables were piled in one of the pavilions but one bench had been left next to a wall facing the stream. She sat down on it and leaned back, closing her eyes. Like a child in a secret hideout, a delicious sense of stolen time came to her. For several long minutes she sat in the quiet pushing the week's worries away, focusing only on the muted rushing of Eight Mile Creek.

She rose reluctantly and started back, pausing again on the bridge and looked upstream to where the creek rounded a bend on its way into Rockford Mills. With the sun sunk lower in the west, the swirling water was now in shadow, gray and opaque. The rainbows had vanished. Some twenty miles to the south the creek flowed past an isolated clearing just off Stone Road. She couldn't help wondering if the spot was still popular among high school kids. In a few more weeks likely the first raft of teenagers would appear launching a new season of beer parties, lighting the night with trash-fed bonfires, pairing off to steam up car windows.

Her hands gripped the railing then as unbidden images stirred in a hidden depth. She turned away and walked briskly up the street, trying to outpace the memory of that dark May night before it could seize her.

"Here's to a great new partnership!" Kim raised her can of diet Pepsi.

Joanna grinned broadly and clunked her root beer against Kim's. "To our great new partnership. Gotta tell you, partner, it sure feels good to get most things settled and find a possible bonus too." They were sitting across from each other in a booth at Sal's Pizzeria. It was nearing eight o'clock. Having spent an hour and a half working out the details of their budget, Kim had suggested they go out to eat and celebrate the agreement. Joanna was feeling especially pleased that at least on paper, she should be actually coming out with a little extra each month.

"I'll be feeling even better when our pizza's done. Working

with money always makes me hungry," Kim said. "I'll bet Gwen's having a good time at her friend's."

"I'm sure she is. She deserved a treat for being so good about all these changes for us. Actually, I have a question for you, Kim. Since we've been getting our arrangements worked out, this would probably be a good time to ask it."

Kim arched her eyebrows. "What's that?"

"With Gwen and me moving in, is it going to put some sort of damper on your social life? The last thing I want is to be in your way. I expected Gary would have been around this week, but he wasn't. He hasn't been staying away because we're there, I hope?"

"No, that's not it at all. He's been busy helping his parents with some sort of remodeling job at their house. And they've been doing inventory at the store. We've got plans to go out tomorrow night."

Joanna didn't know Gary all that well, but she'd always had a good impression of him. He was assistant manager of Napa Auto Parts downtown. They'd been dating for about a year and while he had expressed his interest in getting married, Kim had said she wasn't ready to make things permanent. Considering that he was a hard worker, easy going but with a sense of humor, and not too full of himself for a guy with such dark good looks, Joanna wondered at times what Kim was waiting for.

As if she had read Joanna's mind Kim said, "Actually I've rather liked not having Gary breathing down my neck this week."

"Breathing down your neck?"

"Yeah. When Christine moved out, Gary sort of tried to move in. Not that he hadn't stayed over before when Christine and I shared the place, but after a few days of his being there round the clock, I suddenly realized what he was doing." She toyed with her can of soda, pursing her lips. "It's not like we haven't talked about living together at some point. And I know I told you how he had a ring for me at Christmas, but I won't be rushed. It was just too...too presumptuous of him to think with Christine gone it was the signal to go ahead." She smiled brightly. "So, you can see that I like having you guys with me for more than one reason."

"Well, good. I'm glad we're useful in some sort of way," Joanna said adding, "Really when you think about it, men can be a real pain in the neck way too much of the time."

Kim laughed at this and raised her soda in another salute. "Here! Here! I'll drink to that."

"It's getting a little wild over here, ladies." Sal placed their pizza on the table with a flourish and grinned at them both. "You're sure it's just soda in that can?"

"Careful, Sal," said Kim. "We're busy bad-mouthing men and we wouldn't want to drag you into this."

"One of those Fridays, is it? I've got your message." He retreated with a chuckle.

"Mmm," said Joanna after a few bites of the mushroom pizza, "I don't know if I've ever tasted a more delicious pizza. Guess we'd better count Sal as one of the few good guys."

"Probably so." Kim wiped her mouth with a napkin. "You know, that's part of the problem that there are just too damn few of them. I mean that seriously." Joanna laughed and nodded. This spurred Kim on. "And here's another thing...remember how when we were in high school that's all most of us girls could think about? 'Boys, boys, boys'...'boy-crazy'. All that stuff. All the things we did to make ourselves attractive enough to catch someone's eye. All that emotional energy. And no one tells you until it's too late what the real score is or to watch out for all the rats out there. God, what a bummer!"

"We were sold a bill of goods, all right." Joanna put on a smile. Kim couldn't know the bitter truth that lay behind her response nor how her words lifted a corner of the uncomfortable memory she'd pushed away earlier. It was an incident she kept buried as firmly as she could. Eric Miller all too well fit the description of a rat that someone should have warned her about. "Wolves in sheep's clothing," she murmured, an involuntary shiver crossing her shoulders.

"I'll say. Rats, wolves, they're all the same." Kim said. She studied Joanna closely a moment. "By the look on your face, you've met one or two. Must have been a boy in Berlin?"

Joanna couldn't help but sigh. "Oh yeah. Someone I try to forget." She took another slice of pizza. "After Eric, that was his name, Larry looked like a saint. My mistake was thinking that just because a guy didn't manhandle you and brought home a paycheck pretty regularly, that he was the answer to a girl's prayers. What a dimwit I was." Her laugh sounded hollow even to her.

"Don't be so hard on yourself, Jo. I've made more bad judgements than I care to admit. It's one of the reasons I haven't marched up any church aisles yet."

Joanna nodded. "Mmhmm. I hear you. But if I could play devil's advocate for a minute, Gary doesn't seem too bad a risk."

"Maybe not. Anyway, I'm still hedging my bets. Well, would you look at that." Her gaze had shifted to a point behind Joanna. She turned to see Gary waving through the window at them, a happy grin on his face. Just behind him stood a taller, lanky man whose face was indistinct in the night's shadows. "Looks like we're going to have company, Joanna. I hope you don't mind."

"Hey, good-lookin'," Gary said when he reached their booth, "I thought I recognized your car parked out front. Joanna, nice to see you again. This is my friend, Les Dawes. I'm not sure you two know each other."

She took the hand Les extended, feeling the weight of his blue eyes as he turned to her. "No, we don't. But Kim's spoken of you before."

As he released her hand a slow smile nudged up the corners of his lips beneath a neatly trimmed moustache. "Well, let's hope you haven't believed more than half of it."

Gary said, "Mind if we sit down with you two?"

Joanna moved over to allow room for Les on her side of the booth. Gary slid in beside Kim, slinging his arm around her shoulders and giving her a lingering kiss. Kim was beginning to look happier with the situation. Les stayed mostly quiet sipping his Coke and flipping the top of a cigarette lighter open and shut. Gary wanted to know how the move had gone. Kim gave an enthusiastic description of Gwen and how much she was enjoying having her there.

"You must be a proud mother," Les spoke up, turning towards Joanna. "She sounds like a great kid."

"I'll tell you guys, we should have a lot more parents like Joanna," added Kim. Both Gary and Les looked at her with obvious admiration, and Joanna felt herself blushing.

When they got back to the apartment later, Joanna thanked her for her compliment.

"You're absolutely welcome and you also totally deserve it. Honestly, Jo, I don't know if I could be doing half as well trying to land on my feet like you have and managing to be a good mom all at the same time."

"Better stop now, Kim, before my head gets too big for this place," Joanna said, making Kim laugh. She stifled a yawn. "Well, what I do know is that it's a pretty exhausting business. I'm glad I don't have a heavy date tomorrow night like you do. I'm already looking forward to going to bed with a book by nine o'clock."

"No rest for the wicked, I guess," Kim responded with another laugh and turned to go upstairs. Joanna started towards her room. "Hey, Jo..."

"Yeah?"

Kim was leaning over the banister part way up the stairs. Even in the shadowy light Joanna could see her impish grin. "I noticed that Les was pretty impressed by you, too."

Joanna laughed. "That and fifty cents would get me a ride on the New York subway. Or is it seventy-five these days? But it was sweet of him to say what he did." She waggled a finger at Kim. "Hey, now don't go cooking up anything for me."

"That wasn't exactly on my mind, and besides, he does have a pretty steady friend at the moment. I just couldn't help but notice, that's all."

Joanna took advantage of Gwen's absence to do some reading before she went to sleep.    Before turning off the bedside light she looked over at her daughter's neatly made bed picturing Gwen deep in sleep in her little friend's bedroom. She smiled at the picture it gave her, happy in the thought that Gwen must have had fun that evening.

She switched off the light and pulled up the blanket, blinking until the street light painted its now familiar line across the ceiling. "And she'll have fun seeing Phyllis and George tomorrow too," she murmured and closed her eyes, holding onto that warm thought.

# ~ Five ~

She woke the next morning refreshed from the best night's sleep she'd had in a long while. After picking Gwen up at Julie's, they headed for Berlin. The spicy fragrance of fresh-baked gingerbread greeted them as they entered Phyllis Mannington's kitchen. She greeted them with enveloping hugs, Joanna savoring the moments of being held against Phyllis's ample-bosomed person, her cheek pressed against the her aunt's soft skin. Her bright blue eyes twinkled behind her wire-rimmed glasses when she released Joanna from the embrace, reminding Joanna of her childhood fantasy that she was secretly Mrs. Santa Claus.

Gwen whooped with delight to hear that her cousins Christopher and Allison were due to arrive in a short while. They were Marie's children, Phyllis's middle child.

"I thought you and Mimi would enjoy a chance to see each other," Phyllis said. "If I'm right I don't think you've seen each other since the Holidays."

"I'm afraid that's true, Aunt Phyl, Mimi and I haven't been doing well at keeping in touch." With only ten months difference in their ages, since childhood she and Marie shared a special friendship. She'd graduated a year ahead of Joanna and tried a year of college before opting for what she called her 'm-r-s' degree. She'd married her high school sweetheart, Lonnie Graham, and moved to Syracuse. Their mutual joke was that neither of them had been college material. Phyllis at least could brag about her other two, a son and daughter with their degrees from state colleges. Lynne was an elementary teacher, and Danny, the youngest, was working his way up in a Rochester business.

"Well, here they are," came George's greeting as he entered the kitchen. He gathered them both in a bear hug, planting a whiskery kiss on each of their faces. "Joanna, don't you look good," he said as she stepped back.

"I'm glad you think so, Uncle George. That means I'm doing better than I thought I was."

"How about me, Uncle George?" asked Gwen who still had her arms around his waist.

He touched her nose lightly with a broad finger. "You, my dear, always look like a million dollars." Gwen beamed up at him. "Want to help me with some work I'm doing down in the basement? I could use a helper."

Gwen was all too happy to be extended such an invitation and the two of them disappeared in the direction of the cellar stairs. Phyllis was washing the dishes.

"Something I can do to help, Aunt Phyl?"

"I'm nearly done. You just sit and relax. The tea's probably ready so pour yourself a cup."

Joanna did as she was told, sinking into the kitchen's familiar warm embrace while she listened to family news Phyllis shared. The pot of tea sat steeping under its faded red cozy on the round oak table. Over it hung the green-shaded brass lamp casting its mellow glow against the gray morning. A flurry of geraniums blazed on the wide windowsills.

Phyllis was the glue that held the family together. It had been her endless strength and steadying presence that had gotten them through the ordeal of Sylvia's battle with cancer. Joanna marveled at how she had coped, watching her younger sister who was so dear, fall ill and slip away.

"Well, if it isn't just wonderful to see you sitting here in my kitchen," she said, settling herself across from Joanna. Her smile deepened the netting of fine lines around her eyes. "You know, there are times it doesn't seem possible that you and Mimi aren't teeny boppers planning to go off to see a Saturday matinee in Rockford Mills. And me and your mother sitting here having tea while you were gone, hoping you were having fun but behaving too." She paused, letting the picture warm them both. "Not that I live my life in the past, mind you, but when you came through the door this morning with Gwen who's so grown up and all, it's a reminder of how time's gone by."

Joanna nodded, "If that's not the truth. But I can tell you, Aunt Phyl, it's reassuring to me that your kitchen stays just like it's always been."

"Mimi says the same thing. Your Uncle George and I spend a good part of each day in here which no doubt shows, I'm sure. Of course maybe if I did things differently, say ran up and down stairs a few more times each day, I'd still have my girlish figure." She laughed at her own joke, then lifted her cup and fixed Joanna with a gentle but steady look. "So now, Joanna, what's this your father tells me about you and Gwen moving into the Mills? When we talked last, was it maybe the beginning of February, you told me Larry was still working in Pennsylvania."

Her directness didn't surprise Joanna. What countless times had she sat at this table having arrived with a problem to discuss, knowing her aunt would keep her confidences, and that she'd leave feeling better about things and a key to a solution. Phyllis sat waiting to listen once more.

First, Joanna poured herself more tea and then looked up. "Well, he did start the job. As far as I know he's still there."

"Mmhmm." It was Phyllis's indication to go on.

"You might have guessed things were getting tight for us since last fall." Phyllis nodded. Joanna reflected for a long second, catching her own wavery reflection on the amber tea's steaming surface. "Well," she sighed, "they were worse than that when he left. I thought maybe we'd turned a corner when his first check came in the mail. But his second one bounced and there've been no more." Cataldo's leering grin surfaced. She pushed it aside. "Luckily I had a chance to move in with a girlfriend for a few months which will give me a chance to figure out what to do next."

"You haven't heard from him then?"

"No...and it's gotten to the point, Aunt Phyl, I don't really expect to." She sighed again. "Things weren't good between us when he left.    But probably that wouldn't surprise you either."

Phyllis refilled her own cup before answering. "You're right. It doesn't surprise me. All the same, I never thought Larry was such a bad sort, Joanna. You know that. We've discussed this all before." Joanna nodded. How true that was. She had shared more with Phyllis about her marriage than anyone else. Phyllis' expression grew stern. "But walking away from his family, if that's what he's done, is something else entirely. There's no excuse for that sort of behavior. I think what my first concern is about you and Gwen, and how you're going to manage. Your Uncle George and I will do anything we can to help out, but I'd hope you already know that."

Joanna reached for her hand and squeezed it. "Of course I do. Thanks, Aunt Phyllis. It's awfully reassuring to know you're both here if I need you. For now I think we're managing things okay."

The loud rumble of a car with a questionable muffler signaled Marie's arrival. Her car was an even older rattletrap than the Nova. Gwen came running up from the basement and raced to open the kitchen door. Marie swept in with six-year-old Allison and four-year-old Christopher in tow. She was wearing a suspiciously loose shirt over her jeans. Joanna decided to save the question until the kids were out of earshot. First there was Phyllis's gingerbread to enjoy served around in generous pieces still warm with whipped cream melting invitingly on the top. Soon the girls were off to another room to play with Allison's Barbie dolls.

"Boy, the older those two get, the more they remind me of the two of us when we were kids, don't you think, Jo?" Marie held a complaining Christopher tightly while she finished wiping his hands and face and then he dashed after the girls like a projectile fired from a slingshot. She came and sat down next to Joanna.

"Yes they do.  I hope they have half the fun we did." She reached over to pat Marie's abdomen. "Is this what I think it is?" she asked with a grin.

Marie beamed. "I knew I probably wouldn't hide it from you. Mom didn't tell you then?" She exchanged a bemused look with her mother.

Phyllis winked mischievously. "I thought you'd enjoy surprising her."

"It's a surprise all right," said Joanna. "Hasn't anyone warned you about not letting your kids outnumber you? So when's this newest Graham set to make his or her entrance?" Joanna thought of Marie and Lonnie as likely the world's greatest parents. Lonnie's work as assistant manager of a grocery store yielded only modest wages. Marie's work as a part-time cashier brought in a little more. Still, their schedule was arranged so that one of them was always at home. "We didn't have kids so someone else could raise them," were words Joanna had heard more than once from her.

"October fifteenth, give or take a few days, as usual. We've got to plan on you guys coming to Syracuse pretty soon. It's been too long since we did anything together, your family and mine."

Hesitating only a moment, Joanna said, "You may as well know, Mimi, that Gwen and I have been pretty much on our own since New Year's. We've just moved into Rockford Mills with a friend who had room at her apartment."

Marie's face went blank. "And Larry?"

"I really don't know." Joanna was surprised at how coolly she could speak about it. "He took that construction job in Pennsylvania like he told everyone at Christmas and was planning to send money as soon as he got situated."

"Has he done that?"

"Just one time. Well, twice, but the second check wasn't any good and he hung up on me when we last talked on the phone." Joanna saw Phyllis shake her head. "I'll be honest with you. When he left I had a feeling it might be permanent and the more weeks that go by the more it's looking like that."

Marie placed a hand on Joanna's arm, her eyes troubled.

"Oh, Jo, I'm so sorry to hear this. It must be you knew this, Mom?"

"Yes, Joanna had a chance to tell me before you got here." They exchanged looks.

"I see. Jo, I hardly know what to say."

Joanna gave her a grateful smile. "It's okay, Mimi. In a way it's a relief that you and Aunt Phyl know. Listen, I do need to ask one favor of both of you. As far as my father knows, Larry's keeping in touch. For now please don't tell him otherwise, okay?"

Marie nodded. "And Gwen?"

"I've told her that her father's job makes it hard for him to call us. It's maybe a little early to know, but for Gwen's sake I hope he's going to keep in touch somehow no matter what happens between him and me."

Marie took Joanna's hand and squeezed it. "I hope so too. I can't imagine him wanting to hurt his little girl."

At the end of the afternoon, Marie walked out with them to the car. She hugged Joanna tightly. "Don't get out of touch with me again, okay? I've got your new number so I'll be calling in a couple weeks to see how you two are doing. When the weather gets nicer we'll need to get the kids together."

"That sounds like fun for all of us. Thanks, Mimi, I really appreciate it." Her throat tightened. "Now get back inside out of this cold air before you catch something."

The dining room window was full of people waving goodbye when she backed the car out of the driveway. "Toot the horn, Mommy!" Gwen pumped both arms like a crazed cheerleader.

A gritty snow was swirling from a leaden sky as they left Berlin behind. Gwen hummed happily to herself. Joanna smiled. "I know someone who's had a pretty nice weekend so far. First an overnight with her best friend, and then seeing her favorite cousins."

"Uh huh. And Aunt Phyllis and Aunt Mimi and Uncle George too. Don't forget them."

"You're right. I wouldn't want to forget them. Think you'll have enough energy left to do the dishes tonight?"

"Sure!" She tapped her toes on the car floor. "Mommy?"

"What?"

"If Julie comes over to play with me sometime like you said she could, will she be able to stay overnight with me?" Joanna thought she heard a note of uncertainty in Gwen's voice.

"Probably. As long as her mother thinks it's okay. She's stayed over before." Gwen offered no response right away. "Oh, I think I know what you might be thinking. Are you wondering where the two of you would sleep? Well, we can take care of that."

"How?"

"You and Julie would sleep in our room and I'd sleep on Kim's couch. I'm pretty sure Kim wouldn't mind for just one night. And another thing, I hope by the end of the summer you and I will have our own place again."

"Maybe another trailer?"

"Maybe. Or an apartment." Gwen fell silent and Joanna thought she'd tired of the topic. She turned on the radio.

"Mommy?"

"Uh huh?"

"When Daddy comes back, will there be room for him to stay with us at Kim's?"

Perhaps she should have been, but she was unprepared for that question. She cleared her throat. "Well, if he wants to visit us, I'm sure we'd find room for him. So you don't have to worry about that."

The question she asked herself silently was just how much was Larry thinking about his daughter at all.

The found Kim in the kitchen simmering onions for spaghetti sauce. "Mmm. Every kitchen I've been in today smells great," Joanna told her. "So give me a job to do."

"You'll find the pot I use for pasta over in that cupboard." She pointed with the wooden spoon she was using. "Hey, I've got a favor to ask of you, Jo."

"I'm all ears."

"Now please don't think I've deliberately done this because I haven't. Gary called a little while ago. Les's date fell through for our bowling plans tonight. And so we were wondering if..."

"If I'd be willing to fill in," Joanna finished for her. "Good Lord." She meant the last more as a statement than an exclamation.

"You're mad that I asked you?"

"No, not that. I just saw where you were going." She set the pot in the sink and turned on the water. "Well, for one thing there's no babysitter for Gwen."

"There could be. I called Becky across the street and she said she could do it. Naturally I wasn't sure what you'd say, but I went ahead and checked things out with her. Do you like to bowl?"

"Sort of." She carried the brimming pot to the stove and Kim stepped aside for her to set it on the burner. "Why does this feel just a bit like I'm being maneuvered into something?"

"If you'd rather not go, that's fine. Maneuvering you into anything wasn't the idea, believe me." There was a note of apology in her voice.

"Hey, I was just teasing about that. I guess it's that I wasn't expecting to walk into this when we got here."

"Oh, good. You sounded ticked off at me. But it *is* just bowling and probably drinks somewhere afterwards." She poked Joanna with the handle of the wooden spoon she was using. "Think of it as a chance to enjoy yourself. And anyway, Les has got a girlfriend more or less."

Joanna considered this. "Hmm. A chance to have some fun. Would it be clear to everyone that I'd just be his bowling partner?"

"Absolutely. And I thought of another thing. It would give Gwen and Becky a chance to get to know each other a little before Becky starts watching her after school on Monday."

It had been a long time since she'd so much as gone to the movies. "Well, it's especially true about Gwen needing to get to know Becky."

"So you're considering it?"

"Well, yes, I guess so. Anyway, I'd hate to think I was a stick in the mud at the age of twenty-eight." She laughed at that thought. Suddenly the whole thing looked like a good idea after all. "Guess you've got yourself a bowling sub."

# ~ Six ~

Joanna tried unsuccessfully to stop a yawn. Through the smoky air of the Rusty Nail the clock over the bar showed a few minutes to eleven. The greasy remains of a plate of chicken wings sat on the table along with an array of wadded napkins and mostly empty beer bottles. "Looks like someone's had about enough for one day." Les's husky voice rumbled over the din of laughter and the country and western music booming from the jukebox. "Hope it's not the company," he added, white teeth flashing. He took a last drag of his cigarette and stubbed it out in the ash tray already half full of butts, both his and Gary's. His eyes met hers again.

She raised her voice to be heard over the noise. "No, it's not the company. Mostly it's that I'm not much of a night owl." Both statements were true, even though the first half hour after they'd left Kim's she'd wished she was at home with a book as her original plans had been. But other than having the lowest bowling score that for which she endured good-natured ribbing, the evening had turned out to be surprising fun. Les had proven to be good company in his quiet, laid back manner. He'd showed her a better way to hold the bowling ball and where to set it down on the alley as she released it. A modest improvement in her score resulted but they'd still finished well behind Kim and Gary's score. Though slow-paced, the conversation had never entirely stalled. Somewhere along the line they'd discovered they were both mystery fans and traded suggestions of good books and writers. She had been surprised to find he read at all and silently chastised herself for passing such quick judgement of him.

"Well, let me finish my beer and you two can chauffeur us back to the apartment," said Kim. "I think I'm about ready to call it a night myself." She and Gary had pushed their chairs together on their side of the table. Despite what Kim had said to her the night before, Joanna was struck by how much she clung to Gary and the teasing, playful way they had with each other.

When Gary stopped the car in front of the apartment, Les surprised her by pressing a five dollar bill into her hand. "I want you to put this towards your babysitter, and I won't take 'no' for an answer. Now let's get out and let these two have their fun alone for a few minutes." He took her elbow as she stepped from the car. Once outside, he turned up the collar of his denim jacket and lit up a fresh smoke.

She studied his rugged face as he peered absently into the night. What had spurred his generosity? "That's really nice of you, Les," she said, holding up the folded bill and then tucking it into her pocket. "I'd really like to argue but I guess you won't let me. Anyway, thanks for taking me on as your bowling partner."

He nodded, and blew a line of smoke out of the corner of his mouth directing it away from her. "So, what's a good time tomorrow for me to stop by and check out that car of yours?"

She had almost forgotten his offer. At some point during the evening she'd mentioned being worried by an odd sound from the Nova's engine. It had started just as she and Gwen had driven into Rockford Mills from their trip to Berlin, considerably dampening the good mood the day had otherwise produced. "Really anytime is okay. You're sure you don't mind?"

"Nope. Not at all. Some time around one or two then?"

"That'll be fine. It's really great of you to take the time to do this." Not sure of how to bring things to an end, she shifted her weight to her other foot and pulled her jacket around more tightly against the night's cold air. Kim emerged from the car with a giggly laugh and blew a kiss back inside.

Flicking the rest of his cigarette into the street, Les nodded a last time at her and got into the front seat. "All right, ladies. Behave yourselves now." By the dashboard light Joanna thought she saw him wink as he shut the door.

"So, that wasn't such a bad evening, was it?" Kim asked as they walked up the driveway towards the back door. "You're not still mad at me for setting it all up, I hope."

"No, of course I'm not mad at you. I had a good time."

"Great! I thought you would. And I think you needed a change of pace, Jo."

"You may be right. My Aunt Phyllis would agree with you, I'm sure."

Tired as she was, Joanna lay for a while in the dark listening to Gwen's breathing. Kim was right. It had felt good to just relax and talk about inconsequential things. It had been good to laugh. For a few hours the weight of ordinary concerns had been left behind.

She rolled over and shut her eyes, wanting to drift into sleep and hold that feeling just a little longer.

"I like doing our homework together, Mommy." Gwen had paused in the middle of her arithmetic assignment to grin at her mother who was mulling over her short story on the other side of the kitchen table.

Joanna smiled back. "Me, too, Gwen. How many more problems do you have?"

Gwen tapped her pencil down the margin of the worksheet. "Five. When I'm done can I watch TV?"

"Oh, for a little while I guess, but it's a school night, so only until seven-thirty and then it's bath time."

"Okay." Gwen returned to her work, her lips pressed together, her eyebrows lowered in concentration. Moments like this often transported Joanna back to Gwen's babyhood. How she had loved to tiptoe into the room where Gwen was napping. Leaning on the crib railing, she would study her daughter's beautiful and innocent face with her perfectly-shaped eyebrows, dark lashes closed in sleep, her rosebud mouth occasionally moving as if suckling at the nipple in her baby dreams.

Watching her now, Joanna smiled. Gary had talked Kim into spending the evening at his place. As she left she had whispered to Joanna that she might be gone until tomorrow morning. It had reassured Joanna to know that Kim was keeping up her usual life even with them there.

The pages of her short story were spread out before her. She'd almost hoped she wouldn't be able to find it after all, but the red binder in which she kept her writing work had been at the top of the third box she opened down in the basement. For the first twenty minutes she had enjoyed rereading her class journal and the poems she's written for Scott's course. His penciled comments in the margins were full of helpful and positive comments. The last project had been to write a short story and hers had grown to four and a half pages by the time the semester ended.

Her main character who she had named Cassandra had been modeled on Rachel Lupinski. Certainly the physical details matched Rachel exactly. The story idea had started out as a silly misunderstanding leading to a falling out between Cassandra and her best friend, Renee. Details of high school life as she remembered it from Berlin High fueled the plot. It had been the realism of the characters that had drawn the most praise from Scott and the class when she had read the story to them. But it had seemed like cheating that most of it was based on a real place and real people with only a few surface things changed.

"I'm done now." Gwen placed her homework paper carefully in her folder.

"Good for you. You've got half an hour to watch television."

Once Gwen had gone out of the kitchen, Joanna picked up the last page of her story and read it for the third time. She came to the end and slapped it down on the other sheets. "Shit," she said aloud, staring at the writing glumly. "I don't know what it is he expects of me." She got up abruptly and went to fill the tea kettle, setting it down on the stove with enough force that some of the water sloshed out.

The afternoon had not brought good news about the Nova. Les had had her get in and start the engine and then rev it a few times. After she'd turned it off, he poked about under the hood for several minutes while she hovered anxiously near by. Completing his silent investigation, he had straightened and lit a cigarette before saying anything. She had expected the news to be bad and it was. "Hate to tell you this, but your distributor looks about ready to go," he'd pulled on his moustache, looking sadly into the engine compartment. He'd offered to get the part for her wholesale and install it perhaps the following weekend. She'd asked the likely price and had trouble hiding her distress when he'd told her about eighty dollars. But the worse news was that it could break down on her anytime with little or no warning.

She listened to the water coming to a boil in the kettle. He'd been so sweet about saying he would take care of it for her. As he was leaving he'd told her not to worry about coming up with the money all at once. Perhaps she should call her father and ask if he could get it any cheaper.

"Damn cars." She lifted the screeching kettle from the burner and poured hot water in her cup. She sat down again at the table looking glumly at the pages of her story, dunking the tea bag up and down. When she'd first signed up for the writing course at Alita's urging, Larry had grumbled about babysitting. He bartered the favor, as he called it, into spending Friday or Saturday nights 'out with the boys'. The trade-off had seemed reasonable at first, even useful. Once Gwen had gone to bed, she had the trailer to herself. She'd make a pot of tea and sit at the small kitchen table with her writing pad, working on assignments, taking increasing pleasure in seeing her thoughts grow on the paper beneath her pen. Sometimes Larry would stumble in late and find her still writing. Occasionally he'd be in an amorous mood wanting sex. Usually she'd be ready to go to bed anyway, but sometimes his advances were an annoying interruption and she'd brush them off if she could, breathing a sigh or relief when he stumbled off to bed leaving her undisturbed.

"Damn Larry," she said to the empty kitchen and squeezed the hot liquid out of the tea bag.

Some ten minutes later the phone's ring startled her so that she nearly choked on the last swallow of her tea. Expecting it to be someone for Kim, she was surprised to have her father say hello.

"Dad," she sputtered, and coughed again. "Hi yourself."

"You got a cold?"

"No. Just swallowed some tea wrong. I was sitting here doing some work in the kitchen and when the phone rang, I jumped." She cleared her throat again. "There. Fully recovered, I hope. How are things in Berlin?"

"No major complaints from me. So, how's my granddaughter making out at the moment? Things going okay for you two?"

Joanna gave him the basics of how Gwen was doing and how successful the match with Becky promised to be for after school care. She mentioned their visit to Phyllis's and described how Marie and her family were doing. Gwen came in to ask who she was talking to and Joanna let her talk for a few minutes. By the time she got back on the phone, she'd decided to tell him about the car.

"So this Les you had look at it says it's the distributor?"

"Right."

"Hmm. Does he seem to know what he's doing?"

"Oh, yes. Kim vouched for him."

"And he says he can get it for around eighty?"

"Yes, that's right. Is that a good price? I was wondering if you could do any better."

"Not really. That's a fair price." There was silence for a moment. Gwen would be needing to get started with her bath. Joanna pinched the bridge of her nose, feeling the beginning of a headache. "Tell you what, Joanna. Have him order it and I'll be over to put it in next weekend."

"Okay, Dad. That sounds great. Listen, Gwen's got to have her bath and..."

"Right. Give me a call later in the week so I'll know whether you got the part. Give that little lady a kiss from her Grandpa." He cleared his throat. "And you have a good week for yourself."

"Thanks. You too." After she placed the phone in its receiver she realized she should have thanked him for calling.

It was nearly one in the morning. For two nights in a row now she'd lain awake past midnight unable to quiet the stream of thoughts and memories. Tonight she'd decided to heat some milk like her mother used to do for her when she was a child. This was the day she'd agreed to meet with Scott McFadden which was just one of the things keeping her awake. All she'd gotten done were two half-thought-out paragraphs to show him. The red folder lay on the kitchen counter so she wouldn't forget it in the morning.

The silent kitchen was lit only by the light on the stove. She sat at the table for a while nursing the cup of steaming milk, for the dozenth time moodily assessing her decisions of the past few months.

She had stopped things from sliding too far backwards for them, hadn't she? At least it seemed that way. And everyone was being so nice. Kim, Aunt Phyllis, Alita. And Les Dawes.

There weren't that many reasons to feel anxious, or so alone. But evidently some part of herself had yet to be convinced of that. She drew her knees up on the chair and clasped her arms about them, rocking ever so slightly from side to side.

When her legs demanded to be straightened, she got up and rinsed out the cup, setting it in the drain. Then she turned out the stove light and made her way back down the hall by the dim glow of the night light. She got back into bed.

Tears rose to her eyes and spilled over, almost forcing her back to the kitchen. If she had been any less tired, she probably would have done that. Instead, turning her face into the pillow, she cried as silently as she could manage, falling asleep at last, curled in a ball under the damp-edged blanket.

The next morning Alita picked up on her low spirits. "You're not your usual bright self today, Joanna." Joanna had come into Alita's office to get some files. "Things not going well this week?"

"A little car trouble, but I'm getting that taken care of. Otherwise, no complaints." She stooped to pull the folders she was after from the drawer. "I feel a little like I might be coming down with a cold. Thanks for asking." She directed a fleeting smile at Alita and escaped to her desk.

When Alita suggested that Joanna take a long lunch break, she'd taken advantage of it, spending twenty minutes resting on the couch in the ladies room with her eyes closed. She actually felt a little better and hoped a good lunch might help even more.

There was still Scott McFadden to face. She hadn't been able to think of a polite way to get out of it. At least with the longer time for lunch, she'd been able to get to the snack bar well in advance of his arrival, splurging on soup, a salad, and a sandwich. The red folder lurked on the corner of the table, making her feel like a kid with homework undone. She'd finished the soup and most of the sandwich when Scott appeared, waving to her from the line at the lunch counter.

"Hey, good to see you, Joanna," he greeted her when he reached the table, eyes alight. "Hope I haven't kept you waiting."

"No, you haven't. Alita was in a particularly generous mood today so I have a long lunch."

"She's got to be great to work for. What a fine woman she is."

Joanna nodded her agreement, watching him arrange his lunch on the table between them. Their conversation rambled around for a while, campus news and such. He asked questions about Gwen. How old was she. What grade in school. He

mentioned his own two kids, a boy and a girl somewhat older
than Gwen. Joanna knew he was divorced and wondered how
he managed his parental responsibilities. He asked if she'd
been to see 'Top Gun'.

"No, but it sounds good." She paused, her fork poised over
the remains of the salad. "I think the last movie I went to see
was 'The Muppet Movie' with my daughter. Not that I
wouldn't mind going more often. I love movies. But with
paying a babysitter and the price of a ticket, it's not a luxury I
can afford very often."

He looked at her a long moment as if assessing these facts,
and then he nodded. "I think I can imagine."

The conversation seemed snagged.

*Oh, god. Why did I come out with that? Does he think I
want him to feel sorry for me?* She checked her watch.

"Mr. Mc...I mean, Scott..." She tried not to blush but failed
and reached for her folder needing to do something.

"About to try to escape are you?" His crooked grin caught
her by surprise. "Oh, I saw you look at your watch. Unless you
really do have to get going. Here I've been chatting away when
we were going to look at your story today."

"Well, I...no, Alita doesn't need me back until one." She
mustered a half-smile and opened the folder. "Well, it's a little
embarrassing. I've got to be honest, there's just not much more
I could come up with." She handed the pages across to him.

"Not at all a problem, Joanna. I'm happy you took me up on
my offer. This kind of stuff isn't easy for lots of people." He
indicated her story. "Let's do this and make it a painless first
session. If you'll let me keep your draft, I'll review it and we'll
put our heads together next week. Okay with you?"

"That...that sounds fine. If you really...I mean, if you don't
mind taking the time. I know you're busy with your regular
classes and all."

He shook his head dismissing her words. "Not at all. Unless
you were stringing me along last term, you seemed to get a
kick out of writing. True?" His eyes mirrored a warm sincerity

impossible for her to miss.

"Well, yes."

"Then believe me, Joanna, doing something like this is a real pleasure for me." The fine lines at the corners of his eyes deepened with his smile. She met his gaze for a long moment. Then, to her horror, her eyes filled.

Once more her thoughts tumbled into disarray. She gathered up her things saying she suddenly remembered some work she had to finish by the end of the day. She heard herself agree to meet the following week. Then she was on her feet, heading across the snack bar in what she prayed was a dignified pace, hoping not to fall over a chair leg on the way out. In her head a scenario played in which she had burst into tears and been comforted against the strong chest of Scott McFadden.

# ~ *Seven* ~

Her father released the hood and closed it with a slam. "Guess that will hold you for a while, Jo."

Joanna nodded and blew on her cold hands. The temperature hadn't warmed past the forties despite the brightness of the late March sun. "Good. I need it to get us through the summer at least. I really appreciate both of you taking time out of your Saturday to work on my car." She looked at both her father and Les who had lit up a fresh cigarette. "Kim promised us some coffee as soon as we finished. And Gwen's got some fresh-baked brownies she's pretty proud of."

"You'll have to tell her thanks for me," Les said. "There's some things waiting for me to get to them." He took the greasy towel offered to him by Joanna's father and wiped off his hands.

"You're sure?"

"Yep. Give me a rain check." He folded the towel in half and placed it on the Nova's hood.

Her father spoke. "Thanks for stopping by then, Les."

Les blew out a stream of smoke and took the hand her father held out. "Glad to help. Nice meeting you, Ed." Without saying more he walked off down the driveway towards his car.

"So which way to the coffee and brownies?" her father asked. Gwen pounced on him as soon as he got into the kitchen, impatient to show him around 'my new home' as she was calling it. Insisting he had to clean up first, he stood by the sink washing his hands while talking with Kim.Then Gwen towed him off to her room chattering away like a magpie.

Joanna watched them go, a smile on her face. She warmed her hands around the mug of coffee wondering why Kim had been pacing back and forth since they'd come inside. As soon as her father and Gwen were out of the room, she spun on her

heel to face Joanna. Eyes wide, she hissed the words in a stage
whisper. "You got a phone call while you were outside."

"I did? Why didn't you let me know?"

"I didn't think it was someone you'd want to talk to just
then."

Her stomach lurched. "Larry called?" She knew Kim would
nod even before she did. "What on earth did he... How did he
know to call me here?"

"Your former landlord evidently had this number. I told him
you were out shopping and wouldn't be back until at least five."

Joanna slumped onto a chair, her eyes fixing on the clock,
noting the two hours it would be until five. The last time she
had so much as heard his voice was almost two months ago.
Gwen's high giggle reached the kitchen. She spoke in a low
voice to Kim. "Did he have much to say?"

"No. It was a short conversation. But he did want to know
how Gwen was and I told him 'just fine'. I think he plans to
call you tonight."

Baffled by Kim's news, Joanna could only shake her head.
Kim sat silent, watching her closely. "Guess I'll just have to
wait and see what he has to say. At least he asked about his
daughter."

Nearly the whole evening passed before his call came.
Twice the phone had rung and both times she braced herself,
but the calls had been for Kim. Gwen went off to bed at her
usual eight-thirty bedtime and to Joanna's relief was sound
asleep within a few minutes. Until she knew what he was up to,
she didn't want Gwen to know Larry had even called.

She mulled over his possible reasons. There wasn't one
positive thought among them. Nine o'clock came and went and
she began to feel irritated, wondering if it was deliberate. It
wouldn't be surprising if he didn't call back at all. Actually
she'd prefer that anyway. If she'd decided anything about Larry
or their relationship, it was that she was starting to think of
both in the past tense. Other than wanting him to keep in touch

with Gwen, she'd begun to consider looking into divorce proceedings once their housing situation stabilized.

Kim came back from the kitchen with a bag of pretzels and a soda. "You sure you don't want anything, Jo?"

"No. My stomach's feeling off as it is. I'm beginning to think the rat isn't going to call. What time was it in the kitchen? It's got to be nearly nine-thirty."

"Just past."

Joanna snorted. "This is so like him. He's probably out getting plowed with some friends. At least I don't have to put up with watching that anymore, or wonder how to explain Daddy's behavior to Gwen."

"He did seem interested in finding out how she was doing." She reached for her glass.

"A pleasant surprise, I've got to admit. It's the one thing that's got to be figured out before things go much farther. If it were just me, I could care less if he ever turned back up." She yawned and leaned her head against the back of the couch. "God, I probably sound like a bitter old woman."

"Not at all. You have good reason to feel bitter. I certainly would if I were you."

The phone rang. Their eyes connected and Kim started to get up.

Joanna motioned for her to stay put. "Thanks, but it's probably him this time. I'll get it."

"Okay," Kim said. "Don't take any crap from him, Jo."

It was on its sixth ring when she reached the kitchen.

"Hello, stranger." Larry's nasal twang greeted her. "Hell, I was about to hang up thinking I had the wrong number."

She'd almost forgotten how that tone in his voice could grate on her ears. She kept her voice even. This was not like finding some long-lost friend on the phone, after all. "We were in the living room watching TV. The phone's all the way in the kitchen."

"So you and Gwen moved in with Kim Eddy? How long you been there?"

Was he calling just to chat? "Since I couldn't stretch my money any further."

He seemed to take the hint. "Yeah. I've got to take the heat for some of that. But, hey, I've got some good news in that department."

"Why do I think I've heard this before?" There was no point in hiding the sarcasm.

"Hey, I just said I'm sorry. Listen, Toots, my financial situation went from bad to shit when the job closed up over one weekend back in February and Fran and I both were out of work and owed money by the company on top of that." He paused and sighed. "So, yeah, about then I almost decided to skip out on the whole deal and head South. But I found enough of a job here that will pay for another month. Then I'm looking into a construction job out near Auburn. Anyway, I made up my mind that as soon as the smoke cleared I'd get in touch with you two. Best news is I made enough on the last paycheck to send you guys some money."

She had to give him credit. He'd kept the whine out of his speech. But she wasn't buying much of it. "Funny I haven't seen any sign of this money."

"Well now, considering I didn't have any way of knowing you weren't at the Court anymore, that could possibly explain why, wouldn't you think?"

He had a point. She backed off. "I suppose. No, you couldn't have known. You mean you already sent it there?"

"Right. Cataldo's holding onto it for you and says to stop by anytime to pick it up. Look, I can't stay on the phone much longer. A friend's letting me make the call. Where are you and Gwen in the Mills?"

She hesitated for the space of a second, reluctant to make it easy for him to find them. "82 Lombardy Street. Is there a chance you're going to be sending more than this one check? That is, if this one doesn't bounce?"

Maybe she'd gone a bit too far. There was a long pause on

his end of the line and she wondered if he'd hung up on her. When he spoke again there was a cool edge to the words. "All right, Jo, I know I deserve your spite. Hell, I'll try to send more if I can. But it's not like I've forgotten the kid. I'm planning to get back there by May and I'd like to know how to find you."

"Okay. Okay. I apologize for being...a little nasty." She frowned into the receiver. "It would have helped for Gwen to know she wasn't totally deserted by you. She deserves better than that, Larry." She hoped she'd said that firmly enough. "And one postcard doesn't quite fill the bill."

"Okay. I hear you. I might be a lot of things, Joanna, but you won't see me turning my back on my daughter no matter what things looked like these past two months. I don't suppose she's up at this hour, but I'd like you to tell her that her Daddy said hello and that he loves her. Would you pass that along to her for me?"

Joanna sagged against the counter, rubbing her temple with stiff fingers. "Okay. Yes, I'll tell her in the morning."

"Thanks. Guess I owe you. Look, I've got to go. I'll try to send more money and next time I'll address it to you in the Mills." By now he sounded almost contrite.

"All right. Oh, I talked with your mother a week or so ago and she'd like you to call."

"Fine."

"Larry, one more thing."

"Yeah?"

She closed her eyes. "As far as the two of us go, it ended in January. I want Gwen to have her Daddy, but that's all. Am I being clear?"

"Yeah. As a bell." There was a click on his end of the line. She looked at the dead receiver in her hand. Perhaps she should have said some sort of thank you for the money he had promised even if there was no gratitude to feel.

Kim was hovering at the living room door, the television turned low. After Joanna related all of the conversation, she nodded her approval. "I think you handled that just fine, Jo!"

She leaned over and patted her knee. "You set him straight on where you're coming from, and there's some money in it for you too."

"It looks like it. Now I don't have to wonder how I'm going to pay Les for that car part. I just wish I didn't have to see Cataldo to get it." She leaned back against the couch, relieved to have the conversation behind her.

"Have him send it to you."

"If I didn't need it so badly, I'd be willing to wait. I'll call him from work Monday and stop around there on the way home. Maybe I'll luck out and only have to see his wife."

Joanna smiled to herself. Her Monday morning was going wonderfully well. Gwen had been in an extra bubbly mood, a combination of hearing about her Daddy the day before and anticipating plans for Julie to stay overnight at the end of the week. Joanna was happy to arrange some real fun for her. They'd stood together on the curb waiting for the bus, swinging their joined hands, the morning glowing with pearly light, the air smelling of damp earth. A flock of robins called in excited spring voices somewhere behind the houses across the street. Gwen had reached up for a hug as the bus arrived. Joanna breathed in the faint, sweet smell of her dark hair.  Gwen waved from the window as the bus pulled away.

The Nova started right up when she'd gotten behind the wheel. Hopefully there'd be enough money in Larry's check to cover the cost of the distributor. Les and her father had gone over the engine and found nothing else in bad shape other than the need for a long-overdue oil change.  And that had been set up for the following week, again courtesy of Les. She'd have to think of something she could do to thank him for his kindness.

She was humming as she unlocked the door of the Continuing Ed office. Alita was at a meeting until eleven, so after Joanna checked for messages on their voice mail, she dialed the number for Green Glade, deciding to get that out of the way. Therese Cataldo answered. Larry's check was there, all right, and Joanna should be able to find her home that afternoon. She set the phone back on its receiver and turned to her work, shaking her head. Did Therese know how her husband behaved towards some of the women in the Court? Probably not. Especially with three little kids to keep track of and her in-laws camped on her doorstep every weekend.

The door opened and Joanna turned to see Scott McFadden. "Good morning!" His voice was full of cheerfulness.

She returned his smile. "Hi...Scott. If you're hoping to see Alita, she's at a meeting until eleven."

"Not unless she plans to help you with your story." He grinned and set his battered briefcase on her desk. He took out the paper-clipped pages of her story. "I had a chance over the weekend to read your story again and remembered why I'd liked it so well last fall. I've got some things written down you might try. If this Thursday's too soon to get anything done, we can get together next week."

She took the papers, noting his lengthy written comments on the first sheet. A pleasant suggestion of woodsy cologne reached her. Why he was taking all this time with her, someone who wasn't even a part-time student? "This is really nice of you with all of your regular students. I've got to say though I'm not sure how much I can get done by Thursday." Meeting his eyes, she felt her cheeks color.

He waved away the idea. "Really, Joanna, I'm glad to do it. You've got talent and I like to help people when I see it. And we both work here every day so it's not an inconvenience for either of us. At least not for me." He chuckled. "Of course maybe this is starting to seem like some sort of extra work for you."

She shook her head and looked down, smoothing out the sheets of her story. "No, not really. I just didn't think...I mean I like to write and all," she paused, "but I'd hate to waste your time."

He surprised her by reaching over and placing his hand on her arm. The touch was warm and steady. Startled, she looked up. "Believe me, you are not wasting my time. And remember, if you don't get anything done, we'll just go over my comments on Thursday. I know your days are pretty full. So don't worry if you can't find time. Is it a deal?" He snapped the catch closed on his briefcase.

His earnestness won her over again. Managing a small smile she said, "Well, now that I think of it, it would disappoint my daughter if I don't do it. She thinks it's neat that we can do our homework together. Guess it's a deal."

He beamed. "Great! Remember, just do whatever you have time for and I'll see you then." The office door closed behind him. She carefully folded the pages of her story and put them in her handbag. It looked like Gwen would have company at the kitchen table after supper tonight.

The pace of the day's work picked up soon after. By the time Alita came in at eleven, two people were waiting to speak with her. The pile of transcripts that needed her attention was down to a half dozen when she took her lunch break.

She brought back a sandwich for Alita who worked through lunch. "Thanks for the delivery service, Joanna," Alita said. "Say, I was delighted to hear you're doing some independent study with Scott McFadden."

"Oh, so you must have bumped into him this morning after he left me my homework."

"No, we spoke on Friday. We were both picking up our paychecks at the Bursar's Office. Actually your ears might have been burning since we talked about you for a few minutes."

"Oh?"

"Not to worry, my dear." Alita waved one of her perfect pink fingernails at the chair by her desk. Joanna sat down. "It consisted mostly of my raving about how you're the best receptionist I've ever had and him telling me about your promising writing talent." Joanna found herself blushing. "He did ask me a few questions about you. He seemed genuinely

concerned, so I told him a few things I knew, in a general
way." She paused while unwrapping her sandwich and looked
apologetic. "Now I feel a little guilty since I didn't check with
you first."

Joanna absorbed this revelation, then hastened to reassure
Alita. "Oh, that's okay. It's...it was nice of him to ask, I guess."

"Well, so you know, what I told him was that you had
recently moved into the Mills with your daughter and were
getting your lives stabilized. Also that I admired your energy
and persistence. Probably the most personal comment was
something like, your husband, I guess I referred to him as your
'ex-, was an idiot to give up what he had. You know me and
my opinions on that. All in all I've got to tell you, Joanna,
you've got your admirers out there."

When she got to Green Glade Court she took the right hand
turn to avoid driving past the trailer. It probably would have
been nice to drop in and say hello to Arlie, but she promised
herself she'd get to that as soon as she could. She left the
Nova's engine running to have an excuse for getting in and out
of the office quickly. A light was on. After all, Therese said she
would be there.

A buzzer rang from somewhere inside the house when she
opened the door, but no one was at the desk in the small
cluttered room that served as the Court's office. She was
greeted by the smell of onions cooking. The inner door to the
Cataldo home stood open. To one side was a wet heap of kids'
muddy boots.

"Can I help you?" came Therese Cataldo's disembodied
voice through the doorway.

"It's Joanna Quinn, Mrs. Cataldo. Remember I called this
morning? I'm here to pick up that mail."

"Oh. Right." There was a ringing sound of a pot lid being
set down. "Tony, can you help out here?" she called loudly.
"Mrs. Quinn's here for that envelope." He yelled some sort of
answer Joanna couldn't make out. Therese raised her voice

again. "Well, I'm busy getting supper started. You do it."

Joanna fidgeted with her jacket zipper, bracing herself. There was a sound of someone coming towards the door and then Tony appeared. His usually neatly combed hair was disheveled as if he'd just gotten up from a nap, and he needed a shave. He nodded towards her, expressionless. "So you heard there was mail here for you?"

"That's right." Joanna remained where she was just inside the door.

He began rummaging through papers on the desk, then muttered, "Shit, I thought she said it was right here on the desk. Therese," he called irritably. "Where the hell did you put that thing?"

Therese came through the door going straight to the desk without looking at Joanna. She looked even thinner than the last time Joanna had seen her. Opening the top drawer, she wordlessly handed an envelope to her husband, her eyes downcast as if apologizing for something. There was a child's sudden wail and she hurried back into the house. Joanna almost called "Thank you" after her.

Tony turned towards her, holding out the envelope, a half smile on his face. "Here you go. Looks like that husband didn't disappear after all."

She drew herself up and took it, hoping the disdain she felt for him showed in her expression. "Please thank Therese for me," she said evenly, and turned abruptly towards the door without saying more. If he still stood there with that smirk on his face, she didn't care.


"Mommy, is it okay if Julie and I go down as far as the ball field?" She pointed to the proposed destination at the end of the park.

"Okay. Just don't get too near the water."

Gwen nodded her agreement. "C'mon, Julie." They joined hands and hurried off. Gwen called over her shoulder, "We'll be back in a little while."

Joanna watched them trot away, fragments of their little girl-voices at first drifting back to her, then lost in the silvery clatter of the creek's spring current. She breathed out a long sigh and closed her eyes, luxuriating in the warm sun on her face. How nice to have such a fine day on the weekend. It hadn't taken much urging from Gwen to take them to the park after they'd finished their breakfast. Her night on the couch had resulted in a better night's sleep than she'd expected. Kim had been away at Gary's so there was no concern over the girls disturbing her. Though they'd done a lot of giggling and taken numerous trips to the bathroom, all was quiet by ten. Watching a TV movie all by herself, snuggled on the couch with her pillow and blanket, had been an unexpectedly delightful pleasure in the bargain.

After all the months of upheaval in their lives, Gwen's being able to have a friend sleep over signaled a level of normalcy. Dare she think that things were falling into some sort of place? Even with Larry's unwelcome intrusion, at least he had sent money. And it thrilled Gwen to know her Daddy hadn't forgotten her after all. So that wasn't all bad there.

Even the meeting with Scott had gone surprisingly well on Thursday. With no time to do more than read what he'd written on her papers, she'd shown up timidly at the appointed time. But, just as he'd said, they'd looked over his comments and discussed them, and she vowed to get a start on working with it this very weekend. Their twenty minutes or so together had been enough to do that and allow for some non-threatening chatting as well. She was discovering how easy it was to talk with him. Then he'd smiled a goodbye and wished her luck with the story. Whatever impressions he might have formed about her through talking with Alita didn't emerge in any way she could detect. The last thing she wanted was someone's pity or forced sympathy. Her plan now was to start in on the ideas he'd suggested for her story and have something to show for herself in another week.

"Something to show for myself...." She spoke the words

aloud, turning to watch the girls running towards her from the ball field, a race in progress, unzipped jackets flapping, their excited laughter arching ahead of them. "Something to show for myself."

# ~ *Eight* ~

Joanna sucked on the end of her pen, rereading her last sentence for the fourth time. When she'd first sat down at the table and spread out the pages of her story, she'd focused on a dialogue passage Scott had pointed out to her. It went easily for a time. She filled nearly two-thirds of a page but seemed to have run into a wall with where to next take the scene. Five minutes passed and not another word came to her. "Writer's block," she mumbled and got up to heat water for tea.

From the living room came Gwen's giggle and then Kim's laugh. Gwen had come home from school on Friday with another Amelia Bedelia book. It was like Gwen had two mothers to fuss over her, Joanna thought and smiled. She'd remarked to Kim just that evening that they'd better be careful they didn't wind up spoiling her. Kim laughed that that was nonsense, that likely she would be the one ending up spoiled since she loved having Gwen around, and then went off to read with her.

The water in the kettle started its quiet rumbling. She leaned against the counter, remembering the fall evenings sitting at her own kitchen table working on her writing. Once Gwen was in bed and Larry out somewhere, she sometimes had several quiet hours to herself.  With the cramped trailer reduced to faded shadows beyond the circle of lamp light, she liked imagining she was in a cozy room of her very own house. No one near to make demands or to find fault with her indulging in her 'writing thing', as Larry occasionally termed it. 'What good's it going to do you anyway?' he'd ask.  'No way it'll ever make a penny for you.'

The edge of one of her journals peeked out from under her writing folder. She hadn't yet looked into any of her journals, hadn't dared touch the anger they sometimes contained, or harder to revisit, her flights of fancy confiding her dreams to their pages.

The kettle whistled. She poured the hot water over the tea bag. In some odd way thinking about Larry had shaken loose some more ideas. Fresh memories of Rachel and high school appeared in her mind's eye. She began to write.

When Gwen called for her to come say goodnight she had another page and a half finished. She could hear the two of them chattering away as she came down the hall. Gwen, sat against her propped-up pillow, clad in her favorite pink pajamas, looking freshly scrubbed and shiny. "Goodnight, pumpkin," Kim said, bending down and exchanging hugs.

" 'Night, Kim. Thanks for reading me that story." Love for Kim shone in her dark eyes.

"You're entirely welcome. That Amelia Bedelia's something, isn't she? See you in the morning." Kim gave Joanna a wink and left the room.

Joanna sat down on the bed, and smiled at Gwen. "You're a pretty lucky kid, having two people to read stories to you."

Gwen nodded, hugging Baxter. "Uh huh. Kim's lots of fun. But I like it when you read to me too, Mommy."

"Well, thanks for saying that. You know I love reading to you." She brushed Gwen's bangs back from her forehead. "I know someone who needs to get her sleep for school tomorrow."

"Just four more days until spring vacation. Will I be staying with Grandpa and Aunt Phyllis like I did last year?"

"Yes, I think so. I've got to call and check. Wow! I can't believe it's almost time for the Easter Bunny's visit!"

"Me either. I hope I get to dye Easter eggs with Allison and Christopher again."

"Oh, I'm sure that can be arranged."

Gwen plucked at Baxter's frayed bow tie. "Mommy..."

"What?"

She regarded Joanna steadily. "Is Daddy coming to see us pretty soon?"

Joanna tucked Baxter in next to Gwen. "I'm not sure, Gwenny. He didn't tell me when we talked on the phone, but I know he wants to see you, you can be sure of that, okay?"

"Mmhmm." Gwen nodded, her expression inscrutable. "But I don't think you want to."

"Have him see me, you mean?" Gwen nodded again. Joanna tried not to sigh. How best to explain things? "That's sort of hard to say." She smoothed out the edges of the blanket. "Daddy and I, well, we aren't very good friends anymore."

"Because he was mean to you sometimes?"

Gwen's words dove deep. She managed to keep her face composed. "Well, let's just say he wasn't always as nice as he should have been. If you want, we'll talk more about this real soon. Okay? But for now the Sandman's trying to sprinkle you with dream dust." She wiggled her fingers above Gwen's forehead and then twiddled her nose. Gwen giggled. "Just remember this, Gwenny Penny, Daddy loves you and I love you too. Got that?" She nuzzled Gwen's cheek and kissed her.

She found Kim in the kitchen brewing her own cup of tea. Joanna sat down heavily, drew her mug over, then grimaced to taste how cold it had become. "Any hot water left?" Kim nodded and held out the kettle.

"What's up?" Kim asked. "You look perturbed."

Escaping an explanation wouldn't be easy. "Good word for it, I'd say." She was silent for a moment, watching the steam rise from the tea. "Well, when I was saying goodnight to her, Gwen wanted to know if her Daddy was coming to see us pretty soon."

"Oh, I see."

Joanna wrapped both hands around the warming mug. "For the longest time she hasn't even asked about him so it was easy. I just wanted to push him out of my mind and I did. And then when he didn't contact us for all that while, I wasn't even sure whether he much cared about staying in touch, even with her."

"Now that he's called and sent money, I guess that tells you something."

"You're probably right. I know it's good for Gwen, but to tell you the truth, I was getting really comfortable with the idea of not hearing from him at all." She let that comment hang in the air and took a slow sip of tea.

"You know, I don't have the clearest impression of Larry. Even though you and I have been friends for a couple of years now, I can't say I know him all that well. If I got any impression at all, it was that he was basically okay as a dad."

Joanna set the mug back on the table. "When he felt like it, yes, he was. He didn't know too much what to do when she was a baby, like a lot of guys. It was quite an event if he changed a diaper. Oh, he liked to make her laugh and thought she was pretty cute when she was a toddler. But mostly it was me that did the parent stuff. Not that I minded. When I look back on the last couple years he just got, oh, I don't know, more into himself. He didn't have much time for either of us. He partied more. I never much liked his friends. He'd complain I was a stick in the mud and I'd get angry and try to make him see he had responsibilities to his family. Things gradually got worse, with money mostly, and we were arguing a lot. Sometimes really it was fighting. I did all I could to keep Gwen away from it."

"Uh huh. And you're still doing all the work. I'm probably not the first to tell you this, Jo, but you're doing an excellent job with that sweet little girl of yours."

Joanna gave Kim a grateful smile. "That's nice to hear, although I worry I'm spoiling her." She shook her head. "When I wish sometimes that I'd listened to my parents and never gotten married to Larry, then I think, no, because then I wouldn't have Gwen. Sort of having to take the bad with the good." She sighed. "But I still wish he'd just disappeared. I think I told you that when I talked to him I told him in no uncertain terms that the marriage was over."

"How do you think he took that?"

"I'm not really sure. Even though I don't think he'll want custody of Gwen, I'm starting to worry a little about what he might do. Maybe I should find a lawyer."

"It wouldn't hurt to talk to one. Then when he shows up, you'll be prepared. And remember, you've got people in your corner, especially me. Oh, speaking of people in your corner, I saw Les last night over at Gary's and he asked me to say hello to you."

"That was nice of him."

Kim cleared her throat. "Think you'd want to go out with us again sometime?"

"You mean, go out with Les?"

"Well, yes. Just for fun, like when we went bowling."

"I thought he had a girl friend and that I was just sort of subbing that night."

"I have a feeling that might be coming to an end...not because of going out with you I should add. But I do know Les has got a good opinion of you."

Joanna held up her hands in protest. "That's all well and good, but the last thing I need is encouraging a relationship with another man. I've got my hands full just trying to work my way out of my marriage with Larry."

"I know. Trust me, I know." Kim paused, but Joanna could see she had something else to say. "Some unsolicited advice, Jo, which maybe you might resent, but I think you should keep in mind that all men aren't automatically 'the enemy'. Some can make pretty good friends."

Joanna eyed her for a long moment, then shrugged. "You're right, I guess, about not all of them being enemies. But being good friends, I wouldn't know. Maybe." She got up from the table. "Well, I'd better make a call to my Aunt Phyllis and check on her invitation for Easter Sunday."

As Joanna dialed the number, Kim said 'good night' and left the kitchen.

"Hello?" Her aunt's warm voice made her smile.

"Hi, Aunt Phyl. This is Joanna."

"Joanna! I was thinking about calling you tonight to see how the two of you are making out and then remind you about

Easter dinner next week. Oh, before I forget, Uncle George wants to be sure I've said hello for him. So how are you and Gwen?"

"We're doing just fine, Aunt Phyl. We've gotten pretty well settled in. Gwen's getting picked up for school right here now and I've found someone to be with her after school until I get home. And she just loves the fact that we're living in a real house even if she does have to share a room with her mother."

Phyllis laughed. "Well, that's great to hear. Leave it to children to see the good in things. That reminds me, Allison and Christopher were here the other day and wanted to know how soon they'd be seeing Gwen again. Of course I said, probably Easter. You should know Gwen's invited to stay with us for her school vacation, just like last year."

"She was hoping for that. I've got to check with Dad and see if he'd like her there for part of the time. And how's that daughter of yours doing with baby number three on its way?" She closed her eyes, imagining herself back in Phyllis's comfortable kitchen chatting with her and Mimi.

"So, things are going okay for you then, Joanna?" The conversation was winding down. "Is there anything your Uncle and I could do to help out?"

"Thanks. Things are working out pretty well for now. You'll be sure to hear from me if that changes."

"I should hope so. Well, we'll plan on seeing you soon. And don't worry about bringing anything. Just yourselves is the best thing for us."

"Sounds great, Aunt Phyl. I'll get in touch with Dad and find out how we'll set things up about Gwen. Give our love to Uncle George, won't you?"

Later, as she lay in bed listening to the gentle rise and fall of Gwen's breathing, she thought about her conversation with Kim. She didn't doubt that Les could be a good friend, but some days it was just too much effort to sort out the wolves from the rest.

\* \* \*

Joanna tried not to let her nervousness show while Scott silently read the four pages she'd been able to finish. She plucked at her already wrinkled napkin and then took another sip of her soda. Finally he set the papers down and grinned at her. "Nice new stuff here, Joanna. You've moved the story along, especially with the dialogue."

"Really? You think so?"

"Absolutely. It shows the conflict between your characters is intensifying. Then after they part company, you get us into Renee's thoughts so we see how upset she is by what happened. This is coming along really well."

"Good. Thanks, I mean," she said, feeling both relieved and happy at what he'd said. "When I first started working on it I was sort of stuck, but I went back to it last night and most of it came to me then." She smoothed out her napkin. "I wanted something to show for myself this week."

"Well, that you certainly do," he said, tapping the pages of her story. "You have a good eye for people and what's going on inside their heads. A sign of a good writer. You know, Joanna, I don't want to embarrass you by saying this, but I'm proud of how you've taken on this writing work again. Not a lot of people would have. I hope you can see the talent you have."

She felt suddenly shy. "Thanks. I really like doing it. It's just finding the time and energy that's the problem."

"I'm sure it's hard with all the responsibilities you have."

It seemed an odd remark. Then she remembered that Alita had talked to him about her. "Oh, I manage, just like everybody else." A knot of discomfort registered its presence. She had no desire to air her personal life with him. "Sorry to cut this short, but I'm going to have to get going. Thanks a lot for your time, Mister...oh, sorry...I mean, Scott." She knew her face had gone pink and avoided looking at him. She picked up her papers. "So should I just keep going with things like they are in my story?"

"Yes. That would be fine. See where your characters want to go next. I'll be looking forward to finding out where that is."

"Okay." Holding on to her composure, she finished gathering up her things.

He spoke quietly, as if choosing his words carefully. "Joanna, I think something I said just now may have made you feel uncomfortable."

She risked a look at him. "No, you didn't."

"Maybe you know I talked to Alita about you?"

She half-wished he wasn't being so direct. "Yes. She told me."

"Then perhaps it seems I'm prying into things." His eyes held only concerned kindness.

She had to look away. "Well, yes...it does a little."

"Then please let me apologize, because I don't want to come across as anything like that. I know your life's not an easy one at times. Without being too forward about it, I'd like you to think of me as a friend."

"I...that is, there's no need for any apology. I...I'm not sure of what to say here."

"How about, 'See you next week'?" Things steadied between them.

She found herself able to smile and finally got up from the table. "Okay. See you next week."

Back at the Continuing Ed. office, their conversation replayed itself. First his interest in her writing, and now his apparent concern for her private life. She mulled over his possible motives but reached no definite conclusions other than that male behavior could be annoyingly puzzling.

She lugged two bags of groceries into the kitchen and set them on the counter greeting Becky who came into the kitchen.

"Thanks for staying longer today, Becky," she said to the girl. "Things still okay for you to be here tomorrow all day?" Good Friday was the start of their school break.

"Yes, it is. If it's nice, Gwen wanted to know if we could walk to the park up the street."

"I don't see why not. Just keep her from falling in the

creek."

Becky laughed as she shrugged her jacket on. "I think I can handle that." Gwen appeared in the doorway. "Hey pal, your Mom said we could go to the park tomorrow if you don't jump in the creek. What d'ya say?"

Gwen whooped happily and ran around the table to Becky who danced her around a turn. "We'll have lots of fun!"

"You bet we will. See you bright and early. Bye, Mrs. Quinn." Becky started out the door and then put her head back in for a moment. "Oh Gwen, don't forget to show your Mom that note from school."

Joanna straightened up from putting things in the refrigerator. "What's this note?"

"I've got a note from Mrs. Leahy about my eyes." She reached into her book bag and handed an envelope to Joanna. "I took this eye test today and she says I might need glasses."

Joanna scanned the paper with a sinking feeling. "She wants you to have an eye exam with an optometrist."

"What's that?"

"An eye doctor. I guess that would explain why you come home from school some days with a headache." For a while Joanna had thought her headaches might be due to the stress of the last couple months.

"So I might have to wear glasses?"

"Maybe so. We've at least got to find out if you need them." *Which will be expensive enough for just the doctor's visit*, she added silently. *How we'll manage to pay for glasses on top of that is something else.* "I'll call a doctor from work tomorrow and see what we can do. Don't worry, you'll be fine." *And maybe if we're really lucky, Larry will send another check.*

At supper Gwen enthusiastically announced this new development to Kim. "Some of my friends at school who wear glasses don't like them, but I don't think I'll mind. Mommy says I probably will only need them for reading. That's just like my grandpa."

"Right," Kim answered. "Whatever helps you with reading

is important."

Gwen nodded, spooning some more applesauce on her plate. Some spilled onto the table. "Uh oh."

Before she could stop herself Joanna said sharply, "For heaven sakes be more careful, Gwen. Now go get the dish cloth and wipe that up." Gwen got up from her chair without saying anything and got the cloth. Joanna regretted snapping at her and said in a gentler tone, "Just be more careful with things please, Gwen." She turned to Kim. "Could you recommend an eye doctor in town?"

"There's Dr. Mahoney right downtown. People say he's good."

"I just hope he doesn't charge an arm and a leg. I know this needs taking care of, but this month I'm just barely covering basic expenses. The little extra I have I was planning on maybe spending on Gwen's Easter outfit." Gwen looked up from her plate, a worry line creasing her brow, but she said nothing. "Guess I'll call in the morning and see what can be done."

A call to the doctor's the next morning brought mixed news. She could pay for Gwen's glasses with installments but the exam had to be paid for at the time of the visit. The entire cost was a good fifty dollars more than she'd hoped it would be.

She hung up the phone and sat looking at it as if it might hold answers to her questions. Maybe this was a time to ask her father for a little help. After all, it was for Gwen.

# ~ Nine ~

A festive atmosphere prevailed when Joanna delivered Gwen to Berlin the next morning. Allison and Christopher were already there and hustled Gwen and her suitcase off to the bedroom they'd share for the next few days. Everyone raved over the new Easter dress that Gwen had picked out at Ames that morning.

Though Joanna had been reluctant to do so, she'd called her father the night before and explained her problem about the dress. He offered at once to help out. "After all, Jo, you know how much your mother liked to buy her granddaughter a new Easter outfit every year," he'd said. "I think it's an important tradition for me to keep up."

That thought had crossed her mind too, but Joanna hadn't intended to say anything. She was happy that her father had remembered it on his own. When it came to her mother, there weren't too many things that they found to talk about that left either of them very comfortable.

"She's going to look so sweet in that dress, Joanna," Phyllis was saying as she hung it on the door to the dining room. "I think I'll take the two girls out shopping later and buy each of them a hat to go with their outfits, if you wouldn't mind."

"No, I wouldn't at all. That would really tickle Gwen. It's so thoughtful of you to do that, Aunt Phyllis."

She stirred milk into the cup of coffee Phyllis had poured for her. "I'll try to find the camera and bring it with me tomorrow so I can take some pictures. How nice it's going to be to have everyone here for dinner."

"Yes, it certainly will. Actually there may be someone here you wouldn't expect. I was hoping to have Gwen out of earshot so I could mention it to you first."

"Who on earth would that be?" Joanna smiled, expecting to

hear something about her cousin, Lynne, who usually couldn't make the trip from her home in Wisconsin.

Phyllis drew in a breath. "Well, we got a phone call last night from Larry."

Joanna nearly choked on the coffee she was drinking. "Larry!"

"Yes, Larry. He decided to call here first, since he thought this is where you and Gwen would be for Easter Sunday. He was very polite, wanting to know how your Uncle George and I were doing, and that sort of thing."

Joanna wiped her wet chin with a napkin. "I can't believe this. You mean he invited himself to dinner? Oh, now wait. It could be that his mother talked with him."

"His mother?"

"Yes. I've been in touch with her since we moved and she was planning on giving him a piece of her mind if she could get hold of him."

"Well, he deserves that, I'd say. But no, he didn't ask to come to dinner. I talked with him for a while and I thought he was truthful with me, Joanna, about how irresponsible he's been. I think he was sounding me out about things, how people here felt towards him. I told him pretty clearly how I felt at least." Joanna shook her head in disbelief at what she was hearing. "Joanna, as strange as it sounds, to me he sounded sorry for what he's done. One thing's for sure, he misses Gwen something awful."

"That might be true, but he sure hasn't made a point of letting her know very often lately. Do you mean to tell me he's going to be here tomorrow then?"

"Well, not for dinner. I suggested he come later for dessert which is all I thought would be appropriate. Of course I wanted to see what you thought first, which I told him. He's going to call me back tonight to check. And it would only be for later in the afternoon. I just didn't think him being here for dinner would work very well." Phyllis was looking more and more uncomfortable.

Not wanting to make matters worse for her Joanna said, "I wouldn't have a problem with him showing up for part of the day, Aunt Phyl." She sighed. "Truthfully, Gwen will be thrilled to see him. So go ahead and invite him. After all, it's your home and Uncle George's."

"Only if you're absolutely sure, Joanna." She still looked doubtful. "Your Uncle George and I wouldn't want this to spoil anyone's day, especially yours."

"I'm sure. And it won't spoil my day. After all, I think it's important that Larry involve himself in his daughter's life again. This would be probably a good way to start. But let's not tell Gwen until tomorrow just in case he decides not to show up. He's let her down too many other times."

Having done her best to assure her aunt to go ahead with these plans, she drove back to the Mills to an empty apartment. Kim had gone to her family's for the holiday. She fixed herself a cup of tea and sat with her elbows propped on the table trying to wrestle her thoughts into some meaningful order.

The first time she'd laid eyes on Larry Quinn had been at a party late in the fall after she'd graduated from high school. Rachel had been there. She was home that weekend from college. As things would go, it would be almost the last time they'd see each other. They'd sat and talked together for a while, though the conversation felt perfunctory, and then Rachel had drifted away to another group of people. Even before that school dance the previous April, their childhood ties had seemed to wither. After that spring night she'd somehow endured the whispered comments and sidelong looks for the few weeks remaining until graduation. She'd held a faint hope that at least Rachel hadn't believed all the rumors.

Marie had talked her into going to the party. She knew all of what had happened and had been trying to help Joanna put things behind her. "There are lots of trustworthy guys out there but you'll never know that until you go and see for yourself," was one of her arguments. Joanna had been asked out a few times by boys she met in her classes at Seneca Community but she always said no. Marie tried to set up dates with Lonnie's friends, but Joanna usually found a way to refuse.

On this occasion she had given in since there was no actual date involved and found herself tagging along with them that October night. Other than Rachel, there weren't a lot of people Joanna knew. It was crowded and noisy and after being there a half-hour she wished she hadn't agreed to come. For a while she managed to step back behind Marie, hoping to be less visible. Someone Lonnie knew stopped to say hello and introduced the tall, long-haired man who was with him. With the noise, Joanna didn't catch his name. When the traffic coming through the room caused them to shift places, she found herself elbow to elbow with this stranger. He'd been standing quietly holding his bottle of beer. Joanna wondered if he was feeling awkward too. She caught the scent of English Leather cologne, a fragrance she found sexy, and smiled up at him. Perhaps it was her smile that opened him up. "Know many people here?" he'd asked. She'd shaken her head, and when that mutual fact had been established, they'd made their way to a less congested spot and fell into a friendly conversation. Larry Quinn's dark eyes held a charming twinkle, and though his speech was a bit on the rough side, he seemed amiable and before long had her laughing. At one point she caught Marie's look of approval from across the room.

Riding home in Lonnie's car, she admitted to Marie that he'd talked her in to giving him her phone number but doubted he'd call. And even if he did, she knew she'd say no. And while, yes, she'd been relaxed in his company, it felt far too soon to trust any man enough to go out on a date.

But when he'd called a week later to ask her out for a cup of coffee, there'd been no plausible reason to turn him down, and the hour they spent together had flown by. At nearly twenty-five, Larry had a certain laid back self-confidence that she took to be maturity. Later she was to know that it reflected more of a lack of ambition, but his non-aggressiveness had won her over.

Marie encouraged the relationship and they double-dated often, Joanna still preferring the safety of being with other people. It began to feel comfortable to be with him and she eventually told him about her bad experience. He seemed sympathetic and didn't press her for intimacy. Three months went by. Not wanting to lose this safe relationship, and finding those feelings developing in her, she consented to lovemaking. It wasn't spectacular and never became that, but he was gentle in his approach and told her she was more than enough of a lover for him.

She had finished out her first year at college without much enthusiasm for the business program she'd been in. Attending college had happened mostly to please her parents, and she'd agreed to live at home to save money. Larry had gotten to be a more or less permanent fixture in her life, something Joanna could tell worried her mother. The week of registration for the fall semester was the week Larry asked her to marry him. She was tired of her mother's hovering over her and liked the looks of what she saw in a future as Mrs. Larry Quinn. Not enough compelled her to want to continue in school, so she answered Larry's question with a 'yes'. She barely finished out one more semester. On a brisk January Saturday they were married and she walked out of her parents' house and into what held the appearance of a promising adult life.

Since that night on Stone Road, the question of what men wanted had haunted her. Now she no longer had to puzzle over it. There was a predictability and simplicity to Larry's needs that was what she thought she wanted. For a long time he had not disappointed her in that regard.

She followed Marie into the kitchen, each of them carrying a pile of dirty plates and silverware. The kitchen clock showed it was nearing three. She set things down on the counter and massaged her forehead, closing her eyes for a minute's rest. Sleep had been elusive the night before. Marie returned from the dining room with more dishes.

"You okay, Jo?"

"Oh, I think so. I'll just be glad when he gets here and we can get started with whatever it is
that's going to get started." She started rinsing off the plates. "I wish your mom would stop
looking so guilty like she's done something wrong."

"She told me when I got here this morning that she feels like she's meddling too much. After all, she went ahead and let your father know."

"You'll have to tell her for me that she's not. I, or maybe I should say, "we" had to see him sometime. I'm glad I've got all of you here for moral support. And Gwen's at least happy about it." *Almost too happy*, Joanna thought. Since they'd gotten back from church she'd been parading around in her new dress and hat, saying over and over how much her daddy would like it until Joanna nearly told her to cut it out. But she quickly thought better of saying anything.

"Thank goodness he had the presence of mind to call ahead and not just drop in on us."

"Yeah. It's good to have something positive to focus on. And as far as Dad goes, it was about time he knew how things were. He was more surprised than anything, but I'm sure I haven't heard the last of it."

Phyllis had talked to him before Joanna had gotten there. Shortly after she and Gwen arrived, he'd taken her aside. "Why on earth didn't you say anything about this sooner?" he'd asked point blank, the look on his face half angry and half hurt. Through the kitchen doorway she could see that Phyllis was keeping a discrete eye on their conversation.

She worked to stay calm. "Dad, I wanted to manage this my own way. There was no telling at first that he'd leave me...leave us, so high and dry like he did. I honestly didn't expect it would get this bad."

He appeared to think this over, looking at her steadily. "But if you hadn't kept us all in the dark this long, maybe something could have been done before you had to give up your place."

"Maybe. But that's behind me now. I can understand why you're upset, but I did what I thought was best, Dad." There wasn't much more to say and she excused herself to go back to the kitchen to help with dinner.

"He's here!" came Gwen's happy shriek from the dining room where she'd been keeping watch out the window. Marie put her hand on Joanna's arm.

Joanna forced a smile for Marie's benefit. "Well, at least the waiting part's over."

Gwen tore through the kitchen, holding her hat on firmly, and barreled out the back door leaving it wide open. They heard her excited greeting and Larry's response, "Well, if it ain't my sweet baby girl!" Joanna's eyes connected with Marie's. Only Larry could get away with calling Gwen that.

Moments later they came in, Larry carrying Gwen, her legs and arms wrapped about him, her hat askew. "Mommy, Daddy wants to know if it's time for dessert. Oh! And he really likes my new Easter outfit!" Gwen radiated happiness leaving Joanna no other option but to put a smile on her face.

"Well, I hope you told him yes, it's dessert time. Hi, Larry." His eyes met hers squarely, a strange mix of emotions in them that she couldn't decipher.

"Hello, Jo. Marie." He set Gwen on the floor. At that moment Phyllis came into the kitchen followed by George. Larry looked relieved. "Hi there, Phyllis. George." He came around the table to give Phyllis a hug. She half-returned it, patting his back. Her father, Lonnie and the two kids came in, and for several minutes greetings were exchanged, reflecting various degrees of awkwardness. Joanna stood back watching how Gwen clung to his side. She was relieved when Marie gave her the dessert plates to take to the dining room.

While people got seated back at the table and coffee and pie was served around, Gwen monopolized her father's attention. He seemed happy to give it to her. Phyllis caught Joanna's eye and patted the chair next to her, putting two seats between her and Larry. Joanna smiled a thank you and sat down. Unless she leaned forward she could avoid even having to look at him. People made a show of fixing their coffee and starting in on their pie. Joanna saw her father looking from Larry to her but without any expression. Table conversation limped along for a while until Allison asked her mother if they could change into their play clothes and go outside. Getting the go ahead, she asked, "Gwen, do you want to come out with Chris and me?"

"Go ahead, little lady, I'm going to be here for a while," Larry said to her. "You go have fun
with your cousins."

While things were seen to with the kids, the adults seemed to find a more comfortable level of talking. Joanna heard Larry say to Lonnie that he'd been hired on a construction job for a new outlet mall south of Rochester. He'd be staying with his aunt in Auburn. *I'll bet he has talked to his mother then,* Joanna thought. That would put him about a forty-minute drive from Rockford Mills. Not too near, but near enough to throw a monkey wrench into her new life if he wanted to.

A baseball game on television claimed the men right after dessert. Uncle George led them into the living room. Maybe she'd be lucky and not have to have much of a conversation with him at all. She brought the last of the dirty dishes into the kitchen. Marie already had her sleeves rolled up and her arms deep in soapy water. Phyllis was putting plastic wrap over the leftover turkey. Seeing the appraising looks from both women, she said, "Well, so far, so good, don't you think?"

Phyllis nodded. "It seems so. How are you doing?"

"Well, as I said to Marie, I'm just happy that he's here to see Gwen. The rest we'll figure out all in good time."

After things were finished in the kitchen, the women sat back down at the dining room table with a second cup of coffee. No one stirred from the living room where sounds of the game could be heard as well as fragments of conversation that often included Gwen's voice. She had come back inside and had gone in to be with Larry.

It was Gwen who delivered his message to Joanna later. She

and Marie were upstairs talking in the bedroom where the kids'
things were. "Mommy, Daddy said he's got to go soon but he
wants to talk to you in the kitchen first."

"You can tell him I'll be there in a minute." She stood up
after Gwen left the room and went to look out the window into
the thickening dusk. Whatever he had to say, she was resolved
to hold firm to her decisions of the past few months. She turned
back towards Marie. "Well, here goes nothing."

Marie smiled back encouragement. "Good luck. Just say
what you mean and stick to your guns."

He already had on his jacket and was standing by the
counter when she came into the kitchen. It was the first she'd
noticed he was wearing a pair of new-looking jeans. Maybe
he'd bought them just for today. She stood by the kitchen table
and waited for him to speak. The murmur of voices from the
other room lent her support.

It was easier to look at him than she thought it would be.
She hadn't expected to see such obvious uncertainty in his eyes
and for a second's breadth felt sorry for him. It must have taken
some courage for him to have come after all.

"So, Gwen said you wanted to talk to me."

She saw him swallow. "That's right. But seeing Gwen was
only part of why I wanted to be here."

"Larry, if you think for one minute..."

"God almighty, Jo, don't jump so fast. Can you just hang on
a second?" When she nodded, he went on. "I just wanted you
to know where I was going to be for the next few months.
Maybe you heard me talking about the new mall they're
putting up out near Auburn. I'm going to be living with
Chucky and my Aunt Betty."

"So I take it you talked with your mother?"

He nodded. "She said you and she had talked a couple times
recently. Anyway, I should be making decent money once I get
started. I've got a few debts run up but I still should be able to
send some money for the kid pretty steady before too long."

"That would be awfully good of you." She fixed him with

what she hoped was a scathing look. "She certainly deserves at least that from you."

He raised a hand. "I hear what you're saying, Jo. And I guess I deserve your...your attitude. Heck, my mother really laid into me last week too, so I've paid my dues." Joanna almost rolled her eyes at this. "Think you'll be staying with Kim for a while?"

"That's been my plan. At least until school's over."

"Okay. Least I'll know how to contact you. Let me ask one thing here, Jo."

She tensed. "And what's that?"

"Once I get settled, I'd like to talk to you about my seeing Gwen more or less regular. I've got to think she'd like that, if today's any sign. I've got to tell you, Jo, I wasn't sure she'd be all that fired up to see me after..." He looked away. "After I'd been away for so long." He coughed and cleared his throat. Again, despite herself, she felt a wave of sympathy. "I've really missed her. And I've missed you too, Jo."

She breathed out and rested her hands on the chair in front of her. "I think I've told you how I feel about things, Larry."

"You have. And I certainly don't blame you." He looked at her finally. "But that doesn't change the fact that I've missed you sometimes. Hell, let me at least tell you that you've done a great job with...with our daughter all on your own these last few months. But I'm back to help now, Jo, if you'll let me. That's something I guarantee."

"Something I guarantee..." she repeated aloud as she drove back to Rockford Mills. "Yeah, right, Larry. If that's as good as the 'guarantees' you used to give, I'm not going to hold my breath." She frowned at an imaginary Larry in the windshield. With Gwen staying most of the week in Berlin, she would have some time to sort things out before faced with the questions she knew Gwen would have. Gwen had clung tearfully to her father when he'd left though he'd assured her they'd be seeing each other soon.

She gripped the steering wheel even harder. Regardless of what influence his mother might have had in his turning up now, where did he get off just waltzing back into their lives like this, just assuming he could pick up things like he'd only been away for a week or two? Is that what he actually thought?

"You're in for a rude awakening, Larry Quinn."

His words again, "...I've missed you, too..."

"Men are full of such crap," she said, "just plain full of crap."

# ~ Ten ~

She carried her sour view of men with her for several days.

Kim had been a sympathetic ear when she'd returned from Rochester. "Just stick to your guns when it comes to Larry, Jo. You've survived just fine the past few months, no thanks to him. Let the so-and-so pick up some of the financial burden like he should and you get yourself a lawyer to help you get the divorce-business rolling."

Other than looking at the listings in the phone book, Joanna hadn't gotten any further with that part. "It would have been nice if he'd just disappeared," she'd said, sighing heavily.

"Then you wouldn't have his money for Gwen. Just keep that in mind."

That was a hard point to argue with. And perhaps the financial boost would make whatever struggle was ahead worth going through.

The apartment was too quiet without Gwen. When her usual bedtime rolled around Kim moped about having no one to read with. "I'm just going to have to get busy and have kids so I can have someone to read stories to," she announced to Joanna the second night Gwen was away.

"After your first couple weeks of changing diapers, you might have second thoughts," Joanna had said with a laugh.

"That's where a well-trained husband will come in handy." Then both of them had laughed at the doubtful existence of such a creature. That was the night Kim talked her into their going out and renting *Thelma and Louise* along with picking up a four-pack of peach wine coolers. They popped a huge bowl of popcorn, settled onto the couch with their cold drinks, and cheered on Susan Sarandon and Geena Davis.

Later Joanna drifted off to sleep, replete from the evening's fun. "Who needs men, anyway?" she mumbled, smiling drowsily into the shadowy dark. "Certainly not me."

It was a rainy and dark on Thursday when she drove to Berlin to pick up Gwen. The Seneca Creek was again boiling within its banks from the day's heavy rain. Newly budded willows glowed yellow through the gloom, hinting seasonal promises. Scott McFadden had called that morning to apologize that he couldn't meet with her and asked if she'd like to schedule a writing session for next week. She was glad to agree since she hadn't been in any kind of writing mood since their last session.

Stopped at Main Street's light in Berlin, up ahead she saw the sign for The Beauty Nook. An open parking space right in front of the shop helped make up her mind and she pulled in.

"Joanna!" Thelma's throaty voice greeted her as she opened the door. She put down the towel she was folding and met Joanna halfway across the shop. Her warm embrace, fragrant with the sharp always mysterious hair preparations, assailed Joanna with the memory of her mother's after-school hugs. Tears brimmed without warning, her words snared in a web of memories. There was fortunately no need to speak for the long minute of Thelma's firm embrace. Then she stepped back and surveyed her from head to foot, still holding Joanna's elbows with strong hands. "Joanna Quinn! If you're not a welcome sight to my old eyes! Come, sit down, and tell me everything of how you've been." She directed her to one of the padded chairs backed by a hair dryer, seating herself in the adjacent one. "And I especially want to know how that darling little girl of yours is. I can see she's not with you today to tell me herself."

Joanna brushed at her eyes and smiled at Thelma. "Well, Gwen's been staying with my father and my Aunt Phyllis for a few days this week during her Easter vacation. I've got to tell you she's been wanting to stop in and say 'hi' to you the last few times we've driven by. I'm on my way to pick her up now and decided to come in and see how you are."

"I'm fine, my dear, just fine. You picked a good day. My

next customer's not due for another twenty minutes. So that will give us a good amount of time for you to tell me all the latest news." She patted Joanna's arm and settled back to listen.

Joanna focused on what Gwen was doing in school and on news of Phyllis's family. "And your father, how is he?" Thelma prompted when she paused.

"Same as ever, I'd say. And least I haven't heard any complaints about anything. I wish he'd take a vacation once in a while, but you know him. Only my mother could coax him into taking some time off and even she had trouble doing that."

Thelma nodded. "How well I remember. I was always so glad she talked him into that trip they had to Myrtle Beach that last year. They both deserved that time together." She looked off at some unseen point. It hadn't been long after they'd returned from their trip that her mother had started to feel tired, the first sign of her cancer. Thelma spoke softly, more to herself than Joanna, "It doesn't seem possible that it will be two years in October." She shook her head and then brought her attention back to Joanna. "And what about Larry? How is he?" Joanna hesitated and Thelma immediately looked concerned. She leaned closer and took her hand. "Oh, my dear, is anything wrong."

There wasn't much point in glossing over the truth. Joanna took a deep breath and began by summing up the last few months, Larry's leaving, their move to Kim's apartment, and his recent reappearance. She felt surprisingly calm when she finished, as if the recitation of the ugly matter was making it all easier to handle. "Well, I guess you could say, it's been an eventful winter for me."

"And that would be putting it mildly from all you've said." She was quiet a moment, fingering the St. Christopher medal she had always worn on its silver chain. Then she drew Joanna's hand into hers and gently squeezed it. "Well, here's a thought from an old friend of your mother's and of yours too, I'd like to think. While I was listening to you, Joanna, I couldn't help thinking that your mother would be proud of how you've managed with everything."

"Do you really think so?"

"Oh, my, yes." She paused, looked away for a moment and then back at her. "Now you can go ahead and tell me it's none of my business, Joanna, but I'll ask this anyway."

"Please do, Thelma. You know I value your opinion."

"From what you've said of the present state of things, Larry moving back to Auburn and not into the Mills with you, does this mean that you're thinking about a divorce?"

"Yes, that's what I want."

"And he's going to go along with you on this?"

"He's said as much."

"Mmhmm. Not an easy thing for anyone to do, but sometimes, I know, the only sensible path to take. So you and Gwen have been getting by all right?"

"Well, we've been managing reasonably okay. It was a godsend when Kim came along and offered to share her apartment. That's what has kept us going. Phyllis and George have been supportive too. And of course, my father."

"Of course. Joanna, please consider I want to be of help in anyway I can. Your sainted mother I think of every day. She would be so upset at what Larry has done to you and that darling child by not living up to his responsibility. But you are a strong woman like your mother, so I know you will come out of this just fine."

For a fleeting moment she had a vision of her mother hovering near, concern and worry on her face, pushing her hair back from her temple, the gesture that had always told of her distress.

Joanna got back in the Nova and sat for a minute watching the rain make crooked paths down the windshield. Behind the lighted window of The Beauty Nook, Thelma adjusted the plastic cape around the shoulders of her customer.

She felt in her jacket pocket for the new tube of lipstick Thelma pressed into her hand as they said goodbye, Luscious

Peach. She'd remembered Joanna's favorite shade. Joanna tilted the rearview mirror and ran a line of it over her lips, then looked closely at her serious reflection. How she wanted to think she was looking at the strong woman Thelma had named her to be.

When she got to her father's she found he'd ordered a pizza. It had been Gwen's idea that they have supper together before they started back to Rockford Mills, he explained. When Joanna had come in through the back door to the kitchen, Gwen's welcome had been a quick hug and then she had disappeared back to the living room to watch her TV program.

She watched her father tear up lettuce for a salad. "You sure you don't want some help with that?"

"No, I'm fine. Just sit there and enjoy your coffee."

"Thanks then, I will." She looked around the kitchen, as always mildly surprised how neat he kept things. "I imagine Gwen enjoyed herself at the garage today. Hope she wasn't underfoot too much."

"Nope. She just reigned over the place like the Queen of Sheba, but then the guys always get a kick out of her being there."

Joanna laughed. "Good thing she doesn't get there too often or she'd certainly wear out her welcome. Did she go to bed for you okay last night?"

"Oh, we compromised on a ten o'clock curfew with a story thrown in for good measure." He chuckled as he put the finished salad into the refrigerator, then came and sat at the table. After taking a sip of his coffee, he set the cup down and folded his arms. The sober look he fixed her with indicated he had something on his mind. "She's talked some to me about her father, Joanna."

"Oh, I see." She shifted in the chair. "What about mainly?"

"Mainly how happy she is that he's moved back here. Also that she's missed him a lot."

She studied his expression, wondering where this was

leading. After all, he hadn't known the whole story until a few days ago. Perhaps he was angry. "I guess that doesn't surprise me all that much. Though to tell you the truth, Dad, she hadn't mentioned him that often the past few months."

"Maybe she didn't want to upset you. Do you think Larry has any plans to see Gwen now that he's back in the area?"

Was it his tone of voice that was making her feel defensive? "Well, yes. Just before he left on Sunday he told me that's something he'd like."

"Well, I'm glad to hear that. A child needs both parents if you ask me."

She sat up straighter, keeping her gaze steady. "That may be true, Dad, but the fact of the matter is he pretty much turned his back on not only me but Gwen for nearly three months. Not a single word from him. Even his mother couldn't believe he'd behave that way. Well, I'm not about to interfere in his seeing her, but I've worked too hard trying to keep our lives normal to allow him anything he wants just because he may have finally figured out what his responsibilities are."

"No need to get angry, Jo. Remember I didn't know any of this, at least for sure, until just this past Sunday. And that's something I'm sorry you kept me in the dark about when I might have been more help to you both. You probably could tell me different, but I never thought of Larry as such a bad sort. He always struck me at least as being a pretty good father, and I know that's what your mother thought too."

She looked hard at her father. Was he taking Larry's side in this? "It takes more than that to keep a marriage going, I can tell you that." *And Mom would have agreed with me on that.* "Maybe I should have told you sooner about how things were, Dad, but the truth is he walked out on us. And that's not something I'll ever let happen to me or Gwen again."

The door bell's ring announced that the pizza had arrived. Joanna was glad for the interruption, calling Gwen to come for supper while her father went to pay the delivery person. Gwen came dashing into the kitchen and Joanna got her busy setting the table. While they ate it was easy to keep Gwen talking about her week's adventures so that the topic of Larry was kept at a safe distance.

But later when Gwen was sent upstairs to get her suitcase, her father returned to the subject. She was putting on her coat when he cleared his throat. She turned to look at him standing by the table, his hands resting on the back of a chair. "Joanna, there's one more thing that I'd like to say about this. You can accuse me of sticking my nose in where it doesn't belong, but I think you still can use my advice now and then."

"Go ahead, Dad," she said, resisting an urge to shrug her shoulders nonchalantly.

"I want you to know I'm angry with Larry for doing what he did. God knows he was wrong
to behave that way. Still, some people do learn from their mistakes, and just possibly he's learned some important things. Maybe you should give him a chance to set things right, not only with Gwen, but with your marriage. After all, the facts are that it's not easy being a single parent. At least, Jo, I think you should give things a little time to sort themselves out."

Joanna waited to see if he was finished and then reached for her purse. "I hear what you're trying to say, Dad." They heard Gwen's footsteps coming down the stairs. She adjusted the purse strap on her shoulder. "I'll be sure Gwen sees her father as much as I think she needs to. Me, he doesn't need to see. Nor do I want to see him. You should know that part for me is over and done with and I'm getting on with my life."

On the drive back to Rockford Mills, Joanna kept the conversation focused on what Gwen had done during her stay in Berlin. Always the avid story teller, Gwen described one event after another featuring her cousins, Aunt Phyllis and Uncle George, and her Grandpa Smales. All of that sounded normal enough. Joanna told her about visiting Thelma at The Beauty Nook and promised she'd take Gwen there on their very next visit.

"Well, it certainly sounds like you had a super time this

week, Gwenny Penny. But I've got to tell you, Kim and I really missed you while you were over here having all this fun. Kim didn't have anyone to read with."

"I missed Kim."

"And your mother too, I would hope." She reached across the seat to give Gwen a teasing poke.

"Uh huh," was all Gwen said. "Mommy…"

"What?"

"I miss Daddy too."

Joanna willed away a cold shiver, peering ahead at the lights of Rockford Mills gleaming brighter in the night landscape. She knew she had to make some sort of response.

Gwen spoke again. "Daddy said he wants me to come and visit him real soon."

"Uh huh. He told me that too on Sunday."

"Will he come visit us at Kim's?"

"Tell you what. We'll make sure you can go see your Daddy once he gets himself settled at his cousin's. How's that? Okay?"

"How soon will that be?"

Joanna felt herself floundering. "Oh, I'm not sure. Maybe three weeks, but I don't know exactly." *Damn Larry. He's already intruding in our lives.*

"Mommy," Gwen's voice had grown tiny, directed out into the dark of the damp night, "You don't think Daddy will forget me again, do you?"

A sadness washed over her. "No, of course he won't." She wished she could have added, 'I guarantee it…', but knew she couldn't. After all her efforts to create shelter and security for the two of them, it shocked her to find that Gwen must have harbored such a sense of loss. How could she have not seen this?

The steady, firm place she thought she had reached began to shift out from under her.

# ~ Eleven ~

"Something wrong with my stir fry?" Kim sounded faintly annoyed. Joanna looked up from her plate to see that she was grinning.

"I think it's yummy," said Gwen, scooping up a fork-full. "You make good stir fry, Kim."

"You're right. She certainly does, Gwen. I just don't have much of an appetite tonight."

"Well, thank you for the compliment, Miss Quinn." Kim patted Gwen's arm. "Busy day at work, Jo?"

"Sort of. Although by the time I took Gwen for her eye appointment and then brought her back here so Becky could watch her, I was only there for half a day." The size of the final price tag was going to require several payments. And that hard fact had hung over her all day.

Gwen beamed. "Wait till you see my new glasses, Kim! They're a real pretty blue, and I got to pick them myself."

"Hey, great! I'll bet they look good on you."

"For the money I'll be paying, let's hope so," Joanna said, making an effort to eat more. "Wish keeping our budget balanced wasn't such a tricky thing."

Kim said, "Well, at least now you've got the chance to get away for the weekend and take your mind off it." Marie had called a short time ago inviting them for an overnight visit. Kim was right. She needed a change of scene.

Supper finished Kim shooed them out of the kitchen saying she'd do the clean up so the two of them could pack their things. Gwen's enthusiasm was infectious and they got giggling over what they each should take along.

The phone rang and Kim called to them that Louise was on the phone.

"Grandma Lou! Can I say hi to her?" Gwen asked looking

hopeful.

"Sure. She'd love a chance to talk with you," Joanna said. "Give me a yell when it's my turn to talk." Gwen yelped with glee and dashed out of the bedroom.

After an animated conversation that ran on for ten minutes, Gwen called Joanna to the phone, handing it over with a wide smile. "Grandma Lou wants to know what I want for my birthday this summer. I told her I'd have to think about it. Meet you back in our room, Mommy."

"That's some kid you've got there, Jo," Louise said after Joanna said hello. "So how are things going with you?"

"Just fine, thanks, Louise. Did you have a nice Easter?"

"Not bad, not bad. A bit on the hot side, but otherwise fine." She coughed and cleared her throat. "Excuse me. I should give up those damn smokes. So I hear Larry showed up to say hello to Gwen and you on Sunday."

"Yes. He came to my aunt's and uncle's house in the afternoon."

"Well, I'm glad to hear that. When he turned up at Betty's she had him call me and I did what I could to set him straight on a few things. It seemed like he wasn't too happy with what he'd done. How did he seem to you?"

Joanna sighed. "He did apologize and he said he's going to keep in touch and start sending money for Gwen now that he's got that work in Auburn."

"You're not going to take him back, are you, Jo?"

Used to Louise's frankness, her abrupt question still caught Joanna by surprise. "Well, I…that is, no, Louise." She glanced at the kitchen door, wanting Gwen to be out of earshot. "I don't think Larry and I have much of a future. Probably not any at all to be totally truthful."

Louise coughed again and Joanna waited once more. "Now this might surprise you, Jo, but I'm glad to hear you say that. In all honesty, I don't think it would be the smartest move for you to try and make things up with him. He is my son and all, but he's got his faults and you've put up with them long enough.

Oh I think he'll do right by his daughter, but you deserve to move on with your life."

Buoyed by Louise's words, Joanna returned to the bedroom to finish getting ready for their morning's departure.

They were on the road bright and early the next morning singing along with the radio for most of the hour and a half drive to Syracuse. When they pulled into the driveway of Marie and Lonnie's modest '50s ranch, Allison and Christopher burst from the house with welcoming shouts. Christopher insisted on carrying Joanna's overnight bag, barely managing to lug it up the front steps. Marie stood waiting, holding open the door.

"I hope we haven't come too early for you, Mimi," Joanna said giving her a hug.

"I'm delighted you did. All the more time for us to visit. There's fresh coffee waiting in the kitchen." The three cousins disappeared in the direction of the basement family room.

After putting their things in the guest bedroom, Joanna joined Marie in her sunny kitchen. With Lonnie at work, they had all day to themselves. On the breakfast bar was a plate of doughnuts and a carafe of coffee. Two steaming mugs sat waiting.

"Wow, if this doesn't look wonderful," Joanna said, hooking her heels comfortably on the rungs of the stool. She raised her mug to Marie. "Here's to a wonderful cousin who knew just what I needed this weekend!"

"Here's to a fun time for both of us," Marie said, carefully clinking her mug with Joanna's. "Which I must say we both deserve. After all, the kids had their visit, and it was our turn. You do look a bit on the worn down side, Jo."

"As if I have anything to complain about. Here you are with two little ones and number three due at the end of the summer. How do you do it, Mimi?"

"Oh, I laugh a lot and don't worry if the kitchen floor doesn't get mopped regularly. But seriously, what are those circles under your eyes? I hope it isn't that Larry's already making trouble."

"No. I haven't heard anything from him, but then it hasn't even been a week. Maybe he expects I'll be the one getting in touch about setting up visits with Gwen. Oh, I did hear from his mother again last night. Actually we've talked on the phone a few times."

"Really? She's living in Florida now, right?" Joanna nodded. "And what's her view on all this?" Marie pushed the doughnuts over.

"Thanks," Joanna said, choosing a chocolate glazed. "This should make me feel better. Well, believe it or not, Louise told me I'd be crazy to go back to him. And she's his mother." She took a bite of the doughnut. "Mmm, I was right. This does help."

Marie smiled. "Good. Have all you want. Well, I'm glad his mother said that to you. She always struck me as a pretty perceptive woman."

"That she is. And she knows what she's talking about, I'll tell you. It's a relief to know she understands how things are."

"Mmhmm. How about Gwen? Has she had much to say?"

Joanna sighed and took another bite of her doughnut. "Not too much yet, at least not to me. But when she stayed with Dad this week, she talked to him about missing her father. That's part of what's bothering me, I guess."

"Part? What else, if I can pry a little?"

Joanna tried to explain her father's concerns to Marie. She leaned her arms against the counter. "I think I understand why he feels like he does about my giving Larry some kind of last chance, but I'm a little angry that he doesn't see what a dumb idea that would be."

"Did you try telling him how you felt?"

"Not in so many words. Just that I would do only what was best for Gwen."

Marie nodded. "And he thinks that it would be best for Gwen to have her parents together if at all possible."

"That's pretty much it, I think."

"Well, your father doesn't know the whole story. He'd probably be talking differently if he did. I mean, if Larry's own mother can see that staying together is a bad idea, then he should be able to too, in the long run, at least."

"Maybe. But at the moment I can't help but feel, oh, I don't know, maybe guilty?" She looked at Marie closely. "Please answer me honestly, Mimi. Oddly enough I do think Larry regrets what he did. He's even told me he missed me. But do you think I'm being selfish to want out of this marriage? I mean, would it be better for Gwen if we tried to patch things up?"

"Oh, I'm sure there'd be some who would say you should try patching things up, but I certainly wouldn't. And his mother wouldn't. So there are two no-votes for you." She took a sip of coffee. "You want to know what the bottom line is here? Larry's just not good for you anymore, Jo. There's just no getting around that, as far as I'm concerned."

Joanna frowned, smoothing out her crumpled napkin. "You know, Mimi, when I look back on eight years of marriage to Larry, I ask myself what in the hell did I ever see in him?" She looked up at Marie. "So you really think he's no good for me?"

The thunder of children's feet on the stairs signaled an imminent invasion of the kitchen. "Hold that thought," Marie said. "Let's get these guys their lunch."

Something that Joanna tried not to remember was how her mother had resisted the idea of her daughter's marriage to Larry Quinn. There was never much said, but it was communicated just as clearly through her protracted silences in the weeks leading up to the wedding. Joanna at first thought her objections were more about her decision not to go on with college; she'd certainly made her disappointment in that clear. But with her own uncertain vision of the future, marriage seemed the one definite path to follow. Her twentieth birthday felt like a door opening to adulthood. And Larry, five years older, convincing in his appearance as someone already in control of his life, presented an appealing prospect. What his friends told of his let-it-all-hang-out younger days seemed only amusing stories.

For the first few years, the decision seemed to have been the right one. Gwen's arrival had been a year or two sooner than she would have liked, but it wasn't a hard adjustment and she happily immersed herself in her daughter's needs. And it had mended some fences with her mother.

When she had to return to work, the pace of daily life became relentless. At home, Gwen came first. But then not long after they celebrated Gwen's first birthday, Larry's undisciplined side began to reemerge. It had taken her longer to notice than it should have, she told herself. Maybe if she'd put her foot down sooner. Maybe after all, she was the one that should take the blame for things slowly falling apart.

It was this point that she brought up to Marie once they had the kitchen to themselves again and were washing the dishes. "So maybe I'm the one who did things wrong, at least to start with. You know, the really sad thing is my mother understood the risk I was taking with him, only I totally refused to hear any of it." She reached for another plate to dry.

"Hind sight is always twenty-twenty. Listen, you know I broke my mother's heart too when I dropped out of school to get married."

"Yes, I do. Remember how we called ourselves the 'prodigal daughters'? But you at least picked a decent guy to marry. I'm the one who made the truly stupid choice."

"And where in the world would you be without Gwen?"

"Actually that thought has crossed my mind more than once, especially lately."

Marie rinsed a pan and handed it to Joanna. "So, back to your earlier question about whether I thought Larry wasn't much good for you."

"Right. Was I the only blind and deaf person way back then?" Her smile was rueful. "Except for Gwen, a fatal lapse of sanity when I agreed to marry him."

"Now don't be so hard on yourself. I was there the night you two met. As I recall I was happy you stopped being jumpy long enough to let a guy talk to you again." Marie's offhand remark was not meant to upset her. And it was, after all, the truth. "Not to dredge up too much of the past, but it hadn't been an easy time for you that particular year, Jo."

"No. You're right. Larry was a sort of breath of fresh air." She sighed. "You know better than anyone what it took for me to trust guys again after...well...after Eric. I sometimes wonder if more of what I felt for Larry was kind of like gratitude and wasn't really love at all. And the weird part of that is that we hadn't been married six months when I woke up one day with exactly those thoughts. But by then I told myself it was too late. After all, at that stage of the game, he was as good a husband as I expected a man would be."

"True. He was a decent enough guy in those days. But..." Marie frowned.

" 'But' what?"

"Well, it was when Lonnie and I got married and for a while we didn't see each other much, you remember. By the time we began to get together again, well, Larry just seemed different to me."

"Yeah. For a few months we lived with his mother and that's when he began to hang out with some of his old high school buddies. Here I was, living with people I didn't know well and really didn't like much. Was I glad when he got a job back in the Mills and we were on our own again. If we'd stayed in Auburn, I swear the marriage would have been over seven years sooner than it has. Stupid me, I just thought if we could get back on our own, I could get things right again. And you know, it did work, for a while anyway." She took the wet glass Marie handed to her. "So when did your opinion of him start to change?"

Marie washed another glass and rinsed it under the faucet. "Oh, it was only little things I noticed at first. Once you stopped in at our apartment, I think it was a Friday night, and we'd all had a beer or two. He started to get sort of nasty to you. I can't remember what he said, just that he put you down a few times and you looked pretty unhappy. That part I remember clearly. Oh, I think it was when you were a couple months pregnant, and he was making fun of how you looked only it really wasn't so funny. I remember Lonnie and I talked about it after you'd left."

Joanna dried the glass slowly, remembering exactly the time Marie was describing. Not only that evening but too many other occasions where he made jokes at her expense, a sort of teasing, but too often with a tone of cruelty even when she let him know he was hurting her feelings. A few beers in him always made it worse. "You know, an odd thing was he never acted like that when we were around my parents. When we spent time with his family, he would do that now and then. But then I could tell that not many of his relatives had very happy marriages. Sometimes I'd wonder if we were headed in the same direction."

"Mmhmm. And his friends never seemed much better."

"You're right about that. They weren't. So help me out here. What did I see in him?"

"Well, I don't want to give you the impression I didn't find anything good about him, because that's not true. But when Gwen came along and we'd get together when the girls were little I couldn't help comparing him to Lonnie as far as there both being fathers. Oh, it was clear from the word go that he was just crazy about Gwen, but it never looked to me like he did enough to help out around your place."

"Which I always thought was like a lot of men, unfortunately. And then you have a husband who's really a saint in disguise, Mimi."

"With feet of clay at times, I'll tell you." Marie laughed and emptied the dishwater down the drain. "But, yes, I know Lonnie's unusually helpful, a real 'Mr. Mom'. And Larry wasn't any worse than lots of guys like you said. Just sometimes I wondered why you didn't complain more about things."

Joanna put away the last plate in the cupboard, weighing out what Marie had said. "You know, you've put your finger on something there. That's what I'd tell myself for a long time, that my marriage was no worse than most, so there wasn't any point in my complaining. We just sort of went along with things. And we probably still would be if he hadn't let his carousing get out of control and lost his job at Mulgroves. From then on, well, things just got less and less bearable." She followed Marie back to their seats at the counter. Marie poured them each fresh coffee. "And that's when I think I should have done something about it. Although heaven knows, there were plenty of fights about his being irresponsible."

"And that's exactly what he was, Jo. He was the one being irresponsible. Blaming yourself is wrong when it was what he was doing that was the problem." She leaned towards Joanna. "After all, you were busy trying to keep things going for the sake of your family. And then there was your mother's illness, pardon me for having to mention it, but you had your hands full for quite a while. There weren't any excuses for him. And then his walking out on you and Gwen in January, well, that was just the last straw as far as I'm concerned." She sat back, shaking her head sorrowfully.

There seemed nothing more to say. The silence that fell between them was pierced by children's laughter welling up from the family room.

It had been a long while since she'd spent more than an hour or two in Marie's home. She'd forgotten how warm and loving was the atmosphere that lingered in all the rooms. When Lonnie arrived at suppertime Christopher and Allison pounced on him as soon as he got in the door, demanding hugs. Laughing, he reached out and pulled Gwen in too, planting kisses on all three. The sight went right to Joanna's heart.

He'd brought home the video of "The Lion King" and after

supper they all settled in the family room to watch it. He and
Marie sat snuggled together on the couch. Once Joanna looked
over to see them exchanging a lingering kiss. She smiled and
looked away, unable to stop herself from wondering if she'd
ever again have such moments with someone. Soon after,
Gwen came over and climbed into her lap, lying back against
her mother's chest. Joanna held one of her small hands,
stroking it lightly, loving the feel of the child's delicate fingers
resting quietly in her own. When Elton John began singing
"The Circle of Life", she couldn't stop the tears that slipped
down her cheeks.

Gwen stirred and turned her face up to her mother, a
worried look in her eyes.

"It's okay, Gwenny," she whispered, trying to smile.
"Some movies make me cry." At this, Gwen relaxed and
snuggled closer to her mother.

# ~ Twelve ~

Joanna was getting things together the next morning when Marie came into the bedroom. "It's been great having you two here," she said. "Let's do this again after school's out."

"Absolutely we will. With any luck, I'll have a place to invite all of you to one of these days, or maybe I should say 'years'?" She smiled ruefully at Marie. "I'd like to think I have more than a snowball's chance in you-know-where of that."

"I'm sure you will, Jo. Things are going to work out. You just wait and see."

"I'm planning on it, that's a fact. Talking with you yesterday really helped, Mimi." She put the last of the clothes in the suitcase and zipped it closed.

"Well, I'm glad. You just stick to your guns on doing what's best for Gwen. And no more of this wondering if any of it is your fault. I hope I set you straight on that at least."

"You did. It's good to know I've got your support, Mimi. Heaven knows you've helped me through a few bad times before."

Marie came around the bed and gave her a hug. "That you can always count on. You know your way back here and you don't even have to call to let us know you're coming."

Wordlessly, Joanna hugged her back.

Gwen was absorbed in a book by the time they'd reached the outskirts of Syracuse, heading west on Route 20. Joanna tuned into a classical music station, glad at the prospect of an hour's quiet drive back to Rockford Mills.

Thank God for Marie. This wasn't the first crisis that she had seen her through. Their long talk yesterday helped bring some things into focus, but it had also raised a few ghosts. She'd woken in the middle of the night, gasping for breath, the clutching hands of Eric Miller reaching for her once more from the depths of the familiar nightmare. She passed a shaky hand across her forehead, wanting to be rid of the memory. In the bright light of the spring morning it was still too real.

As long as she lived she doubted she'd ever know if they'd been right when they'd said that she'd probably 'asked for it'. The weeks before the dance had been a dizzying mix of the rush towards the end of senior year, and the intoxication of Eric's attentions. Not that she hadn't tried to be cautious. His reputation was well established by tenth grade.

Over the four years of high school she and Rachel must have talked hours on the phone about Eric and his latest conquest. They always reached the same conclusion, how could any girl resist his darkly handsome charms once he'd turned them on full force. Even the teachers were charmed by him, especially the women. The wildest rumor had been that someone had seen Miss Riley, their eleventh grade English teacher, locked in an intimate embrace with Eric Miller behind the back stage curtain one night after Junior Play practice.

Rachel had landed a steady boyfriend the fall of their senior year, Russ Hopkins. He'd been her secret crush since eighth grade and Joanna was delighted for Rachel, at least for the most part. There'd been attempts to fix Joanna up with one of Russ's friends, but nothing had ever taken hold. With most of Rachel's time devoted to Russ, there was an inevitable distancing between the two friends. None of this came as a surprise. In her heart of hearts she'd long known that she had little to attract the attentions of the opposite sex. This was in some way a continual source of despair, but also a matter of secret pride in her self-honesty.

Then that fall Eric Miller appeared to get a dose of his own medicine. He'd been going out with Elizabeth McIntyre and the story was that she had managed as no girl had before to make Eric behave like a gentleman. No one knew for sure what the real cause was of their breakup which happened over Thanksgiving. Some said he got tired of her resistance, while some said she dumped him for Roger Blake who'd graduated in June and had come home on college break. Neither ever told. Whatever the true story was, Eric had looked woebegone for a long while remaining single for months, apparently chastened by this turn of events.

When he'd struck up a conversation with her during study hall in early April, she hadn't thought much of it. After a week of his showing up suddenly beside her in the halls, stopping by her table in the cafeteria to say hi, and warm smiles flashed across classrooms, she knew she couldn't be imagining this attention. Others began to take notice. Rachel advised caution even if Eric looked to be a reformed Casanova. They'd double-dated twice with nothing more alarming than the fact his kisses goodnight were long, wet ones. He certainly seemed respectful of her in every way.

Perhaps there was a subtle pressure building up which she missed. Or maybe it was a yielding on her part which god knew she thought about but was ever so careful to not reveal. They'd proceeded to holding hands whenever they were together. Once in a while he maneuvered her up against the lockers, not hard, but teasingly insistent that she let him kiss her. His kisses when they were alone sometimes strayed down her neck where he'd nuzzle the hollow of her throat and she'd hope he wouldn't try to go further. He never had, though she was pretty sure he wanted to.

Spring was early that year bringing long, mellow April twilights night after night. There was a May Day dance, the last dance before the prom. Rachel had come down with a heavy cold, canceling their double date. Joanna had talked to her on the phone just before Eric had arrived to pick her up. Her last words were, "And I'll just bet he's planning on asking you to the prom tonight. So enjoy yourself but remember to make Eric behave himself." They'd laughed and then hung up.

A pink glow still edged the horizon when they'd gone out to get in his car. He'd stopped and put his arm around her while they both stood and looked at it. She shivered with happiness; almost not believing how perfect everything seemed.

It was crowded at the dance. Most of the senior class was there reveling in the heady sense of June's being just around the corner. They'd joined a large, raucous group and staked out one end of the gym, spilling out onto the floor to dance in loose groups for all the fast songs the DJ played. For a while Eric had gone outside with some of his buddies. When he came back, the smell of beer on his breath was unmistakable. He pulled her out on the floor for a slow dance. When she protested about his drinking, he kidded her about being uptight until she smiled back. She liked too well how he was holding her and moving in close when they twirled slowly around. When not much later he'd whispered to her about going off alone somewhere, she surprised herself at how quickly she'd said yes.

The April night had grown dark but the air was balmy and fragrant as they left the lights and noise behind. She found herself not caring where they wound up and would have just possibly driven around all night with him. He produced two bottles of beer from under the front seat when they got in the car. "What do you say you and me find a place to enjoy these together? The word is there's a party planned at Eight Mile Creek."

She remembered that she'd giggled and nodded her agreement. After all, it wasn't as if she had never had a beer. She and Rachel had snuck a bottle out of her father's refrigerator a time or two. Concealed in the haymow, they'd passed it back and forth amidst fits of giggling until it was gone. Then they would stash the empty bottle in a dark corner where they figured it would never be found and had gargled mouthwash to cover any telltale sign. And she'd been to a few parties where she'd managed to hold down a few and still keep control. The more amazing part was how she had been able to hide this from her mother's vigilant eyes. If she was going to hold onto Eric Miller she knew she'd have to comply, at least this once.

They drove into the velvet dark. She'd leaned back against the seat and watched the streetlights and houses slide by. Then they were out in the country, the dark outlines of trees sweeping past.

"I thought we'd beat the crowd out to the Creek. A bunch of them are coming out pretty soon. You and me can have ourselves a little private party before the rest get there."

While the events of earlier in the evening had grown hazy over the years, her memory retained every minute of what happened once they'd turned off Stone Road. She remembered how her heart had started to beat faster. The headlights picked up the shadowy figures of trees, the beams traveling far into the woods in two long funnels of light. The car bumped along the rutted dirt track sending up sudden splashes as they hit rain-filled mud puddles.

Neither spoke. They'd stopped talking a mile or so back. Joanna glanced at Eric's face, the dashboard lights shading hollows on his cheek and throat. He stared watchfully out the window. An ominous voice whispered in her head. "We should have stayed at the dance."

A final lurch and then they were at the end of the road. The car's lights played briefly on the stream beyond the parking area. Then Eric cut the engine and the lights died. The radio still played, the Beach Boys softly crooned the lyrics of "In My Room." The ripple of water could be heard above their voices.

She jumped when he spoke, "Yep, there's going to be a pretty good party here tonight. What do you say we get it started?" His short laugh was probably meant to make her relax. He fished out the two bottles from under the seat along with a bottle opener. When he handed her one, he toasted her. "Down the hatch!" Over her raised bottle she watched with an increasingly stricken feeling as he chugged half of his. Praying that she'd be more at ease once she'd had some herself, she managed to drink half of hers.

He placed his arm along the back of the seat, his thick fingers coming to rest on her shoulder, not exactly a grasping touch, but with a proprietary, confident weight in his hand and arm. She suddenly had a vision of all the girls who had sat in exactly the same spot she was now sitting and knew it was a practiced move. The weeks she had spent in his polite company vanished leaving her with a cold certainty that she was in the presence of a powerful and menacing stranger.

She couldn't get her breathing right. Wild thoughts crossed her mind of saying she felt sick, or of jumping out of the car and running into the darkness, but her senses were fogged by panic and the beer. So when he had leaned into her and placed his hand on her breast, she retreated to the hope that he would at least not hurt her too badly.

Five minutes? Was it ten minutes that passed? His suggestion that she remove her stockings and panties herself so they wouldn't be ripped had made sense as he had begun unfastening his pants. He'd actually talked a lot, the only part that she couldn't recall completely because some of it was mumbled against her breasts while he mouthed them beneath her pushed-up sweater. At least once he'd said something of how marvelous her body was. She would have liked to have been able to say she enjoyed it, but the reality was it had hurt. The traces of blood she'd found on her panties the next morning told the reason. He had worked himself into her with a few grunts followed quickly by a moan and then he sat back against the seat, silent.

Perhaps he had meant to say something more, but car lights wavered through the trees towards them and she had barely managed to rearrange her clothes before the others arrived, all but her stockings that she stuffed in her purse. The hour that passed once the rest arrived was largely blank in her memory. She did remember the chill of the night air. Standing with her jacket pulled tight about her, her bare legs pressed together, she felt cold and exposed. She also couldn't forget that Eric paid practically no attention to her for all of that time.

She had been grateful when he gallantly remembered she had a strict 12:30 curfew. He had her home at 12:25. Not until she entered the silent house and passed the telephone did she realize with mild surprise that there'd been no invitation to the prom. There wouldn't be one.

At school on Monday he'd stopped by her locker only briefly. He had said something like he hoped she'd had a good time on Friday. She remembered mumbling something inane and then he'd turned away with an odd, satisfied smile. Watching him go, she suddenly wished she'd slapped him. Except for the Elizabeth McIntyre episode, Eric's exploits were too well known for her to be surprised by his rapidly cooling attentions. She knew the signs, and in a week he put out the word to his friends that she had broken it off with him. A protest from her, even if she could muster one up, would have only prolonged the agony.

Other than Marie, Rachel was the only other person with whom Joanna shared the entire story of that night. Rachel was properly horrified and sorry for her, and extended as much sympathy as she had time for what with all she had to do to get ready for the prom. It was Marie who listened with quiet, supportive sympathy and had always been at the end of the phone line to reassure her things would get better.

Clinging to her shredded pride, she'd weathered the snickers and sidelong looks of the next few weeks. Thankfully, prom-frenzy descended, diverting everyone's attention. It hadn't mattered that she had no date, much to what she knew was her mother's puzzlement. The protective numbness that had settled on her there in the front seat of Eric's car lasted until the day after graduation. That part had been a blessing.

That, and the great relief when her period came at its usual time some three weeks later.

When they reached the apartment Kim greeted them with the news that Larry had phoned that afternoon. He hadn't left a number, saying he'd call back. Gwen had whooped with delight, certain that he'd called to make arrangements for a visit. She begged to stay up past her usual bedtime so she could talk to him and pouted when Joanna had said no. Reminding her there was school tomorrow, and promising to give her every detail in the morning, she'd given her mother a perfunctory kiss but glared at Joanna as she pulled the door closed.

She sat reading in the kitchen waiting for the call, not wanting the ring to wake either Gwen or Kim who had gone to bed early. She'd looked in on her before going upstairs. "Jo, if you want to come and talk after Larry calls, you just feel free to get me up."

Joanna looked up from her book she and smiled. "That's awfully nice of you, Kim. Maybe I will."

Nearly an hour had gone by. It was almost ten-thirty. Her thoughts kept wandering from the romance novel. Parts of her conversation with Marie kept intruding, and it didn't help that the heroine's love-interest reminded her of Eric Miller. She frowned over at the phone thinking how typical of Larry to inconvenience her this way. If she went to bed now, probably that would be about the time he'd call. Even though she was looking at it, the sudden loud ring made her jump. She grabbed the receiver before it could ring again, hoping it hadn't woken Gwen.

"That you, Jo?"

"Well, I should hope so, or you'd be disturbing some other poor soul in the middle of the night."

"Sorry, I guess it is a little late. Chuckie's been on the phone with his woman." He cleared his throat. "So how are you and Gwen doing?"

She wasn't in the mood for conversation. "About the same as when you saw us last week."

"Uh huh. So did Gwen have a good time with her cousins and your father? She was pretty fired up about that when she was talking to me last week."

"Yes. She had a good time."

"Uh huh. Good. Well, I know she's not up to talk to me, but I wanted her to know that maybe in another two, three weeks I'll have time for her to come for a visit, that is if it's still all right with you. Aunt Betty said for me to tell you it's just fine with her. So what do you say?"

*You don't want the real truth here.* "She's counting on seeing you, I can tell you that. I suppose you're going to need me to bring her over?"

"I might be able to borrow a car. I'll get back to you on that. Okay?"

"Fine. So you'll be calling Gwen in another week or so?"

"Yeah. Tell her Daddy loves her, all right?"

"Uh huh. Anything else?" *Like are you planning to send us some money soon?*

"Not that I can think of. So, you take care, Jo."

She hesitated. "You too," she said and hung up before he had a chance to say more. She poured out the tea that had grown cold and then reached for the light switch. "Next time I'll ask the cheapskate about money," she said to the darkened room.

Gwen had come down with a bad cold, something Joanna suspected she picked up from Christopher who had been sniffling when they visited over the weekend. She tried to stave it off with warm baths and early bedtimes, but by Friday it was clear she needed to stay home from school. Alita clucked concern when she called to request the family-sick time telling Joanna not to worry about anything there. Her small number of allowable days off would have to be hoarded more than ever.

By noon, Gwen had perked up some and chattered away while they ate lunch together on TV trays in the living room. Once they'd finished, Joanna got her settled on the couch for a nap. She plumped up the pillow and tucked the afghan in at her sides. "There. I think you'll be comfortable." She felt Gwen's forehead. "You know, I think your temperature's almost back to normal."

Gwen smiled up at her. "I think I'm feeling a whole lot better."

"Wonderful. You know what I might do while you're sleeping? I'd like to go for a quick walk around the block for some fresh air. Okay with you?"

"Uh huh. But you'll be here when I wake up?"

"Absolutely I will." She started to pick up their lunch things. "I'll only be gone for fifteen minutes tops. You don't mind, do you?"

Gwen shook her head. "Nope. If the phone rings should I answer it?"

"No. You just let it ring. Whoever it is will call back later. Now close your eyes and I'll see you later." She started for the hall.

"Do you think Daddy will call this weekend?"

The hopeful note in her voice was plain to hear. "He might, Gwen. He said he'd be calling this weekend or next. You just need to be patient. Okay?"

"Okay. I'm closing my eyes now, Mommy." She promptly closed her eyes.

"Sweet dreams, Gwenny Penny."

She peeked in on Gwen in another ten minutes and saw she was asleep. She let herself quietly out the kitchen door, hoping a walk would shake the restless, unsettled feeling that had nagged her much of the week. The warm breeze definitely had the feel of summer in it. She joked once with Kim that while some people could afford to pay a therapist, she at least could take 'therapy walks' for free.

The conversation with Marie, and Larry's Sunday phone call had shaken loose old memories. Even when she was able to push them away, their intrusions left a lingering residue of unease. She yearned for something concrete to grasp, for some sort of clues as to what direction to take now for herself and Gwen.

Gwen's hoping for Larry to call was no surprise. Knowing her daddy was planning on seeing her, she was less anxious and had only mentioned him a few times in the past week. So for her peace of mind, Joanna hoped he'd be calling soon. She'd become convinced that some sort of reconciliation was important and was resolved to pursue it as long as she could keep some control of the details. Her father was right at least in insisting Gwen needed both her parents. It would be selfish of her to think otherwise. But for herself, she knew for certain that that was the only link she wanted any longer to Larry.

A question that persisted was figuring out what she had ever seen in Larry. Youthful inexperience aside, twice within one year she had made poor judgments about men, both times with lasting consequences. Was there a chance now to undo the damage of those decisions?

It was a consolation that her mother would be pleased she was moving Larry to the margins of her life. Memories of Eric were more cumbersome baggage.

At times she fervently wished she'd been able to keep the events of that night from her parents, especially from her mother. When she made it to graduation without too many wounds to show for what happened, she had felt safe. Then came Rachel's graduation party. It had been an unpleasant surprise to find Eric was there too, but when she'd first seen him, he'd appeared to ignore her. Against her better wisdom, she decided it was okay to stay longer. The Lupinski's patio was thronged with people milling about the picnic tables laden with refreshments. She'd just filled a cup with soda when she turned around and nearly bumped into Eric and a couple of his friends.

It was Tim Jeffers who smirked at her and said loudly, "Well, Eric, look who we have here. If it isn't your little Miss Spring Fling." His remark set off raucous, back-slapping laughter, and a wave of nudging and whispers seemed to ripple to the edges of the crowd on the patio. She stood frozen to the spot, her face burning with humiliation. Before her legs finally obeyed her and she fled, she thought she saw an apologetic look on Eric's face. Even if it was, it didn't lessen the blow delivered in those endless seconds.

By some miracle she had managed to reach her parent's car without collapsing. She drove home through a thick curtain of pain and nausea. When she stumbled into the kitchen, her

mother had been making supper and turned towards the door as
Joanna came in. A smile of greeting froze on her face. When
Joanna tried to rush past her, she stepped in her way. Caught in
her mother's arms, the dam broke and Joanna sobbed out the
story of the party and then of that dark April night. Her mother
stroked her hair and held her for a long time. There was no
harsh judgment in her mother's eyes, only a look of sadness
that reminded her of the times she knew her mother was
thinking about Paul.

Her sympathy had seemed genuine, but in a subtle way it
was as if she held Joanna at fault for what had happened.
"When it comes to this sort of thing, Joanna, men and boys
usually can't help themselves. It's got to be up to the woman to
hold the line. I hope in the future you won't allow yourself to
get into a similar predicament." That had summed up her
mother's advice. The next day she had taken Joanna to the
Planned Parenthood offices in Auburn where a doctor
examined her and offered her birth control counseling. He'd
been kindly in his treatment and the nurse who spoke with her
afterwards offered sympathy for her ordeal and advice on how
to avoid future problems. She had been sent home with a piece
of paper containing a hot line number and another number for
free counseling.

Her mother evidently thought that had been enough, and
with the exception of one time, nothing more was ever said.
She was never certain whether or not her father knew what had
happened. For a while he had seemed more silent than usual. A
few times she thought he looked at her with a somewhat
baffled or troubled expression. She put the paper with the
phone numbers in her dresser drawer and once almost called on
a night when she'd woken shaking from a nightmare, clutching
her sheet tightly around her.

The only other reference her mother had ever made came
when she and Larry had been dating for a couple months. She
was getting ready to go out one evening when her mother
stopped at the open bathroom door. There was an unreadable

expression in the mirrored reflection of her mother's face when she said, "I hope you've got yourself on some sort of birth control this time, Joanna," she said.

The words 'this time' nearly made her flinch. Without turning around, Joanna answered, "Yes, Mom, I am," and then leaned forward to finish putting on her mascara, hoping her mother didn't see how her lower lip had started to tremble.

# ~ Thirteen ~

Kim was away with Gary for the weekend in Atlantic City, his present for her Wednesday birthday. Joanna wanted to do some spring-cleaning to surprise her. Gwen had woken up feeling almost herself again, so Joanna had her busy washing windows while she cleaned the kitchen cupboards. Gwen worked diligently, motivated in part by the promise of supper at Sal's pizzeria and maybe a walk to the park on Sunday if the weather cooperated.

Joanna stood back from the cupboard she'd just finished and looked at it with satisfaction. She thought how nice it would be if it were her own kitchen she was setting to rights and felt a fleeting pang of nostalgia for the trailer at Green Glade. She'd been particularly zealous about keeping its small kitchen tidy and in order. Larry used to tease that she'd nag him if he so much as put the salt and pepper shakers back in the wrong order. Whether it was due to the kitchen's cramped quarters or to how neat her mother's kitchen had always been, she never was sure.

The phone rang while they were having lunch. Gwen hurried to answer it.

"Daddy! Mommy, Daddy's on the phone!" Joanna cringed inwardly, but pasted on a smile for Gwen. Gwen's side of the conversation indicated Larry was inviting her to come to Auburn the following weekend. She hopped from one foot to the other, directing happy looks at her mother as she talked.

Clamping her hand over the receiver she said, "Daddy wants to know if you can bring me over there because he's having problems with the truck. You can, can't you?" Joanna nodded. "She can, Daddy!" Gwen shrieked happily into the phone. "Okay, I'll put her on." She beckoned to Joanna. "Daddy needs to give you the directions in case you don't remember how to get there." She handed the phone over and dashed from the kitchen.

"Hope it's not too much trouble asking you to drive up here, Jo" Larry said by way of greeting.

"Let's just say it would be worse to keep Gwen home and hear her complain all weekend about not getting to go to Auburn."

"Damn thing needs some major work and I'm still trying to line up the right place to get it done. Probably should tell you that it might end up taking a bite out of my pay so that there'll be less to send you for Gwen for a while."

"How long is a while?" she asked in a sharp tone, making no attempt to hide the irritation she felt.

"That all depends on the bottom line. I'll do my best to make it short."

She sighed loudly. "Just give me the directions then."

She wrote them down on the back of an envelope and ended the conversation with that. Gwen yelled from the bedroom that she couldn't find her suitcase.

"It's down in the basement, Gwen," she called back to her. "Listen, we've got plenty of time to bring it upstairs." She sighed and heaved herself up out of the chair. Something told her it could be a long week. Her other thought was that getting hold of a lawyer was something she shouldn't put off much longer.

Joanna gave the swing seat a big push, sending a giggling Gwen off on another swooping arch. "Okay," she laughed, "You go on your own for a while and I'll watch." She sat back down at the picnic table where they'd had their lunch, smiling at the child's tireless energy carrying her back and forth, an animated pendulum. She'd shed her sweater, the temperature approaching sixty. Her slender pale arms pulled rhythmically on the swing chains. The bright warm Sunday had brought out several other families buoyed to their own picnic tables with variations of the same picnic items. A lively assortment of kids was playing baseball on the diamond at the far end of the park. Every so often someone jogging or walking their dog came along the park's meandering sidewalk.

Joanna lay back on the sun-warmed bench and closed her eyes. The rustling gurgle of Seneca Creek wove together the sounds of people enjoying the May afternoon. Relishing the day's warmth, she sank into a daze of contentment.

Their determined cleaning efforts yesterday had the apartment sparkling, and they could hardly wait to see the expression on Kim's face when she got home that evening. Gwen had spent a whole hour that morning working on an elaborate birthday card that was now safely hidden under her socks in her top dresser drawer. Joanna splurged on a copy of the Rochester Sunday paper and had spent a luxurious hour at the kitchen table, her feet up on another chair, reading and sipping coffee.

While packing things to bring on their picnic, the thought occurred to her that the park might be a good place to work on her story so she'd brought it along. She thought of it now and after another few minutes lolling in the sun, roused herself and drew the papers out of the tote bag. She scanned the most recent pages she'd written, smoothed the papers flat, and began to write.

"Mommy, watch this. I'm going to jump!" Joanna looked up in time to see Gwen leap from her swing. She teetered as she landed but kept her balance, trotting over with a triumphant grin. "Did you see that?"

"Sure did, Tarzan-woman. You're quite the swinger."

"I still like your swing in Grandpa's yard the best."

"Oh you do, do you? Well, I think you've got good taste in swings then."

Gwen grinned and leaned against her mother's shoulder. She was flushed and warm, sweet-smelling from the swinging. Joanna encircled her narrow waist with one arm. Gwen pointed to the papers. "Mommy, will you please read me your grownup story now?" Other times when she'd asked Joanna had told her it would probably only bore her. Obliging her now, she read her the story's last two pages along with the half page of narrative she'd just written in a scene where her main characters met at the local teen hangout after school.

"Hmm," Gwen said when Joanna finished reading. "Is that girl Renee going to be friends again with the other one?"

"She's hoping to be, but they haven't worked everything out yet. Do you think they should?"

Gwen nodded emphatically, eyeing her mother. "Oh yes. I don't like it when people are mad at each other." Joanna studied her earnest expression, struck by the thought that Gwen might be thinking about her parents.

"That's a good point. Neither do I. Thanks for your idea, Gwenny, I'll keep your suggestion in mind when I get a chance to work on my story some more." She tidied up the papers. "But now I think it's time we packed our things up and got home so we can be ready for Kim. What do you say?"

"I say, yes." Gwen scurried around to the other side of the table to collect the cups and juice bottle. "Can I still stay up until she gets here like you said I might be able to?"

"As long as it's not after nine o'clock."

Gwen pirouetted around the room in her new bright yellow tee shirt. "Oh, I just love my shirt, Kim! I can't wait to show it to Julie at school tomorrow." She fingered the iridescent lettering across the front that spelled out Atlantic City.

"I'm so glad you like it, Gwen," Kim said. "You know, Gary's the one who saw it first."

"Boy, I'm glad he did."

"Me too." She winked at Joanna. "And I can't get over how great the apartment looks with all the cleaning you guys did while I was away. I don't think this kitchen's been quite this spick and span before." Her happy smile had been nonstop since she and Gary had come in a little past seven, practically glowing. Gary had stayed long enough to watch Gwen open up the gifts they'd brought her. Besides the shirt there'd been a net bag full of sea shells and a pencil with a pink-feathered end. They'd brought Joanna an oversize coffee mug decorated with blue waves and dolphins. Then Gary had given Kim a particularly long kiss and said goodnight to everyone.

"Well, it sounds like your birthday trip was even more fun than you thought it would be," Joanna said to her now. "It was sweet of you two to bring us both back such nice things. Thank you so much."

"You're entirely welcome. We wanted you to have a little momento of this trip too." She seemed about to say more. The odd expression on her face reminded Joanna of Gwen when she was trying to keep a secret. Joanna was beginning to suspect what that might be.

Gwen had stopped her dancing and was perched on Kim's lap. "Well," Kim started again, "I guess maybe now's the time to show you guys what made this an extra special weekend." She reached into her shirt pocket and took out a gold ring. A large diamond sparkled in the overhead light.

"Wow!" Joanna said, her breath squeezed out of her.

"Ooh, Kim," said Gwen, her eyes big, "That is the prettiest ring I've ever seen. Did Gary buy that for you?"

"He sure did, sweetie." She winked at Joanna again. "But it has a very special meaning, too."

"Oh, I know what it is!" Gwen looked pleased with her understanding. "He wants you to get married to him, right?"

Kim nodded and slid the ring onto her finger. "Yes, he does."

Joanna knew she needed to say something. "Well, congratulations, Kim. Congratulations to you both. You must have been surprised."

"Flabbergasted!" She told them how Gary had talked their waiter into perching the ring on top of the cake they'd had for dessert, and he'd done so, serving it on a silver platter with two complimentary glasses of champagne courtesy of the restaurant. People near their table had clapped and Kim had cried.

"That's so neat, Kim!" said Gwen. "I hope some day someone will give me a ring that way."

"Wouldn't that be nice," Joanna said. "But right now you've got bedtime calling you. It's almost nine o'clock. Give Kim a hug, and then it's straight to our room."

Gwen put up a mild protest, wanting to have more fun, but then dutifully gave Kim a big hug and followed her mother down the hall. While she got Gwen into bed, Joanna's head swam with thoughts. Kim's good news had implications that crowded in almost the moment she'd seen the ring. But she'd already resolved that tonight was not a time to be unhappy.

She snapped off the bedroom light and returned to the kitchen determined to be upbeat. Kim wasn't there, but Joanna's new mug steamed with hot tea and Kim's favorite cup sat across from it with a tea tag hanging over the edge. Joanna sat down heavily and traced the dolphin's outline with cold fingers. She welcomed the feel of the tea-heated china.

As Gwen had said, how Gary proposed was pretty 'neat'. She had always enjoyed hearing the story of how her daddy had proposed to her Mommy at the top of a Ferris wheel at the county fair, which was exactly how it happened. She'd been giddy with happiness all night and for the next few days. The memory of that special happiness was still vivid. Thinking of that now, she silently vowed to not spoil this time for Kim

"Hey there," Kim said quietly, coming back into the kitchen.

"Hey there, yourself." Joanna was stuck for more to say. The tea steamed. When she started to speak, Kim did too. They both laughed, easing away some of the tension that had silently invaded the kitchen.

Their eyes connected. Kim's cheeks were pink. "You go ahead."

In an instant Joanna knew Kim had likely already considered how this would affect Gwen and her. But the last thing she wanted was for her to worry about it, at least not now. She held onto a smile. "Well, I was starting to say that I'm really happy for you. I mean, anyone can see that Gary's wild about you. So you turning him down at Christmas evidently didn't discourage him then."

Kim shook her head, smiling. "No, I guess it didn't. Thanks, Jo."

"Well, I can see where he thought your birthday was a good time to give it another try. What a sweet thing it was to have the waiter in on the surprise. I can just picture the whole thing." Words came easily after all. "Do you know that Larry proposed when we stopped at the top of the Ferris wheel at the Seneca Fair?"

"He did? What a nice place to get proposed to."

Joanna nodded. "It was. I've always thought that. I like your story even better."

"You know, Jo, I never suspected anything. At first I couldn't believe what was happening. Who could say 'no' after something like that?" She laughed and swirled the tea bag around in her cup, her smile bemused. "And to think just a few weeks ago you and I talked about the glories of independent living."

"We did sort of bash men that night, didn't we? Well, when the right one comes along, I think that changes everything."

"I'm glad to hear you say that, Jo. I think Gary's the right one for me."

"Then there's no point in holding back if you ask me." She gave Kim another smile. But there was something more she needed to know. "So, have you two set a date?"

"We're thinking about a Christmas wedding."

"Christmas? How nice that will be." More of the weight lifted. December was months away. She and Gwen would probably be settled somewhere else long before. "Things are so festive that time of year anyway."

Kim nodded. "Yes. They are." She was studying her mug intently as if it held some answer. A small furrow had appeared between her brows.

"Hey, you don't sound too enthused. Lots to plan for, I'm

sure, but there's plenty of time."

"That's not the problem."

Joanna blinked. Kim's discomfort was making her feel ill at ease. "What sort of problem could there be?"

Kim cleared her throat. "Gary's been offered a job in Rochester. It starts next month."

"Oh. But that sounds like good news to me. I..."

Kim leaned against the table. "He wants me to move up there with him. And I told him that probably I would but I had to have some time to think about it." Her expression was deeply troubled. "Joanna, I'm really torn about what to do because I know if I go that it would make things harder here...for you and Gwen, I mean."

Joanna felt herself nod numbly. Needing something to do, she took hold of the still-warm mug with both hands. She took a deep breath. "Oh, don't be so quick to think that. I could maybe see about getting another roommate. Probably I can find someone at the college. Or I could...I could maybe ask my father for help. And for that matter Larry's back in the picture now too." She conjured up a smile and drank some of the tea, congratulating herself at how steady her hands were. "So you see, you don't have to worry about us, Kim. We'll be fine."

Kim looked doubtful but somewhat brighter. "Well, I want to think so. I talked with Gary about it for quite a while on the ride back here. It's not until July that he wants us to go. There'd be time for me to help you find someone else to take my place here."

"That would be great. So stop your worrying, okay?" But without warning, she shivered.

She woke with the same shiver the next morning. She'd been dreaming that she was walking along a city street trying to find a grocery store. She and Gwen needed food. Daylight was fading into murky gray. Hunched against a cold wind, she clutched the few dollars in her pocket. Then, a half block ahead, she saw the store sign and started to hurry towards it, but it was as if she was walking through deep sand that dragged at her feet. Others passed her swiftly, their pace unhindered. She redoubled her efforts and finally was at the door. Just then the store lights blinked out and she stood numbly looking in at the food out of her reach. She yelled out "No!"

"Mommy?"

Joanna opened her eyes. Gwen was peering down at her with a worried expression, Baxter clutched tight.

"Mommy, are you okay? You were making funny noises in your sleep and the alarm went off but you didn't hear it so I turned it off."

Joanna pushed herself up on her elbows and smiled to reassure Gwen. "Oh, it was just an old nasty dream, and you rescued me from it. Thanks, sweetie pie. Let's snuggle for a few minutes and then I've got to jump in the shower." Gwen climbed in beside her and tucked her head beneath her mother's chin. Joanna closed her eyes, letting the child's warmth drive away the chill.

Joanna reached the kitchen somewhat later than usual. Kim had helped Gwen get her cereal and juice. Between spoonfuls of corn flakes she was talking to Kim about going to visit her father at the end of the week.

There were circles beneath Kim's eyes. *Probably they match the ones under mine pretty well*, Joanna thought.

"I'll just bet you're going to have a nice time in Auburn, Gwen," Kim said. "So you're driving her over on Friday, Jo?"

"And back on Sunday, likely. Larry's truck is acting up as usual, and he doesn't want to drive it too far."

"Want me to ride along and keep you company?"

"That'd be great, Kim!" said Gwen before Joanna could answer. "Then you could meet my Daddy!"

Joanna returned Kim's smile over Gwen's head and rolled her eyes. "Sure thing. I'm sure you'll find it an interesting encounter."

"I'm sure I will. Did you sleep okay, Jo? I think I see circles under your eyes."

"Oh, it took me a little while to get to sleep is all, thanks," Joanna said. "Lots of excitement around here lately."

"And Mommy had a nightmare too. She didn't even hear our alarm clock so I had to turn it off, and then I helped her wake up." Gwen seemed pleased to report this to Kim.

"Well, I'm sorry to hear about that. Good thing you were there to help out," Kim said. "What sort of bad dream did you have, Jo?"

Joanna shrugged and mustered up a smile. "At this point I can't remember. But at least Gwen rescued me from it."

She'd like that to have been the truth. Any sort of rescue would be welcome now.

# ~ Fourteen ~

Rainy weather much of the week only reinforced Joanna's
bleak frame of mind. Each morning she had to endure Gwen's
enthusiastic countdown to Friday. At the breakfast table she'd
announce the number of days left and once more revise what
she was planning to take with her. She'd lugged her suitcase up
from the basement after school on Monday. It irked Joanna to
see it, but she only went so far as to insist Gwen keep it out of
the way under her bed. As much as she disliked the thought of
her spending the weekend with him, she had to hope Larry
wouldn't renege on the plans. It would be so like him to cancel
at the last minute.

Celebrating Kim's birthday on Wednesday provided some
diversion for everyone. Gary had come over and helped
prepare a spaghetti dinner. Kim oohed and aahed over Gwen's
card, pleasing her no end. On Thursday morning Joanna woke
up with a headache. When she'd gotten to the kitchen and
started to pour herself a cup of coffee, Gwen asked gleefully,
"Mommy, guess how many days are left now?"

Joanna set her lips in a firm line, then turned and glared at
her daughter's smiling face. "For God's sakes, Gwen, do we
have to hear this every morning?" She regretted her words as
soon as they left her mouth. Gwen's face fell, her smile wilted
like a flower withered by hot wind. Kim looked up from
reading the paper. Joanna went around the table and ruffled the
child's hair. "Oh, Gwenny, I'm sorry I said that. I've got a
headache and it's made me feel grouchy. How many days are
left now?"

Gwen stirred the soggy remnants of her corn flakes before
looking up at her mother, her eyes holding some caution.

"Don't tell me you don't know!" Joanna coaxed.

Gwen stayed hunched over her cereal bowl. "It's…it's just

one."

"So how many hours does that make it then?" Kim joined in with a wink at Joanna.

Gwen wrinkled her forehead and sat up straighter. "Twenty-eight? No, wait. Mommy, how many hours in a day?"

"Twenty-four," Joanna answered, glad to move things back to center. "So, this time tomorrow morning will be twenty-four hours from now. And then in about another eight hours after that, Kim and I will be driving you over to Auburn. What's twenty-four and eight?"

Gwen puzzled with that for a minute before arriving at the right answer, and then with this new time frame in mind, went to recheck the contents of her suitcase.

With Kim as navigator reading off the directions, they reached Auburn around 6:30 the next evening. A few minutes later they pulled up in front of a gray-shingled house. Larry appeared on the porch and was nearly bowled over by Gwen as he came down the steps. Joanna busied herself getting Gwen's suitcase from the trunk.

"Daddy, this is Kim!" Gwen was hanging tight to Larry's hand by the time Joanna came up the walk.

He put the lit cigarette he was holding between his lips, and reached out to shake Kim's hand. "Hey, Kim. Haven't seen you in quite a while."

"Hi. Yes, it has been a long time."

"Right. Time flies, doesn't it?" His eyes met Joanna's. "Any trouble finding the place?"

"No. The directions were fine, and I thought I remembered how to get here."

"Good. You just missed Betty. Maybe you'll be able to see her on Sunday. She and I have plans to take Gwen to the circus tomorrow." He smiled down at Gwen. "What do you think of that, little lady?"

Gwen's eyes lit up. "Oh, boy, Daddy! Really? Mommy, did you hear that? I'm going to go to a circus!"

Larry looked pleased with himself. "You guys want coffee
or something before you go?"

"No," Joanna said, studying his pale blue eyes. She had no
desire to linger. Beyond a faint smile, there was no sign of
what he was thinking. "Kim and I thought we'd stop for
something on the way back home."

They stayed long enough for Larry to show Gwen where she
would be sleeping. She was thrilled with the roll-away bed
which had been set up in the room next to her father's. As they
drove off she waved goodbye from the porch. Larry stood
behind her, his hands on her shoulders. The image lingered.
Now that he literally had his hands on her again, would it be
hard to get her back?

They'd found a diner that advertised a fish fry. The place
was busy with the Friday night crowd. Joanna waved away the
cigarette smoke that drifted from the adjoining table. "God, I
hate the thought that Gwen's going to have to suck in Larry's
second-hand smoke all weekend." She coughed and then
sighed, contemplating the stale smell that would likely be on all
Gwen's clothes when she got back. "So when was the last time
you saw Larry, do you think?"

Kim stirred the ice in her Coke. "It must have been three
years ago. He seemed the same as I remember him. I've got to
say he did seem happy to see his daughter. And he had made
plans for the weekend that sounded like fun for Gwen."

"You're right. He does deserve some credit, and I do want
Gwen to stay in touch with him and that side of her family."
She sighed. "It's not that I think she shouldn't be there. It's just
that..." She cast about for the right words. "I'm not sure if
Larry's influence on her is, well, healthy. You saw how she
was behaving this week. At times she hardly listened to me.
Before he stuck his nose back in our lives, things were starting
to shape up for us. I've worked so hard these past months to get
things settled."

"I absolutely agree with you there. You have worked hard
and if you ask me, it's paying off. Gwen will be fine, Jo. This

weekend's a novelty for her so of course she's been a little wound up the past few days. I know what a good child she is, and that's thanks to her mother. You're worrying for nothing, I truly think."

"I hope you're right, Kim. It's not like I thought this day would never come. But now that it's here, I mean now that he's actually trying to weasel his way back into her affections, I'm dreading what the consequences might be."

"My grandmother had an expression about not borrowing trouble. Half of what you're worried about probably won't happen."

The waitress appeared and plunked down two plates laden with steaming haddock fillets.

"Thanks," Joanna said to her. "You're probably right there too, Kim. But there's that other half which I don't know if I'm prepared for." She poked at the fish with her fork. "Wish I had more of an appetite."

"You want to pass me that ketchup please?" Kim doused her fries with it and set the bottle between them. "Now don't take this wrong, Jo, but would you listen to yourself whining? Think about having the weekend free to have some fun. Hey, how about I call Gary when we get home and see if..."

"Stop right there." She waved her fork at Kim. "You're right about my whining, but I don't think I'm up for another double date with Les Dawes."

"And why not, pray tell? He's not such a bad guy."

"No, he's not. There's a lot I like about him. And anyway, where's this girl friend of his?"

Kim grinned. "Oh, I think that's cooled off in the past few weeks. And Gary said he'd asked about you just recently."

Joanna groaned. "Kim, give me a break. I've got enough to deal with with my soon-to-be ex-husband. I'm looking forward to being a free agent for a good long while if not permanently."

Kim rolled her eyes. "Well, you don't have to marry the guy. You're just in desperate need of a good time. And it would keep your mind off of worrying about Gwen. So when we get home, I'm going to call Gary and have him set something up for tomorrow night, and that's that."

Joanna found herself smiling at Kim's persistence. She started to butter her roll. "Well, I can see you won't leave me alone until I agree."

"Super! So you'll go?"

Joanna faked a groan. "Well, all right, I guess. You win."

"That's great," Kim said, laughing. "You'll be glad you changed your mind, I guarantee it."

"Hope so. Hey, you know, something just occurred to me. If I sat around all weekend and moped, it would be like I was letting Larry spoil things for me all over again."

Kim nodded vigorously. "I'd say you hit the nail on the head there, girlfriend."

"And what's more, I'm not going to tolerate that sort of thing anymore."

Kim reached out her hand, palm up for a high-five. "Way to go, Joanna!" They smacked hands together loudly. People around them looked their way sending them into a fit of giggling.

She did her best not to let her thoughts dwell on Gwen or where she was when she woke the next morning. Grocery shopping provided a few hours distraction. They hadn't been back ten minutes when there was a knock on the back door. Joanna went to answer it and found her father standing on the steps. "Dad, what a surprise to see you here," she said.

"Hope you don't mind an unannounced visit," he said, sounding a note of apology. He'd only stepped part way inside when she'd held the door open. "I was over this way trying to find a truck part and thought I'd stop in for a few minutes."

"Well, good. I'm glad you did. Come on in." She followed him into the kitchen where Kim greeted him.

"Hope I'm not interrupting anything," he said.

"Not at all, Mr. Smales," Kim said. "We were just going to put on a pot of coffee."

"Have a seat, Dad," Joanna said, pulling out a chair at the table.

"Your daughter's got the weekend off from her Mom-duties," Kim told him, standing at the counter measuring out the coffee.

"Oh? I was just about to ask where Gwen was. Is she at a friend's house?"

Joanna was setting out cups and napkins. At his question, she turned back to get the spoons from the silverware drawer. "No, she's visiting her father." She counted out the three spoons a second time.

"Oh, really? Where was it he was living now?"

"Auburn." Despite the flat tone of his voice, Joanna knew he had to be surprised. She told about Larry's plans for Gwen's visit. He listened, his face showing little expression. Joanna fiddled with her cup, running her finger around the rim.

"Mmhmm," he said when she'd finished. "Sounds like she'll have a nice time there. Thanks," he said with a smile to Kim who poured him some coffee. He blew on it and took a sip. Joanna braced herself for the comment she knew he was likely preparing to offer. There was no mistaking the solemn look he gave her as he said, "I'm glad to hear she's spending some time with her father."

Lost for a response, she could only look at him.

Kim stood up, catching Joanna's eye. "What do you say we break into that package of Pecan Sandies, Jo?" Joanna wanted to hug her. To her relief, by the time the cookies had been located and passed around, the conversation had shifted to a more neutral topic.

The phone rang. It was Gary. Kim excused herself to take the call in the living room.

After she'd gone, Joanna told her father, "Gary's Kim's boyfriend. Actually I should say her fiancée." *Damn, why did I let that slip out? What will he think?* But her father only nodded. If she was headed for hard times, she wanted that to be known only when it was absolutely unavoidable.

She asked for news of Phyllis and her family; he'd heard nothing new. He asked how school was going for Gwen. After a few minutes more of half-hearted efforts at conversation, there was a noticeable lag. He drank down the last of his coffee and said how he should be on his way back to Berlin. She walked out with him to the back steps.

He turned and looked up at her, then ran a hand through his hair. "Well, I've got to say it again. It's good to hear Gwen's seeing Larry this weekend."

She stiffened. "Let's hope you're right, Dad. I'll be glad when he can afford to get his truck in decent shape so I don't have to drive back and forth to Auburn."

"I hope you didn't let on to Gwen about things like that. Kids pick up on attitudes pretty quick."

His comment irked her all the more. "Please give me some credit for common sense, Dad. I don't bad-mouth Larry in front of her."

"Uh huh. That's..." He hesitated, jingling his car keys, looking off in the distance. He still hadn't moved to go. She felt frozen to the spot, like a child waiting to be excused. Finally he started to turn away but paused and caught her eye. "I can't help thinking, Jo, that Gwen having both her parents back in the picture is a good thing for her. Just give it some time, okay?"

She only nodded in answer. "Have a safe trip home, Dad." She turned away abruptly before he could say more and managed to resist the urge to slam the door shut behind her. Back in the kitchen she busied herself putting away the remaining groceries.

Kim reappeared. "Oh, your Dad's gone?" She began folding up the empty paper bags.

"Yes, he just left. I didn't expect him to stay long, especially with Gwen not here. He asked me to say goodbye to you. Gosh, Kim, thanks for coming up with the cookie thing when you did. It probably saved me from hearing more of his ideas about that whole Larry and fathers-being-important-deal.

Although I didn't escape it entirely."

"Meaning what? But wait, sit down with me first and let's finish the coffee." She topped off Joanna's cup and gestured at the chair.

Joanna sat, moodily stirring more cream into her coffee. "Oh, he started in on it again when I went out to the driveway with him. He said he hoped I hadn't put up a fuss about letting Gwen go see Larry, and then he said something like 'You'll see. This will really be good for Gwen to have both her parents back in the picture.' For a second I was afraid he was going to say 'back together', and if he had, I'd have had to say something. As it was, I just nodded like I agreed." She rubbed her temple where a throbbing had set in. "God, this business is starting to give me a headache."

"Try not to let it get to you, Jo. So let's change the subject. Aren't you glad we've got some fun to look forward to tonight? Gary said they'd be by around seven. Oh, and they want us to decide where we'd like to eat."

Joanna made the trip back to Auburn by herself. Kim had given in to Gary's request to go off somewhere. She apologized several times for leaving Joanna to drive back alone. She'd assured Kim she didn't mind, and that the drive would give her time alone to think. A bright May sun poured in through the windshield as she left Rockford Mills behind. Meadows and lawns showed a vibrant spring green and wooded hillsides were luminescent with a gauzy haze of delicate golds, greens, and pale bronzes. She felt her spirits rising as she drove along.

Kim had been right. The double date had been a happy success. She had kept up an animated chatter while they got ready, and they joked that it was like being two college girls preparing for a night on the town. Determined to get into the spirit of things, Joanna started humming to herself while she was getting dressed. Standing in front the bathroom mirror applying her eye makeup, she paused, surprised at her half-smile, and had to admit she was truly looking forward to the evening after all.

There'd been plenty of talk and laughter during dinner. By the time the after-dinner coffee came around, she knew she hadn't felt so relaxed in a long, long time. Perhaps it was the two glasses of Chablis, but whatever the reason, Joanna decided to savor it. Les was more dressed up this time with a tailored black vest worn over his pressed denim shirt and his cowboy boots showing obvious signs of a careful polishing job. His moustache was neatly trimmed and his musky aftershave quickened her pulse ever so slightly each time she caught its scent. When he'd gone up to buy the movie tickets and then started back towards her through the crowd in the theater lobby, she was startled to find herself thinking how positively sexy he was. Maybe she was glad to hear he and his girlfriend had split. When they'd said goodnight at the end of the evening, he'd given her a polite but warm-feeling kiss. Joanna knew she wouldn't have minded one or two more.

*We'll see what the future will bring*, she thought to herself. She passed a highway sign indicating eight more miles to Auburn. *For now there's still a lot left to work through.*

## ~ *Fifteen* ~

Joanna blessed her good fortune at how quickly she'd been able to get in and out of Larry's Aunt Betty's. There'd been a polite but short conversation with Betty whose sweet, unassuming nature Joanna had always appreciated back in the days they'd gone to Quinn family gatherings. She had high praise for Gwen's manners, crediting it to her good upbringing. She nodded towards Joanna when she said this and Joanna allowed herself a moment of maternal pride.

Though it could have been her imagination, she thought Larry looked a bit haggard. All weekend with a seven-year old might well have been more than he bargained for. The only reference to another visit had been when Betty said she hoped to see Gwen again "before too long". Larry said nothing about it.

After giving a hug to both her father and Betty, Gwen seemed glad enough to get in the car. Once started on their way, she talked for a while about the circus and then sat quietly. When Joanna looked over at her a few minutes later, Gwen had fallen asleep. She reached over to prop her head more comfortably against Baxter and then gently brushed back some hair that had fallen across her face. She allowed herself a deep sigh. She had her daughter back and apparently none the worse for her weekend with Larry. "Now you can relax," she said aloud.

Later she wondered if she'd spoken too soon. After they'd gotten back to the apartment she was decidedly cranky when Joanna asked her to unpack her suitcase and sort out dirty clothes from clean ones. Ten minutes later she returned to check on her progress, finding Gwen sitting on the floor playing with her dolls, the suitcase open on the bed and untouched.

Kim came home but Joanna wouldn't let Gwen come out to say hello until she'd gotten it done. She finally called out that she was finished and that her mother could come and see. Gwen stood in the middle of the room, arms folded, her chin set defiantly. Joanna ignored the thundercloud look while she inspected things. Though she had done the job less than neatly, Joanna decided to leave it at that and told her she could go out to the kitchen where supper was waiting.

Gwen's mood improved as soon as she reached the kitchen and got a hug from Kim. She chattered away happily about her weekend visit with especially animated detail about the circus. Joanna listened carefully for hints of what else had gone on. After they'd gotten back from the circus they'd had pizza and then Aunt Betty had taken care of her while Larry had gone out for the evening. Gwen said Betty had let her stay up to watch a movie but that she had fallen asleep on the couch. When she woke up in the morning someone had put her in bed. No one had gotten up for the longest time, so she had gone in to wake up her father. Here she stopped and looked down at her plate. Joanna and Kim exchanged looks. In a lowered voice, Gwen told how he'd been mad at being woken up, but that afterwards he'd told her he was sorry he'd yelled. Then he'd taken her out to buy some doughnuts.

"You know what, Mommy," her eyes were round and somber, "when Daddy got mad at me, I remembered when we were living in our trailer and you used to tell me not to be loud on Sunday mornings. And sometimes I'd forget and then he'd yell. Remember?"

"Yes, Gwen, I do," she said quietly. Kim sat motionless.

"But it was okay this time, because Daddy said so." Joanna knew Gwen was attempting to reassure her with this. "And I want to go back pretty soon and Daddy said that would be all right. So can I?"

"I would imagine so," Joanna answered, offering a smile. There was no sense in making an issue of anything now.

Kim stirred at last and picked up her coffee cup. "Well, it

certainly sounds like you had yourself some fun, young lady."

"Uh huh. I did," Gwen said, nodding her head. "Want me to help you with the dishes, Kim?"

"Well how nice of you to offer, but I've got an even better idea. Your Mom and I worked out a deal since I've missed you so much these past two days. After you have your bath and are ready for bed, how about reading a book together, you and me?"

"Could I do that, Mommy?" She turned to Joanna, her eyes bright once more.

Banishing the memory of her earlier unpleasantness, Joanna nodded but shook her finger at her. "On one condition, young lady, and that's if you'll get started towards the bathroom pronto. Supper was late tonight and there's school tomorrow. Do we have a deal?"

Gwen nodded her head vigorously. "Yes! Thank you, Mommy." She jumped up out of her chair and hurried to take her dishes to the sink.

Once she'd disappeared from the room, Joanna eyed Kim. "If I'm not careful, she's going to wind up spoiled. By that I don't mean that it's a bad idea you're going to read to her."

"Well, good, I'm glad you don't think so," Kim said, getting up from the table as well. "But I knew what you meant. As long as you're her mother, spoiling is not going to happen to her." She began rinsing the dishes. "You know something, Jo, I'm starting to realize how much I'm going to miss that sweet child of yours. I hope you'll let her come and stay with me once in a while."

"Only if you promise to set a good example while she's with you," Joanna laughed and swatted at Kim with the dish towel. "Now go on and have your fun and let me get my chores done."

After finishing the dishes, she sat for a while at the kitchen table with a cup of tea and the paper, glad for some undisturbed time. When Kim and Gwen appeared together hand in hand, she looked up, puzzled by the pinched look on Gwen's face.

Kim nodded for Gwen to go ahead.

"Mommy, I think I left my new glasses at Daddy's."

"You're kidding."

Kim spoke. "I'm afraid it's true. I helped her look through her things and we couldn't find them."

Joanna slapped down the paper. "Good Lord, Gwen." Her earlier exasperation instantly rekindled.

Gwen drew back against Kim, her face paling. "I'm sorry I forgot them, Mommy. I didn't mean to."

Joanna drew in a breath and smoothed out the rumpled paper, avoiding Kim's eyes. "Well, I'm sure you didn't, but now we'll have to figure out how to get them back. There's nothing we can do about it tonight. So you go read your story with Kim, if you haven't done that yet, and then you need to get to bed."

They went out without another word, Gwen holding on to Kim's hand for dear life, Joanna knew. She sat for a long minute after they'd gone, staring fixedly at the light over the table. What was left of her tea had grown cold and she got up and dumped it down the drain, bright spots of yellow swimming in her vision. She watched the amber liquid swirl down through the strainer and disappear. "Shit," she said aloud, and went to find Larry's phone number.

Alita handed a small piece of paper to Joanna. "After our talk yesterday I looked this up. This is the number of a good legal service group in Syracuse. You'll be able to get all the help you need with divorce proceedings and it won't cost you more than you can afford. Was it today that you said you were seeing Larry?"

"Yes. He's meeting me in the parking lot before I leave for home." The kind concern in Alita's expression was hard to miss. The day before Alita had found her browsing through the yellow pages looking at lawyers' ads. She'd asked Joanna about it and this led to a half hour's talk where it seemed nearly all her problems had spilled out. Larry's reappearance in their lives, the divorce stalemate, Kim's impending move. When Joanna apologized for taking up so much time, Alita gently scolded her, saying this was important. She counseled Joanna to take things one at a time and to have faith that she was going in the right direction with all of it. "And remember, big changes in our lives take time, so practice patience, especially with yourself." Joanna left the office at the end of the day with a much-restored sense of confidence.

"Thanks for this," she said, looking again at the paper. "Maybe I should show it to him."

"Not a bad idea, I'd say. Now, I'm not trying to tell you what to do, Joanna, but I want to encourage you to call them today and do it from here. Save yourself the long-distance fee on your home phone. And then you could let Larry know that too when you see him." She flashed one of her mega-watt smiles and started back towards her office.

Joanna found her voice. "Are you sure that it's all right? I mean, taking time to do this?"

Alita paused at the door and smiled again. "It's not only all right, my dear, it's something I think you *need* to do." She turned and went into her office.

The phone rang at Joanna's desk before she could take any action. Somewhat relieved, she transferred the call to Alita and turned back to the work on her computer screen. Alita buzzed her a few minutes later. "I'm off the phone now, Joanna. There's no time like the present if you'd like to make that call." She chuckled. "Talk about being an old mother hen. Once you get done talking, I'd be glad to go over anything with you that you heard." She clicked off without waiting for a reply.

"Might as well get this business started," she said under her breath. She placed the paper squarely before her and studied if as if it contained a secret code. *What on earth do I ask when someone answers?* She looked at the phone, cleared her throat, and picked up the receiver. After a few moments more, she dialed the number with trembling fingers.

\* \* \*

The pine trees at the edge of the parking lot lengthened their shadows in the late afternoon sun. Joanna paced once more around the Nova. She didn't know if she was angrier with Larry for being late or with Gwen for carelessly forgetting her glasses and causing this mess. Well, at least she'd gotten the ball rolling on their divorce. The woman she'd spoken with had been patiently helpful and set an appointment for the following Thursday. Alita had even said she'd arrange it so the half-day off would be with pay.

When she'd hung up the phone her first reaction had been one of great relief at having taken the first real step. She returned to her work with fresh energy, smiling frequently to herself, and at four o'clock she left the office humming.

Now it was nearly quarter to five and her spirits were deflating. She had yet to decide whether to tell Larry now about the lawyer or wait. She shaded her eyes with her hand and again searched the traffic for some sign of a green truck he said he'd be driving. Telling him would be admitting that she intended to follow through on matters her phone call was setting in motion, that she intended to permanently sever connections with the man she'd been married to for going on nine years.

She bit her lip and studied the pavement. Now that she'd taken the first step, why was she wavering? Was there a chance her father was right?

The place was emptying out at the end of the day. Joanna caught sight of Scott McFadden approaching the parking lot. She thought of ducking into her car so he wouldn't see her. She had no desire to explain why she was standing there. But he waved and walked towards her.

"Hi there, Joanna. You having car trouble?"

The last thing she needed at the moment was his interested concern. "Hi Scott. No, I'm meeting someone is all."

"Oh, good. I'm glad that's what it is." He shifted his briefcase to his other hand. "So tell me, are you considering signing up for my summer course I hope? I'm planning on making it lots of fun if you need further convincing."

"I'm not too sure yet, but I'm keeping it in mind." She saw a green pickup with a sign on its door turn onto the campus drive. Her heart started thumping. "Well, I think they're coming now. I promise that as soon as I figure out my summer I'll let you know." Praying he wouldn't linger, she went around to the passenger door and pretended to be getting something from the front seat.

"You be sure to do that then. Have a good one."

"You too. Take care."

To her relief he strode briskly away with a wave back to her.

She was just able to catch her breath when Larry pulled up. She risked a quick glance in Scott's direction. He stood by his car, the door open. To her annoyance, she felt her face flush and was thankful Scott wasn't close enough to see.

Larry got out, spit on the pavement, and came around the truck carrying the glasses' case. She heard a car door slam followed by an engine starting.

Focusing on Larry, she met his smile with a stern look. "I was beginning to wonder if you were going to show up today." The words came out more sharply than she'd intended them to but she couldn't think of a reason to apologize. After all he'd said he'd be there near four.

She was glad to see his smile fade. He handed the case to her and pushed back his faded Buffalo Bills cap. His lank hair hung untidily below his ears. But then he had no one to get after him to keep it cut. "It took longer picking up the order than I thought it would. Not much I could do about that." He shook a cigarette out of the crumpled pack he took from his shirt pocket and lit it up, folding his thin arms across his chest. "Hey, at least my having to come to the Mills today saved you a trip all the way back to Auburn."

That much was true. She relented and chose another approach. "Yes, you did. Thanks. Gwen should have packed her things more carefully to come home."

"She say she had a good time with her old man?" Joanna found herself analyzing his expression as he said this. The upturned corners of his mouth hinted at his satisfied smugness that she'd have to admit Gwen had enjoyed herself.

She'd give him as little satisfaction as she could. "She had a lot to say about the circus."

He nodded and took a drag of his cigarette. "Gwen tells me you're going to be losing your roommate pretty soon. Kim's moving out in July, I think she said?"

His question caught her off guard. Her stomach knotted. Pretending interest in something across the parking lot, she tried to sound offhand. "She and Gary are getting married at Christmas." Then she looked back at him.

He blew out a stream of smoke, squinting at her for a long moment. She willed her face to remain blank and tried to anticipate what he'd say next. "You going to be able to stay in the Mills?"

"I should be able to find someone to take over Kim's place. Or I might be able to handle the rent on my own. There's a raise coming our way here in August." The lie slipped out easily inspiring another thought. "And then there's the fact that with you earning better money these days I've got to assume you're in a position to help support your daughter again."

He hesitated before answering. "Well, you've hit upon a point there, and that's that you and I should sit down and discuss a few things about the future, especially as far as Gwen goes." His evasive response was better than the argument she half-expected.

She decided to stop prodding and looked meaningfully at her watch. The business about the lawyer could wait. "Well, you're right about that, but we're going to have to save that for another day. I'm already late getting home." She turned away and opened her car door. "So, thanks again for bringing Gwen's glasses down. I'll call you in a week or so and we can plan some things out."

He got back in the truck without another word and drove

off. She waited until he'd reached the exit before she backed the Nova out of the parking space.

Supper was on the table when she reached the apartment. Gwen had an apron tied high above her waist and Kim reported that she had made the macaroni and cheese almost single-handed. Joanna rethought the scolding she had in mind to give when she handed over the glasses, only saying pointedly that it had better not happen again. Gwen vowed that that would be the case and went off with them straight to their bedroom as Joanna told her to do.

"That damn Larry was almost an hour late," she said to Kim when Gwen had left the room. "But you'll be glad to hear what I did this afternoon at work. I called a lawyer Alita told me about and I have an appointment for next Thursday."

"Good for you, Joanna. That's great!" Gwen's footsteps could be heard coming back down the hall. "You can fill me in all about it later, okay?"

"Absolutely I will," she managed to say just as Gwen returned to the kitchen.

She half-listened to the supper table conversation, answering a question when asked, but was preoccupied sorting through her jumbled thoughts of the afternoon. Larry's words kept echoing, 'Gwen tells me you're going to be losing your roommate...You going to be able to stay in the Mills?'

"Earth to Joanna." She looked up to see Kim's amused smile accompanied by Gwen's giggle. She winked at Gwen. "Well, now that we've got your mother's attention, shall we tell her we're ready for some ice cream?" Gwen laughed even harder.

Joanna laughed too, glad to shove Larry out of her mind. "All right, stop picking on me, you two. Since when have I ever refused ice cream in this house?"

"Your tea, madam," said Kim, placing the mug down on the coffee table with a flourish. She settled herself in the easy chair across from Joanna. "From the sound of the snores coming from your bedroom, I think it's safe to talk now."

"For a little girl I can't get over how she can saw wood, as my father would say. I even had to get out of bed the other night and turn her over so I could sleep. What a kid," Joanna said, shaking her head. She sipped some of the hot tea. "Mmm. Thanks for making the tea. It sure does hit the spot."

"You're entirely welcome." Kim leaned forward. "So now, tell me what you found out from this lawyer you called today."

"Well, in a way, nothing too specific. The woman I spoke with, Angela Lindsay, gave me an idea of what the process would be. Then she asked me a few things like what was I after, and whether my husband had agreed to it. Stuff like that."

"Uh huh. That means that you're after an uncontested divorce, I think. The only tricky part is probably arranging Gwen's visitation with her father."

Joanna nodded. "That's right. Gwen's custody. And she said hopefully that wouldn't be hard to work out. I sure want to think so." She watched steam rise from her tea. "There's a year's waiting period to go through. But she made it sound like it wouldn't be all that complicated, not even the money end of it. They work on a sliding scale. Boy, that will be nice."

"Well, good. I'm sure you were relieved to hear that." Kim drank some tea and then cleared her throat. "Jo, there's something I've been thinking about and this would probably be the best time to say it. I don't want you to take this wrong." She hesitated. Joanna looked at her curiously. "But if my moving out makes it harder financially to swing this divorce this summer, I want you to let me help you out so you can go ahead and do it."

Joanna blinked. "Kim, I...I..." She frowned, searching for an appropriate response.

Kim leaned forward again." Listen, if it would help, you could think of it as a loan. But I'd rather you just let me..."

"No, I wouldn't want..." Her words stalled. Joanna could feel color rising in her cheeks. It suddenly dawned on her why

Kim might have been doing extra things lately, insisting on washing the dishes every night, offering to do a load of their laundry, bringing home ice cream. She was probably feeling guilty over pulling out on them.

Joanna found her voice. "Yes, that's exactly what I'd want it to be...if it turned out I needed it. After all, it's..." She'd almost said '... it's not like I'm some sort of charity case.' She smoothed out a wrinkle in the couch cushion, surprised by the anger Kim's offer had aroused.

"Joanna, I'm sorry if I made you feel uncomfortable. I didn't mean to do that at all."

Joanna stood up, just wanting the conversation to be over. The distress on Kim's face was plain. "You haven't. Really, you haven't done that. And I do appreciate your offer, Kim. I'll...I'll keep it in mind. Okay?"

"Okay." She made no move to get up. "If you want to get in the bathroom first, feel free."

Joanna paused by the hallway door. She tried not to think this was just one more nice gesture. "Thanks, I think I will. I only need a quick shower so I won't be long." She turned to leave.

"Jo?"

"Yeah?"

"I think it's great you're seeing that lawyer next week."

"Me too." She backed herself out of the room, wishing for some graceful way to end their conversation. "Like the old saying goes, just maybe there's some light at the end of the tunnel."

Kim's words followed her down the hall. "I think there is, Jo. There's some light."

# ~ Sixteen ~

She decided to circle the park a second time just to savor more of the soft spring evening. With Memorial Day only a week away, light lingered until nearly eight. An older couple approached hand in hand. She thought of Arlie and Edith and their custom of walking around Green Glade Court on nights like this one. "Beautiful evening," the man said to her when they drew abreast. The woman gave her a cheery smile. A pair of sparkly barrettes gleamed in her silvery hair.

"It certainly is, isn't it?" Joanna responded, returning a smile. She entertained a picture of them going home and enjoying a cup of tea together, sitting on their front porch.

She finally headed back, swinging her arms like a kid, enjoying the thought of returning to the quiet apartment. Gwen was away on an overnight again at Julie's, and Kim was out with Gary probably until the morning.

On the way home from work she'd splurged on take-out Chinese, and then ate with the kitchen door propped open to better hear the robin singing in their neighbor's yard. The May evening had proven irresistible, beckoning her out of doors for a walk to the park. As she tied on her sneakers, she caught sight of her writing folder under a magazine on the night stand. She took it out with her to the kitchen table, deciding she might be inspired to do some writing after she got back.

She set off for the park with a bounce in her step, breathing deeply of the balmy, spring-scented air. It had been a busy but productive week at work with nearly all the registrations completed for the summer session. At home Gwen had been working feverishly on a science project on volcanoes. For three nights the kitchen had been the scene of construction, the table littered with cardboard, markers, scissors, and papermache makings. That morning Joanna had driven her to school, Gwen cradling it on her lap. Mrs. Timian had been full of compliments when they'd gotten it to her classroom. Gwen wore an ear to ear smile when she gave her mother a hug goodbye.

Best of all was the boost she'd gotten yesterday from her appointment with Angela Lindsay. Despite Alita's assurance that things would be fine, she'd reached the Syracuse office with some trepidation. When she'd walked out a half hour later, it felt like a huge weight had been lifted away. With her were some papers that Larry needed to review and eventually sign. They would have to appear in court together to agree to custody, but it was the only thing they'd have to do together. Even with the required year's wait, the process was relatively straightforward. A year's time wasn't too much to get through.

On Wednesday Kim had news that a young woman in her office, a student intern she knew vaguely, had expressed interest in the apartment. There'd been no response to the notice that had been posted for nearly two weeks on campus bulletin boards. Maybe she'd be lucky finally in this matter too.

Shadows were deepening when she turned the corner onto Lombardy Street. A car was just backing out of their driveway. "Les!" she called, lengthening her stride. He stopped and waved a greeting.

"Well, this is a surprise," she said when she reached him, curious as to why he was there.

He flashed a boyish grin. "Kim told me you'd be rattling around the apartment by yourself tonight so I thought I'd stop by and see if you wanted any company."

Her mind worked fast. Was Kim behind this?

"How does a cup of coffee sound?" Her words came out almost without thinking, as if another part of her brain had taken sudden control.

His pleased smile answered the question. "Sounds just fine. I'd offer you a ride, but you look like you're enjoying your exercise." He winked and drove his car back up the driveway.

\* \* \*

She got up from the table to pour each of them a second cup and noticed with surprise that it had grown dark outside the windows. An hour had flown by while they'd sat talking in the kitchen.

When they'd first come inside, she'd felt suddenly awkward at being there alone with him. So she'd purposefully taken extra time getting the coffee made and selecting mugs, silently telling herself to stop being so silly. After all, they'd been out together twice and he'd been a perfect gentleman. And then he'd been so kind in helping her out with the Nova. By the time she'd sat down across from him, the fluttery sensation in her stomach was at least subdued.

Once the coffee had finished perking, he'd gotten up to help and she'd sent him to the refrigerator to get the creamer. His shirt sleeve brushed her arm as he poured some in her mug. She tried to decide if the denim shirt he was wearing represented a deliberate choice for the evening. The sleeves were folded back revealing his well-muscled forearms. Her eyes were drawn to them more than once. When she found herself wondering if he might have the same dark chest hair, she had to work quickly to banish that notion from her mind. It was all she could do to keep from blushing at her unspoken thoughts.

Despite this oddly disturbing incident, finding things to talk about had been easy. She'd begun to realize that he spent more time listening than talking. He had a way of asking questions and then sitting quietly, nodding thoughtfully at what she'd say. He chuckled over her description of Gwen's science project, pointing out that a bit of he papermache was still stuck to the edge of the table where he sat.

"Your daughter sounds like a pretty fine young lady, Joanna. One of these days maybe I'll have the chance to meet her." He reached for his cigarettes. "Now answer me honestly, would you mind if I had another smoke?" Earlier he'd politely asked if he should smoke outside, but with Gwen not home, she couldn't see the need for that.

"No, I don't mind, Les. Go ahead."

"Well, thanks for obliging me." He flicked open his lighter. "I've been giving some thought to quitting. Probably will when I'm through being on my own."

"Oh? Some lucky lady have designs on your future?" She grinned, happy she felt relaxed enough to tease him gently.

He laughed, tilting his head back. "Not that I know of. But that does bring around me around to something I've been wondering." He cleared his throat. "With Kim and Gary getting themselves together this summer, I know you're going to be on your own here with your daughter." For a moment he studied the cigarette he held in his hand.

His sudden seriousness caught her off guard. She tried to weigh the meaning of his words. "Well, I'm hoping I'll find someone to move in with us," she said, wanting to sound upbeat. "As a matter of fact, someone in Kim's office has asked about it and she's maybe going to stop by this weekend to see the place."

"That's good to hear." He shifted forward on his chair and set his elbows on the table, directing a level look at her. Kindness and something else she couldn't identify was in his eyes. "But if you and your daughter ever need anything, whatever it might be, I want you to know that I'm here to help."

She dropped her eyes. "That's...that's awfully nice of you to say, Les. Thanks."

He said quickly, "I don't mean to upset you by saying that, Joanna."

"You haven't." She looked at him again, knowing he saw how her cheeks had reddened.

"So you'll keep that in mind?" He spoke even more gently, like he was coaxing a shy child.

She nodded and managed a small smile. "I certainly will."

He smiled and looked relieved to have that said. "Good. I'm glad to know that," he said, stubbing out his cigarette. "Guess I'll get myself out of your way now. You probably had some plans to enjoy the evening all on your own."

"Oh, nothing definite, but I thought I'd spend some time on my writing." She pointed to her folder. "I got started on some last fall when I took a writing course at the college."

"Sounds interesting. I've always admired people who can do that sort of thing." He got up. "So now I really will get going so you can get something done with your writing."

Not sure of the best way to end the visit, she trailed him to the driveway stopping at the bottom of the steps. He stood an arm's length away, his hands in his pockets. Someone seeing them might have mistaken them for two teenagers at the awkward end of a date, she thought and smiled, the image dispelling her discomfort. "Thanks for stopping by, Les," she said.

"Hope I wasn't a bother," he said, grinning, a twinkle back in his eyes.

"You weren't at all. It was nice to have the company." She hoped he understood she wasn't just being polite. "Or maybe I should say, it was nice to have *your* company."

"I'll take you at your word." He turned to go and then stopped. There was that serious look again. "Not to make a pest of myself more than I already have tonight, but there's one more thing on my mind and I might as well go ahead and say it. I know things aren't really settled for you yet with...with Gwen's father. But when they are, I was wondering if you'd be interested in going out together now and then. By that I mean, just the two of us."

This time she didn't look away and her quick response surprised her. "You know, Les, I think I'd like that." Behind her the phone rang in the kitchen.

"Well, good. Hey, there's your phone. Take care of yourself, Joanna."

"You too, Les. Goodnight!" She hurried back inside, carrying with her the pleased look she saw on his face as he turned away.

"Joanna, hi...it's Marie."

"Mimi! I was thinking of calling you tonight."

"Oh, really? From the sound of your voice is there some good news?"

"For a change, yes there is. Let me start by telling you where I went yesterday."

Marie was delighted to hear she'd been to the lawyer's. "In my opinion, it can't come soon enough, but then you knew I'd feel that way."

"You probably thought I was dragging my feet."

"Not really," said Marie. "It's certainly a big step for anyone to take. Now that you've done that, the rest should be pretty manageable. So tell me what else is going on? There's a lot of enthusiasm in your voice for a Friday night."

Joanna told her about the person who might look at the apartment. "So of course, I'm keeping my fingers crossed on that." She paused for effect, smiling to herself as she thought back over the last hour and a half. "Oh, yes, and I should probably add that I had some...well, shall I say, pleasant company this evening."

"Jo! What have you been up to?" Marie sounded intrigued.

"Well, do you remember my telling you about the guy Kim set me up with to go bowling a while back?" She filled her in on Les, up to and including the present evening.

"I'm so glad to hear about this," Marie said when she finished. "He sounds like a really great guy, Jo."

"He is," Joanna said. "I'm finding more to like about him all the time. But he needs to know I'm a long way from any sort of relationship other than being friends."

"That would be my advice, too. You know the old phrase about leaping out of the frying pan. But I'm really glad to hear you've struck up this new friendship. Listen, other than finding out how things are, I wanted to let you know the kids are going to be spending next weekend with my mother so I can have a breather. She wanted me to call and see if you'd bring Gwen over for at least Saturday and that she's welcome to spend the whole weekend there if you'd like."

"Gosh, your parents are saints, Mimi. I'll have to give it some thought, especially with Gwen's being at her friend's this weekend. I'd love a chance to see you though."

"Same here. Hey, here's an idea. How about meeting me at Mom's on Sunday afternoon? After all, it's a long weekend. Memorial Day's on Monday."

Joanna couldn't resist that prospect and it was left that they'd see one another in Berlin in a week's time. She hung up the phone and looked at the clock. It was nearly ten. Too late to call Phyllis. Her writing folder lay untouched on the table. Maybe she'd find time for it in the morning.

She yawned and stretched, sighing with a contentment she hadn't felt in a very long time.

"But I want to go to Daddy's," Gwen said, scowling at her mother.

Joanna tried to remain patient. "But we've already told Aunt Phyllis that you're spending Saturday and Sunday at her house. Allison and Christopher would be disappointed too. Think of that." They'd been going around the question for five minutes. After plans had been set for her to go to Berlin, Larry had called just that evening and said he wanted Gwen to spend the holiday weekend with him. Gwen had answered the phone and he'd filled her with all sorts of fun-sounding plans, so that by the time Joanna had gotten on the line Gwen was hopping around the kitchen like a maniac.

"And Daddy even said he could drive both ways this time because his truck is fixed."

"Don't whine to me, Gwen."

"I'm not whining. I want to go to Daddy's." She stamped her foot.

Joanna raised her voice. "You most certainly are whining, young lady. And if you continue another minute more, you won't be going anywhere this weekend. You'll just stay here. Now you go and start your bath and we'll finish talking about this later. I need to think things over some more." She turned back to the dishes in the sink. Gwen didn't try saying anything else but left the kitchen dragging her feet, passing Kim without a greeting.

"That damn Larry," Joanna said to her, hoping Gwen was out of earshot, "I'm already sick to death of him being in Auburn. And that's even with the fifty dollars he finally sent me this week."

"He sure is throwing a monkey wrench into things," Kim said, picking up a dish towel. "I've never known Gwen to be so irritable. But on a different subject, what did you think of Marcie? It seemed to me she liked the place."

"Gosh, I'd almost forgotten she was here." She pictured the girl who had come to look at the apartment just as they were putting supper on the table. She had stood with a slouch smacking her gum while Kim introduced them and then had gone off for a tour of the apartment, Gwen tagging along. Joanna frowned. "She seemed awfully young, maybe twenty-one, do you think? I'm not sure she'd want to put up with a seven-year old."

"Well, as I said, she seemed to like things when I showed her around, including what I told her about the rent. And from what she's told me, she needs to find something soon. She won Gwen over as soon as she said she'd be bringing a cat with her. Of course, it would be up to you to okay that part of it."

Joanna was comparing the lackluster dullness this girl had projected with Kim's sunny personality. She sighed. "Well, if no one else comes to look at it, I guess I can't be too choosy, cat or no cat."

In the end, Joanna decided to let Gwen spend the weekend with her father. There was the fact that she needed to talk with him about the divorce proceedings and there was also the fact he could take Gwen there and back. After Gwen had gone to bed, she negotiated with him on the phone. They'd agreed to do their talking when he arrived Friday evening, and then he'd see to it that Gwen was at Phyllis's house on Sunday morning.

"I think you definitely won this round, Jo," Kim said when

Joanna told her the outcome of their phone conversation.

Joanna smiled at herself in the bathroom mirror as she got ready for bed. Kim was right. She had won this round. She'd gotten nearly all the arrangements for the weekend set up on her own terms. And even if gloomy Marcie became their apartment-mate, it at least meant that if nothing else worked out about their getting another place, they could stay on in Rockford Mills. She'd have things settled with Larry in a few days more and be able to lay the groundwork for where she and Gwen would go from here.

Maybe all she had to do was hang on a little longer.

When Larry had finally shown up on Friday nearly an hour and a half late, Joanna's patience with Gwen had been worn to the breaking point. She'd been pacing from one end of the apartment to the other. Larry was apologetic saying that he'd been held up first at work and then by traffic. With the hour's drive back to Auburn, it hardly seemed the time to get into a serious discussion. Gwen wasn't likely to give them much chance to talk alone either, so they'd agreed to meet in Berlin on Sunday morning and go out for coffee. As much as Joanna had wanted to get this discussion over with, it made better sense to tackle it when they both were more rested and didn't have to feel rushed.

This unanticipated hassle spoiled some of the happy mood she'd been in when she came home from work. That morning Alita had presented her with an intriguing possibility. She suggested they take their morning break together and Joanna had gotten their coffees from the cafeteria. She carried them into the inner office and settled in the chair across from Alita. Her ever-present smile seemed even brighter than usual.

After a few minutes of general conversation, Alita leaned forward in her chair. "Let me ask you something, Joanna. Now that things are going forward with your divorce, I hope you don't mind my saying so, but I'm curious to know what your long term plans might be. As much as I love having you as my assistant, I hope you're not planning to spend the rest of your working career here in the Continuing Ed. Office." There was something of a twinkle in her eye.

"Well, actually, my long range plans are sort of sketchy. For quite a while I've had to focus on day to day for Gwen and myself. Once things get more stabilized, then I can look ahead more."

Alita nodded. "That's an approach I can well understand. I've wished for a long time there was more pay connected with the excellent work you do."

Joanna blushed. "You know how much I like working here."

"Yes, I do. Well, I've got what might be some very interesting news. I could hardly wait to tell you about it this morning." She leaned forward again, exuberance spilling out. "A good friend of mine at Onondaga Community College got in touch with me yesterday and told me about a year-long program they're offering starting next semester. It would lead to certification as an administrative assistant. There's some grant money involved that will supply some special funding for two or three students. She asked if I knew of anyone who might qualify. I said I knew of just the ideal candidate." She stopped and beamed at Joanna, obviously waiting for her to supply the next words.

Joanna looked at her, practically speechless. "You wouldn't be thinking...you couldn't mean..."

"Why of course!" Alita couldn't contain her enthusiasm. "You would be just perfect for this, Joanna. Or should I say, it's absolutely perfect for you."

While Joanna sat nearly stunned, she outlined just how she thought Joanna could take advantage of the opportunity. The year's program would mean having to leave her work at Seneca Community, but the skills and degree she would gain through it would practically guarantee a better-paying job than was possible for her now. She made it all sound manageable and when Joanna left at the end of the afternoon, she promised

Alita she'd give it careful thought.

Just before she left the office, Marcie appeared to say she was interested in moving into the apartment. Not wanting to risk having no one else show up to take it, or have someone even less desirable, Joanna had been glad to agree. How any decision about the OCC program would affect this new agreement would remain to be seen. One thing at a time, she told herself as she started the Nova and cranked down the window to let out the day's trapped heat.

She reported this news first to Kim who arrived right after Gwen had left. "So at least one thing's been taken care of. And you know, maybe it's just me being optimistic, but I thought Marcie was a little more likeable today than she was last night. She smiled more and didn't chew gum in my face."

Kim laughed. "Well, I'm glad to hear that. She and Gwen can have bubble gum blowing contests. Speaking of Gwen, did you remind her to keep track of her glasses this trip?"

"Nope. Something better." Joanna grinned and pointed to the shelf above the refrigerator. "This time I didn't let her take them with her."

"I've got to hand it to you, Jo, at this rate you'll have everything set to rights in no time at all."

"Don't I wish," Joanna said, shaking her head. "Only time will tell. But wait until you hear what Alita had to tell me this morning. It's the most unbelievable thing." Joanna gave her the details of the OCC program and the grant money offered with it.

Kim seized both of Joanna's hands when she finished. "Oh my God, Jo! That sounds so fantastic!"

"I know it does. But I keep thinking about all the things I'd need to figure out in order to do it."

"Uh huh. As if you couldn't do that. Here's what I want you to do. Give me one good reason why you should ignore this opportunity."

"Well, I..." She looked at the delight in Kim's face and then laughed. "I guess I don't have a good one."

Kim held up her hands. "I rest my case. So now that we've eliminated that obstacle, tell me what your next move will be."

"Well," she said, grinning broadly, "as much as it all seems pretty unimaginable, the least I should do is to give it some careful thought. I'm going to guess that you'll be seeing that I do that."

"Without a doubt, Joanna, my friend. You can count on that."

# ~ Seventeen ~

Gary came by in the morning wanting Kim to drive up to Rochester with him. She left with orders to save some of the weekend's housecleaning for her and to "keep thinking". Joanna watched them drive off with a twinge of envy at their happiness in each other. Then, annoyed at herself, she went to get the vacuum.

Rain set in by the afternoon canceling the plans she had to go to the park and maybe work there on her writing. So instead she brewed herself a pot of tea and spread out her papers on the table, planning to put in a lengthy writing session. Within a few minutes she wrote several sentences. She reread them, erased a phrase and rewrote it but liked it no better. Frowning, she crossed out a word and tried another. Ten minutes crept by but her mind was depressingly blank. She scowled at the marked up paper. "God, will I ever get this thing done?" She got up and stood at the window watching the rain fall outside.

Despite her promise to Kim, she knew she was avoiding having to think about the OCC program. After yesterday's burst of enthusiasm, doubts and inescapable facts had been chasing themselves around in her head. There was no denying that it was a unique opportunity and she was flattered beyond words that Alita thought she could do it. But could she? Money considerations aside, it had been a long while since she had been a student. She wasn't so sure she had that sort of discipline to handle serious college work and she'd be carrying at least three courses each semester. But beyond all of that was a bigger problem. How on earth would she support Gwen and herself for the year, even with the financial assistance Alita had described?

She turned away from the window and went to get her jacket and pocketbook. A trip to the grocery store seemed a good solution for the moment.

With some additional browsing time at K-Mart, she managed to kill nearly two hours before returning home to fix an omelet for her supper. The television evening news was followed by a rerun of "Bewitched". *Wish I could wrinkle my nose and change a few things around here*, she thought as the credits came up.

Just as she was hoping for her return, Kim called to say Gary had talked her into staying at his place. "Hope you don't mind being alone. But hey, this will give you more time to get that thinking done, which I trust you've been doing."

Joanna turned her hand over and studied her nails. "Oh, I'm thinking up a storm here, no pun intended what with all the rain today. And I've just been inspired by Elizabeth Montgomery for the last half hour."

Kim laughed. "Well good. There are far worse influences. I guess you're keeping out of trouble then. Speaking of influences, maybe you should give Les a call and see what he's up to. He just might be glad to keep you company."

"I don't think so and don't you call him either, please. I'm in the mood to curl up with that book you lent me. That's enough company for me tonight." Actually Les had crossed her mind, but this wasn't a time to try and see what more might lie in that direction. And then what made Kim so sure he'd drop whatever he was doing to come over? She didn't voice that question to her but said goodnight and went to find the book.

After indulging in a long, warm shower, she finagled with the clock radio until she figured out how to set the timer for sleep mode, and found a radio station playing soft rock. Turning the volume down low, she borrowed the pillow from Gwen's bed and settled herself to read. Kim's latest romance novel proved to be absorbing and she half-worried she'd have trouble falling asleep. But an hour or so later her eyelids began to droop and she turned off the light.

Her sleep was disturbed by troubled dreams. Often it seemed Gwen was in some sort of distress, its cause never clear. Once her mother's shadowy figure had been present. Had she intended to help? Coming fully awake at last, the window held gray-hued light. The clock dial showed a little past five-thirty. Nearby the robin was already in full-throated song and Joanna closed her eyes, letting the sound of it flow over her.

The day dawned clear and mild after Saturday's rain. She left the apartment at seven-thirty, glad to be on her way. People were already out on the highway taking advantage of the good weather predicted for the rest of the holiday weekend. A minivan passed her with two kids and a dog in the back seat. A jumble of beach gear showed in the rear window. Probably they were headed for the state park on Seneca Lake. She pictured them with their lunch spread out on the picnic table, the dad happily cooking hamburgers and hotdogs on the grill, the smell of burning charcoal perfuming the air. They'd drive home late in the day, tired and perhaps a little sunburned, beach sand harbored in the seats of damp swimsuits, the watery remains of bagged ice clunking around in the cooler; a day brewed full of family memories.

She sighed and took the Dunkin' Donuts cup from the holder finding the coffee had cooled enough to drink. She squinted against the glare of the sun as she rounded a bend. Would there be some future Memorial Day when she and Gwen and some sort of stepfamily would be happily traveling somewhere together?

The sign for Maple Grove Cemetery was small but she saw it when it was still a quarter mile further ahead. A half-formed intention had been in the back of her mind when she'd gotten ready to go that morning, so now she slowed and put on her blinker. It was a half-mile off the county highway down a narrow side road.

Maybe it was that her parents had seldom visited their son's grave, and more rarely allowed Joanna to go with them. But even now with her mother there too, Joanna had only come here twice in the two years it had been since the funeral.

Gwen had wanted to go one of the times. Joanna didn't

hesitate to have her come along. She had picked a bouquet of wildflowers and placed it on her grandmother's grave. They'd said a prayer together for both Grandma Smales and baby Paul, and then walked back to the car, Gwen's hand in hers. On the way home they talked some, Joanna following Gwen's lead. Mostly she wanted to know what her mother thought about where Grandma and Paul might be now, and they agreed that certainly both were in heaven. Beyond that Gwen seemed content. She hadn't asked to go again.

Though it was still early, the gates were open. New American flags placed on veterans' graves for Memorial Day waved their bright colors in the light breeze. She passed one other car pulled off to the side. A white-haired woman leaned on the arm of a young man. They stood close together looking down. Joanna glimpsed the flag in its holder by the gravestone. Someday there'd be one at her parents' grave silently memorializing her father's service in the Korean War.

Their family plot was at the back of the cemetery. She carefully parked the car off the roadway and got out. The grave was in the last row. Just beyond was a wide, sloping hayfield and a view across the valley to wooded hills. One of the rare comments she recalled her mother making about the cemetery was that it made her happy her little boy was buried in such a beautiful spot.

The sky overhead had turned a brilliant blue and there was the promise of balmy heat in the weight of the full spring sun. It would be a good day at the beach.

She stood before the gray granite headstone with its single rose carved in the upper left corner. It had been a day very similar to this that her parents brought her to visit her brother's grave that first time. Her father had stayed by the car while she and her mother walked over. She had wanted to kneel down and run her hands over the letters of his name, Paul Edward Smales, with the single date carved beneath it. When she looked up at her mother to ask, she was looking off at some far-distant point, her gray eyes filled with unnamable sorrow.

Joanna knew she must remain silent. At length her mother had knelt and motioned her to do the same. "Say a prayer for Paul, Joanna," she had whispered and closed her eyes. The grass stubble pricked uncomfortably at her bare knees after a few minutes, and she'd been glad when they rose and gone back to the car. There'd been no comments, no conversation at all on the whole drive back to the house. The Smales family was never much for that sort of thing.

She knelt down now and traced the letters of her mother's name. "Maybe it would have helped if we'd talked more, Mom," she said. She paused and then ran her fingers over her brother's name. "At least you did finally bring me here to visit Paul."

Spring birds called. The wind crossed the field, whispering. She sat back on her heels to be more comfortable and looked out at the swaying grass. "Heaven knows I could use a little conversation with you right now, Mom." She felt a catch in her throat. "I want you to know that I'm starting to get somewhere at long last. At least it feels that way. Larry and I are really through. Boy, that would certainly make you happy." Her eyes filled, but she smiled. "Yes, I finally figured that part out. I just hope I'm smart enough to get through the rest before I'm forty. You think that will happen?" Her chest heaved with a ragged sigh and she looked down at her hands resting on her lap. She blinked, losing herself for a moment to the past. She turned her hands palms up, studying them. Her voice was barely a whisper. "Guess I know the answer to that one. You always said if a person had two good hands and an ounce or two of persistence that there wasn't much they couldn't accomplish."

She let the tears come then. When she rose some time later, she reached down and touched the stone again. "Thanks, Mom," she said, her voice wavery but more certain, and then she started back to the car.

They'd been talking for the better part of an hour. The waitress circled back again with the coffee carafe. Joanna placed her hand over her cup. "No more for me, thanks."

"You can just reheat mine some, young lady," Larry said, giving the middle-aged woman a wink. She chuckled and winked back.

For a Sunday morning, a day off, his appearance was exceptionally neat. His short-sleeved shirt looked pressed and his face bore signs of a careful shave. Even his ball cap looked new and he'd placed it on the seat of the booth when they'd sat down. The gesture wasn't lost on her. It had often been a source of irritation when he'd leave it on no matter where they went. It had been a struggle to have him take it off even on their few visits to church.

To this point in their conversation, he'd been agreeable to about everything she'd suggested, surprising her with his lack of argument.

"So, we need to set up an appointment to see this lawyer of yours together sometime," he said now, stirring more sugar into his coffee.

"Yes. I'd like to do that soon. As I said, she has late afternoon appointments."

"And I don't need my own lawyer as long as the two of us agree on everything."

She nodded. "That's right. Angela is what's called a 'lawyer-mediator'. As long as you and I can work things out, most all of it can be handled through her."

He took a slow drink of his coffee, gazing out the window. "It's mostly the money thing for Gwen that needs some figuring out. I think we're pretty much in agreement about the visitation part." He looked back at her, his expression solemn.

She'd suggested twice a month on weekends to him, which Angela Lindsay had told her was standard. "Yes, I think we have agreed on that. As far as money, I've told you what her suggestions were and to me that sounded reasonable." She paused and then added, "You're lucky I'm not after you for any back payments that Gwen's entitled to. But from this point on if you don't help out, that likely could be different."

It was the most pointed comment she'd made. He lit another cigarette. Maybe she'd finally hit a sore point. "I'm going to give you my word this time, Jo. I'll do my best to send forty a week and more when things improve for me, and I hope that will be sooner rather than later. Hell, I'm not proud of the way I acted the past few months." He tapped off ashes into the tray. "I don't suppose you have some new guy in the wings who wants to hook up with you?" This he said with a trace of a grin.

"No, I sure don't. And I'm not in any hurry either." Thinking of Les, she felt the smallest twinge of guilt at this half-truth. What was he getting at?

He smoked silently for a long minute. "Well, I can't say the same thing for myself. I might as well tell you before Gwen lets you know. I've started going out with someone up in Auburn and she's not interested in seeing me much more as long as I'm still married."

"Oh, I see." For a several moments she couldn't think of what more to say. Then she asked, "Does Gwen knows about this person?"

"Yeah. She met Jennifer this weekend."

"Oh, I see," she said again, surprised at how uncomfortable he looked. She wondered at her own lack of reaction at this revelation. "So you're dating someone."

"That's right. Jennifer thought Gwen was a pretty neat kid. She's got a daughter who's almost five. Reminds me of Gwen when Gwen was that age. If things go along okay, I think they'll get along fine together.

Joanna pictured a future day with Larry being driven crazy by two adolescent girls, one his daughter, the other his stepdaughter. Serve him right, she thought to herself, hiding a smile. He was expecting some reaction from her she knew, and looked at him now squarely. "Well, Larry, I can't say that this is all that surprising. After all, you've been out there on your own for a while." For several long seconds neither of them spoke. "It's not like either one of us expected to put the pieces back together," she said, and then added quietly, "At least, I don't think we did." The hard truth of her words hung in the air between them.

He regarded her steadily, his face for a moment's breadth, open and vulnerable. Something unspoken passed between them, honest and deeply sad. He took a last puff of the cigarette and stubbed it out. "No, we don't. I pretty much knew that when I saw you at Easter." He cleared his throat and then spoke, the trace of a broken edge in his voice, "That's just the way things are, I guess. Though likely we'd both agree that life goes on, no matter what." He didn't look at her.

For a brief moment she wanted to reach across the table for his hand, but she didn't. She said softly, "Yes, you're right. Life does go on."


Phyllis arched her eyebrows. "So, Larry's dating someone. Well, I guess I'm not too surprised to hear that."

"Me either," Marie said. "The good news about that to me is that it shows he's not going to be angling to get back together with you."

They were sitting at Phyllis's kitchen table, a half-empty pitcher of ice tea within easy reach. Larry hadn't stayed long once they'd driven back to the house. He'd given Gwen a quick hug and left. Over lunch Joanna related the main points of their morning's talk.

"No, he's not. It's a relief to know that for sure. Actually I think I'll feel better about Gwen going to visit Larry if this Jennifer turns out to be someone worthwhile." Marie and her mother exchanged looks.

"Well, let's hope she is," Marie said. "If he's looking for someone like you, then that will be fine. After all, I rather think he's sorry he let his marriage go to hell."

Phyllis nodded. "I certainly agree. He threw a wonderful family away. Still I have to give him credit for returning and promising to help support his daughter."

"Whoever this Jennifer is, I wish her a lot of luck," Marie said, then smiled mischievously. "But now, tell us a little about this nice sounding person named Les who had just left before I called you last Friday."

"That's sort of an interesting topic, I'll have to admit." To her surprise she knew her cheeks had turned pink. "Well, he's a friend of Kim's fiancée. He's helped me out with the Nova's aches and pains, and he's been a good person to talk to when I've needed that."

"No need to feel put on the spot, Joanna," Phyllis said, reaching over to pat her hand. "And what's more, you should feel perfectly free to form friendships with whomever you wish from this point on."

"I'll say." Marie caught her eye and smiled. "He sounds like a really nice man and I hope you'll get to be better friends."

"I hope the same, so you both know. Let's face it, though, I think Marie found the last good guy available. So for the foreseeable future, it's just going to be Gwen and me."

Raucous yells and laughter from the kickball game going on in the backyard had been punctuating their conversation. The kitchen was suddenly invaded by the three kids and a perspiring Lonnie, all in search of something cold to drink. Gwen announced they were looking for anyone who wanted to take a walk around the block with them. If they promised not to go too fast, Marie said she'd be glad to join in. Joanna said she'd stay to help Phyllis with the salads for the afternoon's picnic.

Phyllis protested that she should go too, but Joanna held firm. She watched them troop off down the sidewalk, Gwen and Allison tugging Uncle George along, Lonnie and Marie walking together holding hands, and Christopher leading the way, skipping. "Isn't it something how much noise three kids can make?" Joanna said, turning back from the screen door. Two handsome Bermuda onions stood waiting on the cutting board set out on the table. She chose a knife from the drawer.

Phyllis was working at the counter. "Just like old times. Your Uncle George and I will take all of it we can get. Sometimes I'm sorry your father doesn't have more chance to see them all together like this and get in on the fun."

"Uh huh. Too bad he's not here to go off on the walk with everyone. He always seems to enjoy Gwen's company, but if I didn't initiate it, I swear he wouldn't see much of his only grandchild." She shook her head and began to chop up the onion, sniffing its sharp smell.

"It's been hard for him since your Mom died. But you know that. Quite often men just find it difficult to get on with life when they lose their wives. Oh, that's not to say he's not managing his day to day affairs; some men can barely keep a house running. He's done better than most. What's sad to me is how he's...I'm not sure how to say it...how he's closed up in himself."

Joanna looked over at her aunt. "Well, truth to tell Dad's never been one to talk a lot. But then it's going to be two years this fall. You'd think he'd be moving ahead finally." She sighed. In the living room the grandfather clock struck two. "On my way here today I stopped to visit Mom's grave. It had been too long since I've done that." Saying this to Phyllis felt like a confession.

"It's a beautiful spot where she is, I've always thought." Phyllis tucked plastic wrap over the tray of deviled eggs she'd finished and set it in the refrigerator. "Don't ever be hard on yourself about how often you go there, Joanna. You do what feels right. Your mother wouldn't want it any different."

Joanna smiled at her. "I appreciate your saying that. And you're right, that is what she'd say about it." She tipped the bowl towards her. "Do you think that's enough salad dressing on this?"

"That's fine. It just needs some celery. I'll get it out of the fridge. Why don't you just have a seat since this is the last thing that needs doing?" She waved Joanna away from the counter.

Joanna knew better than to protest and sat down. She weighed the idea of telling her about the OCC program but decided against it. There was time for that. Phyllis was humming as she rinsed the celery at the sink. Joanna watched her. Her mother had often hummed to herself when she worked in the kitchen. At times Phyllis would do something that would vividly remind Joanna of her, a simple gesture or figure of speech, and memories would flood in.

She traced a pattern in the water beads on her glass of iced tea. "You know, going there today helped straighten something out for me, Aunt Phyl. And I think it was the first I'd been able to really understand it. It was what we were just talking about...about Dad." Phyllis stopped chopping the celery. "Since Mom died there have been so many times I've felt...well, I guess it's anger towards him. Just when I think it's totally gone, something will happen and there it is again. Now I think I know why." Phyllis just nodded, allowing Joanna to continue uninterrupted. "This may sound harsh, but I can't help thinking that if...well, if people in my family had talked more, shared more, then maybe Mom would have had more of a chance to...to survive. I remember being angry at her when it first came out about her cancer, and the fact that there wasn't much the doctors could do. I know she should have said something sooner to someone, but I've always thought..." She paused, hesitating to voice this long-buried thought. "I've always thought Dad should have known, should have noticed something. And if he did, why didn't he do anything?"

Phyllis came and sat down across from her. Her shoulders sagged. "He tried to, Joanna."

Joanna studied her aunt's face, hardly believing what she'd heard. "He tried to? When? When was that?"

"Nearly six months before she went to the doctor. I guess you never knew."

Joanna sat back in the chair, stunned. "Six months? No, I never knew. But how..."

"He came and told me that he was worried about her, that he'd tried to convince her to see a doctor but she wouldn't go. He asked me if I'd speak to her and I did, but she just dismissed it. I never knew why. And she didn't want you to know we were concerned." She sighed deeply. "Oh, maybe he should have been more persistent, and maybe I should have been too. I've told myself that more than once, believe me. But you should know, Joanna, he did try."

Joanna took a breath. "And for so long I've had this resentment towards him when maybe I shouldn't have."

"You shouldn't anymore. I'm sorry now I didn't say something to you before this."

Joanna reached across for her aunt's hand and squeezed it. "How could you have known, Aunt Phyl? I'm just glad that now I do know."

From the front of the house they heard Christopher yell, "I'm going to be the winner!" Racing feet thundered towards the back door.

Phyllis squeezed Joanna's hand back, enveloping her with a gentle smile. "Things always happen for a reason, Joanna. The longer I live the more I see this is true. Have faith in that."

# ~ Eighteen ~

The last rays of the sun were setting the horizon ablaze as they left Berlin behind and headed for home. "Wow, isn't that a beautiful sunset?" Joanna said.

"The sun looks like a giant red ball, doesn't it, Mommy?" Gwen said. "Grandpa told me that when you see a red sunset that it's going to be a nice day the next day."

"Grandpa's right. Did he teach you the rhyme about 'Red sky at night, sailor's delight.'?"

"Yes! I know it all. Listen, it's 'Red sky at night, sailor's delight. Red sky at morning, sailors take warning.' He said that means there's going to be a storm if the sun comes up all red, and if you were a sailor that would be bad. So tomorrow's going to be a nice day then, right?"

"Right. And probably a hot one too as far as what the weather man's saying."

"So Grandpa taught you that when you were a little girl like me?"

"Uh huh. He did."

She was still marveling at the things Phyllis had told her about her father, and the new perspective now unfolding itself. When he'd arrived for the picnic and gotten his usual hug from Gwen, she'd stepped forward and given him a quick hug too, an uncustomary gesture. "Nice to see you, Dad," she said, feeling oddly shy, but no less glad she'd done so. "Nice to see you too, Joanna," he'd answered, looking surprised and pleased at the same time. Later she'd found herself watching him when he was sitting on the porch talking with George and Lonnie. It was if she was seeing him with new eyes, like looking through a child's kaleidoscope when, with just a slight turn, the bright-colored pieces fall into a startling new and brilliant pattern.

They passed the turn for the cemetery. She glanced in its

direction and glimpsed long shadows cast by the trees along its edge. The sunset's rosy glow illuminated the hills beyond. The next time she stood before her mother's grave it would be with a new awareness. She clicked on the car's headlights against the dimming light.

Approaching the outskirts of Rockford Mills, Gwen pointed to the blinking lights of Gilligan's Ice Cream Isle. "Mommy, can we please stop for some ice cream?"

Joanna smiled and put on the turn signal. "Sounds like a nice way to end the day to me."

"To me too!"

The place was crowded, no surprise on the summery night, but they managed to find a spot to sit down with their cones. Joanna grinned at Gwen across the picnic table. Vanilla ice cream moustached her upper lip. "Looks like your vanilla tastes pretty good."

Gwen nodded. "Mmhmm."

"So tell me what you did while you were in Auburn this time."

"I helped Aunt Betty make some chocolate chip cookies yesterday. I have some in my suitcase for you and Kim."

"Yum. How nice. Did you and Daddy go anywhere?"

"We went to a park where they had some swings and a slide and Daddy pushed me on the swings." She looked like she was about to say something else but went back to licking the rapidly melting ice cream. Was she considering whether or not to tell her mother about meeting Jennifer? The people who were sitting at the table with them got up and left. Gwen ate her ice cream down to the cone.

"Mommy?"

"Yes?"

"Can I tell you something else?"

"About being in Auburn, you mean?" Gwen nodded, her eyes solemn. "Why sure you can. Tell me anything you want." Joanna tried her best to make this sound encouraging.

"Well, I think Daddy's got a new friend where he lives. It's a girl named Jennifer."

Joanna smiled gently at her daughter. "Yes, I know, Gwen. He told me that you'd met her this weekend. He told me that she had a little girl too, but I don't know her name. Did you meet her?"

Gwen shook her head. Joanna waited for her to say more. She nibbled on her cone and then looked up again. "Mommy?"

"Yes, Gwen?"

"I think that Daddy wants Jennifer to be his girlfriend."

Gwen's perceptiveness was beyond what she expected. She reached over with her napkin and daubed off some ice cream on Gwen's cheek. "I think he does too, Gwen," she said, rubbing gently with the napkin. "Did you like her?"

"She's sort of pretty, but not as pretty as you." A troubled look came to hover around Gwen's eyes. She looked down at the cone that had sprung a milky leak. "I don't want any more of this, Mommy," she said, holding it out to Joanna.

Joanna wrapped it in a napkin and got up from the bench. Her throat was tight. "I'll just take care of this and be right back. Want a cup of water?" She was glad for the chance to order her thoughts. A water cooler and paper cups stood on a ledge beside the service window. She wet a napkin with a little water and filled a cup. Gwen sat waiting at the table, her eyes fixed on her mother as she approached. *Please God, what do I tell her tonight?*

She sat down on the bench beside Gwen. "Here, use this napkin to wipe your hands and face," she said. Gwen did as she was told and then took a sip from the cup. "Mind if we share this?" Joanna asked and then drank some herself. "Gwen, did Daddy talk to you at all about...his friend, Jennifer?"

"He did a little."

"Gwen, Daddy and I had an important talk this morning after he brought you to Aunt Phyllis and Uncle George's house. We talked about what was best for all of us as a family, you, me, and Daddy. Sometimes...sometimes when people start out as a family it doesn't always stay that way forever. Sometimes that changes."

Gwen was looking deeply into Joanna's eyes. There was a moment's silence. "Is it because Daddy went away for a while?"

Joanna slipped her arm around Gwen's waist, pulling her close. "Yes, that's part of it."

Gwen leaned against her and ducked her head against her mother's shirt. "He told me he's sorry he did that." she said, her voice muffled. She held very still.

She spoke softly against Gwen's hair. "I know he is, Gwenny, but there are other reasons. Most of them are grownup things which would be hard for you to understand right now."

"Is one reason about him wanting to have a girlfriend?"

"No, that's not one. I'll explain the other ones to you someday when you're old enough to understand, I promise. But what I want to tell you is that Daddy and I have decided..." For a moment she wasn't sure she could go on. She breathed in. "...we don't want to be married to each other anymore. So, we're getting something called a divorce." She waited for Gwen to say something, but she remained motionless in her arms. "What that means is that Daddy can have a girlfriend and maybe that will be Jennifer. Then he and Jennifer could get married if they wanted to someday. And if I met someone I liked a lot, he could be my boyfriend too, if I wanted that." Les's image made a fleeting appearance. "Do you understand what I'm telling you so far?"

"Yes." Gwen stirred and looked up. "If Daddy got married to Jennifer would I live with them?"

"No, you'd still live with me just like we're doing now. You would go and visit them a lot though. And Jennifer's daughter would be your step-sister."

"She'd be my sister?"

"Yes, what people call a 'step-sister.' That probably would be really nice, don't you think? I know I would have loved having a sister when I was growing up." She smiled. Gwen searched her mother's face. "So there's going to be some changes for us, Gwen. Daddy and I will do the best we can to make them good changes. But there's one thing you can count on always, and that's that your Daddy and I love you very, very much. You're always going to have two parents that love you no matter where we are and no matter where you go." The thickness in her throat made the last words hard to say.

"That's just like how Grandpa feels about you too, isn't it?"

Joanna nodded. "Yes, it is," she said, her voice whispery.

"And like Grandma did too."

"Yes, like Grandma did too," she said, hugging Gwen to stop the tears threatening to spill over. "Let's get ourselves home now, okay?" she whispered into Gwen's sweet-smelling hair.

A soft stirring of insect sound drifted in from the warm May night. A few houses over some sort of gathering was going on, faint sounds of music and occasional laughter reached to where she was sitting on the front porch. Through the open screen door she heard Kim laugh. She and Gary had moved to the kitchen when Gwen had gone to bed.

Tired from the day, she'd protested little when bedtime arrived. She had wanted an extra hug and then lay back on the pillow, hugging Baxter close. Joanna smoothed the sheet over her and Gwen had closed her eyes with a soft sigh. Then she turned off the bedside lamp and lingered for a few moments looking at her daughter in the half-light, at the slight rise and fall of her breathing beneath the covers.

Now she settled more comfortably on the porch chair, sorting through the day's events, marveling at how much had occurred, pondering its meaning for the future. Her talk with Gwen had had to come sooner or later, and while it hadn't been easy, Joanna was glad to have some things said at last. She wouldn't have trusted Larry to have gotten things right. If she could believe his reaction during their morning's conversation, she was beginning to hope that the divorce would go smoothly.

Whether or not she could count on his financial support for Gwen still wasn't clear, but there'd been more of a willingness on his part than she'd expected. If anything had gotten clearer in the past few weeks, it was that he wanted to resume a permanent part in his daughter's life. That was something to be glad about, at least.

And so now he was seeing someone. What was this Jennifer like? For some reason she pictured her as younger than herself. Was she prettier too? If she'd insisted that Larry get out of his marriage first, that said something about her standards. That part Joanna liked about her.

There was the rusty screech of the back door being opened and then Kim and Gary's voices in the driveway. In another minute he started his car and backed it out onto the street, waving goodbye to Kim through his open window. She sighed. In just a few more weeks they'd no longer have to part company at the end of the day. "Lucky them," she said aloud wistfully.

She heard Kim coming through the living room towards the front door. "Hey there. Want some company?"

"Hey yourself. Sounds nice to me."

Kim stepped out onto the porch carrying two cans of soda. "Thought you might want something cold to drink," she said, handing her one and then going to sit in the other chair. Her blonde hair shone in the half light.

"Gee, thanks. I was feeling thirsty." She popped open the tab and took a sip. "Yes, that hits the spot. Thought I'd try out this porch furniture we brought up from the basement yesterday. You know I can picture myself sitting out here quite a bit this summer."

"I'll be thinking of you doing that some hot July night. The apartment we're getting doesn't have a porch. I'm sure going to miss this one. And I'll miss you too, of course!" They both laughed. "So how did your talk go this morning with Larry? You kept crossing my mind all day."

"Better than I thought it would, I'm glad to say. There

really wasn't anything he didn't agree to with the exception of how much child support he could afford. At first I couldn't figure out why he was being so accommodating, then he told me he's dating someone in Auburn."

"Oh really? And how did you feel when you heard that?"

"Well, I guess I wasn't all that surprised. The interesting part to me was that this person, her name's Jennifer, doesn't want to see him much as long as he's still married. So for him, getting this divorce started has gotten to be a matter of the sooner the better."

"So it sounds like it all went well. I'm glad for you, Jo."

"Yes, it feels like there's real progress happening." She slowly swirled the soda around in the half-empty can. "You know it's odd though, Kim. When I was sitting there across from him and we were just about through with stuff, for some reason I started feeling sad." She paused, recalling how she'd wanted to reach for Larry's hand. "As much as I'm glad to get out from under this marriage, there's something sad about finally, oh I don't know, finally reaching the end of it, I guess." She sighed. "I know the day we sign those papers I won't be doing any sort of victory dance."

Kim reached over and placed her hand on Joanna's arm. "No, of course you won't, Jo. And I'd be surprised if you didn't feel sad about it. I don't think there's anything strange about that reaction. You and Larry did have some good years together and I'm sure there are happy times to remember."

"You're right. There were some good years, especially when Gwen was a baby. And for her sake, I'm happy he's promising to keep up his connection with her. On the way back here tonight we stopped at Gilligan's and I had the chance to tell her about the divorce."

"Oh my. That must have been hard to do. Was she upset?"

"Mostly sad, I think." She took a last drink of the soda and set the can down. "I hope I said things the best way there was about it. Divorce isn't easy for anyone, but I want to spare her as much as I can. I'm hoping he doesn't pull another disappearing act on her."

"If he settles down with someone whether it's this person he told you about or someone else, then no doubt he'll be more reliable."

"Possibly, if he's reformed some of his bad habits. I'm almost feeling a little sorry for this woman. After all, she's got a daughter, too."

The chair creaked as Kim leaned forward. "That's really not your worry, Jo. If she's like you, she's learned a few things from life at this point."

"Boy, I'd like to think I've learned a few things so far, especially in this last year." She reflected again on what Phyllis had told her, how her view of the past had so swiftly changed. For a moment she considered telling Kim all about this. A car drove by, its headlights slowly sweeping along the houses on the other side of the street. "It's been quite a day. After Larry brought me back to my aunt's house it struck me that divorcing him is really going to happen. There's been all this time when I've been waiting for it to get here and now it's just about here. Even though he left in January, I was still connected to him in a way and not very independent. But now, I'm really on my own." She turned towards Kim. "It's nice but sort of scary at the same time."

Kim nodded. "Naturally. But look at all you've accomplished in the past few months. You're ready for this, Jo. You're one of the most independent and self-sufficient people I know. And look at the OCC program Alita's told you about. There's a door opening for you. And what's more, I just know you're going to enjoy what's waiting for you when you go through it."

Kim's words echoed the ones she'd said to herself kneeling by her mother's grave that morning. A small secret fear that had been menacing loosened some of its grip. "Listening to you makes me almost believe it for myself. You're right, I know." She got up and went to lean against the porch railing. Bright stars shone overhead. "If my mother were here, she would say to me, 'Joanna, have the courage of your convictions.'" She took a deep breath. "I guess it's time I got hold of them then."

Kim came and stood close to her, looking up at the night sky. She spoke softly. "And you know what my mother would say to that? She'd say, 'And don't forget, the sky's the limit.'" She nudged her shoulder against Joanna's. "Hey, and if we can't believe our mothers, who can we believe?"

The next day was Memorial Day and, as planned, she devoted it to just having fun with Gwen. They went to the parade downtown and in the afternoon saw the new Muppet movie at the Capitol Theater. She found herself watching Gwen closely trying to detect if yesterday's news was having an impact. But there was no sign of anything out of the ordinary and Joanna thought it best to leave things as they were for now.

When she wasn't focused on Gwen, she was preoccupied with what to do about the OCC program. There seemed to be an equal number of positives and negatives. But weighing against all the advantages it might bring, it would be a monumental task rearranging their lives for a year or more so she could go to school. Having the courage of her convictions might not be enough.

She was no closer to a decision when she reached the Continuing Ed. office the following morning. Alita understood and told her that the end of the week was soon enough to decide in order for Joanna to take advantage of the grant.

One thing was definitely under her control and she placed a call to Angela Lindsay to set up an appointment. She was heartened by Angela's telling her a positive outcome meant essentially all that was needed to conclude the rest was a brief court appearance later on. "By mid-July you'll be on your way to being an independent woman again," were her parting words to Joanna.

The holiday-shortened work week sped by. On Thursday she went ahead with her plans to talk with Becky about watching Gwen during summer vacation just around the corner. Larry's promised money at least eased that need. After Becky left, Gwen danced around the kitchen for ten minutes at the prospect of being with her all day. The phone rang. It was Kim calling to say she'd be home late and not to hold supper. Tuna wiggle was on the menu, a dish Gwen loved to help prepare. While they worked together, she chattered away about all the things she and Becky could do during vacation.

Once supper was over, Gwen took her new library book out to the front porch to read while Joanna sat at the kitchen table with paper and pencil working out a prospective budget for the summer months. The week had produced one item of positive news. The college was closer to providing a pay raise to full-time employees beginning in September. And Larry's bottom-line figure of forty dollars a week child-support gave them a thin cushion.

Friday loomed ahead and the need to have her decision to give Alita. Her thoughts about OCC had increasingly been playing to a theme of misgivings and her inadequacies. She felt less and less willing to uproot Gwen again so soon. And when she'd gotten more specifics from Alita on how much the grant would be, the figure sounded too meager. It would all be such a scramble just to get things in place by the first day of classes. But by far the largest question was what would be done about school for Gwen in a place as big as Syracuse, especially based on where they might find an affordable place to stay. Staying put in Rockford Mills at least for another year was looking more and more like the only sensible choice. She tried not to think how disappointed Alita would be to have her turn down the opportunity.

A car pulled into the driveway. "Kim's home," Gwen announced from the porch. She came in with several boxes to add to the others she'd been bringing home. Her move was barely more than a week away.

Joanna looked up from her work. "Need some help carrying any more of those in?"

"No. These are all I have for today. I'm just going to put them in the basement."

Gwen came into the kitchen. "I'll do that for you, Kim."

"Thanks, sweetie. Was that you I saw out on the porch just now?"

"Uh huh," said Gwen, grappling with the boxes. "I thought you saw me!"

"You be careful on the stairs with those," Joanna said. "Maybe take one down at a time because they're big." Gwen clunked off down the hall.  Kim was looking into the refrigerator. "That's a fresh batch of iced tea we made for supper. Oh, here's my last check for you for June's rent." She tore the check out of her checkbook.

"So I see you've been working on some math, though by the looks of it it's not Gwen's homework." Kim sat down at the table with her glass of tea and took the check Joanna handed to her.

"I wish it was as simple as that. But as far as this particular homework goes, the good news is that, barring a catastrophe, if I decide to stay where I am, we should be able to get through the summer even with the extra money I need to pay Becky. I worked things out with her today.  And if we get that raise they're talking about, I'll have even a few more options going for us."

"Does that mean you've decided not to enroll in the OCC program?"

"I can't say I have entirely." She tapped her pencil on the paper. "I wanted to figure out where things stood if I decide to just stay here."

"Well, maybe you..." Kim started to say something but paused when Gwen came back into the room.

"All done."

Kim held out her arms. "Come over here, you good kid, and let me give you a hug." Gwen hurried over and wrapped her arms around Kim. "Boy, I'm going to miss having you around, Gwenny Penny. I know I say that a lot because it's so true."

She planted a kiss on her cheek and Gwen smooched her back. "You are going to be coming to see me during your summer vacation, right?"

"Uh huh. Mommy's going to bring me sometime. Right, Mommy?"

Joanna started to pick up the papers she'd been working on. "I think that's pretty certain. I wouldn't want to disappoint either one of you. But for right now what's certain is that it's bath time. So on your way, young lady."

Kim gave her one more squeeze. "And I'd like to read a story with you afterwards while I still have the chance to do that, okay?"

Gwen was headed towards the doorway. "Okay! I want to show you the one I was reading when you came home just now."

"Sounds great. Let me know when you're ready for me." Kim sipped her tea. "Say Jo, want to sit out on the porch with me while your kiddo has her bath?"

"Good deal. I'm just going to take these papers to our room and then I'll meet you out there. Save me a seat." She checked to be sure Gwen had things started in the bathroom and then went out to the porch.

"Lordy, what a gorgeous evening," Kim said. She'd pulled the chairs up near the porch railing and had her feet propped up. "I hope I manage to adjust to big city life after being spoiled by this."

"Oh, you'll manage, especially considering who you'll be hanging out with up there in Rochester," Joanna teased, tipping her own chair back on its rear legs. "Gwen and I will be lost without you at first, that's a fact. So you'll find us on your doorstep a time or two. Maybe you'll even get more of our company than you bargained for."

"I'm sure I can handle it. You just be sure to get there."

Joanna nodded. "You can count on it." They sat together in silence for a time watching people pass by who were out enjoying the early June evening.

Kim began to tap her fingers on the arms of the chair. "Jo, I've got some news I need to tell you." Her tone of voice had changed.

"Is something wrong?"

"I hope not. I really do. It's...what Chuck Perkins told me when I stopped to give him the rent money on my way home today."

"He's not happy with how we arranged for someone else to move in? Or is it her cat?" Kim's apparent discomfort was alarming her.

"No. Neither of those things." Joanna saw her frown. "He told me he's planning to do some remodeling to the place this summer."

"Oh, I see." She was able to push the panic away. "So he's maybe concerned that Gwen and her babysitter will be in their way?"

"No, not that." Kim's voice was more and more pained. "Joanna, he wanted me to let you know that he's...planning to raise the rent. I told him that probably wouldn't be easy for you and so he at least agreed to keep it as it is until September and maybe even October. Gosh, I hated to come back here and have to tell you this. But then I thought, well you do have that OCC program to consider. And, you know, I got thinking that maybe this is some sort of sign you ought to go for it."

Joanna lowered the legs of her chair to the floor, unsure of what she was feeling beyond surprise at this news. What she needed to do was not give in to the panic that she could feel already nibbling away at her once more, its faint, sinister whispering nearly audible. "Well...I'll just have to see what we can manage, that's all." Her mind raced. "For one thing, I'd be splitting the increase with Marcie. Of course I'll have to let her know right away. How much did he say he wanted to raise it by?"

"Eighty dollars."

Joanna winced despite herself. "Wow. That much. But then it wouldn't be until the fall thanks to your going to bat for me.

By then Gwen will be back in school and I won't be paying Becky so much. It's certainly not good news, but there are worse things like if the Nova decides to blow up on me." That thought was actually pretty awful, but she tried to pass it off as a joke. "Geeze, I hope I haven't just cursed myself."

"Let's hope not. Gosh, I'm so sorry this has happened right at this point, Jo."

"Well, it's not the best news of the day, but I'll just have to do the best I can. Don't worry about it. We'll be okay."

"I'm sure you will." Kim looked doubtful but somewhat relieved. "And remember there's the OCC program to think..."

"I know. You don't have to remind me again about that." Joanna interrupted her, speaking more sharply than she intended and then didn't know what to say next. She kept her eyes focused on the house across the street trying not to feel guilty for having snapped at Kim.

Kim hadn't moved for several seconds. Then she got to her feet. "Listen, you just sit here and be a lady of leisure and I'll go see if Gwen's ready for that story." She spoke in what could only be a mock cheerful voice.

"Okay, I will. Thanks." Kim was already inside. *Probably glad to get away from me.* She raised her voice and called after her. "Give me a yell when you two need me."

Then she slid down and rested her head on the back of the chair, closing her eyes against the evening darkness.

# ~ Nineteen ~

The Nova's engine sputtered when she turned off the key but then subsided into silence. It had threatened to stall at the last stoplight before campus too. "Please, old buddy, don't do this to me," Joanna said, patting the steering wheel. "All I need is a car repair bill thrown in on top of everything else." With warm temperatures predicted for the day, she left the windows half rolled down and started for the administration building. She felt wrung out before the day had even started. At least the aspirin she'd taken had begun to work on the headache she'd woken up with. Kim's news had kept her awake well into the night. A glass of warm milk at two-thirty had taken enough of the edge off to allow sleep to come.

"Hey there, stranger." Scott McFadden's voice hailed her as she was part way across the main quad. She turned around and squinted at him in the bright morning sun.

"Oh hi, Scott. How are you?" She was pleased that for once his name had come out easily. He fell into step beside her.

"Just fine, thanks. On your way to work, I imagine?"

"Yes, I am. You too, I suppose."

He laughed. "There's always a pile of student papers awaiting my attention. Hey, when you didn't show up for the first class last week, I've got to tell you I was a little disappointed. Feel free to drop in this Thursday if you get the urge."

"That's nice of you to offer." She glanced at him. "It might sound like a lame excuse but it really has been a little hectic for me lately. But I will think about it, I promise." They paused at the entrance of her building.

He grinned. "Well good. I hope you will. Say, I saw Alita last week. She told me about a program at Onondaga Community College that she thinks you'd be a perfect candidate for. Are you giving it some thought?"

"Yes, I am. It certainly sounds interesting, but I'm not sure how I'd manage something like that even if I was accepted."

"In her opinion you would be a shoo-in."

"Thanks, but I..."

He waggled a finger at her. "No 'buts' about it, Joanna Quinn. You owe it to yourself to think seriously about it. And if you need any sort of faculty recommendation, I'd write you a dandy one. Well, I'm holding you up. See you around" He gripped her elbow briefly and started on his way before she could think of something more to say.

"Bye, Scott. I'll think about Thursday."

"Good deal," he called back. "Hope to see you then."

By the time she let herself into the Continuing Ed. Office she'd decided to at least look for the pamphlet Alita had given her on Tuesday. She'd set it down somewhere with the intention of looking it over, but never had. Alita wouldn't be in until later in the morning. Likely things would be quiet until then. Summer session was underway creating a lull for them in their office. A slow morning would suit her just fine.

She sat down at her desk and surveyed the work left from yesterday. A few letters to address and a stack of papers to file was all. Beyond that there wouldn't be much new work until Alita got in. The conversation with Scott replayed itself. It was flattering that he considered her equal to that kind of challenge. She allowed herself a private smile and reached for her cup of Dunkin' Donuts coffee. Something about his confidence in her made it all look more possible again. Alita had mentioned something yesterday about how relatively easy it was to obtain student loans. And the program could be completed in three semesters if need be.

Then thoughts of the costly repair work possibly looming for the Nova intruded upon this rosy vision. *Probably I should give Les a call and ask if he'd come and take a look at it. Maybe I did curse myself last night,* she thought, sipping at her coffee. *Why is it things can't stay even more than a few weeks at a time? Every time things start running smooth, something pops up and throws in a monkey wrench, like a damn house of cards falling down for the umpteenth time.* She sighed and closed her eyes, holding the warm Styrofoam cup against her forehead.

She let herself drift for a while, wishing she could just go home and curl up in bed. Outside the closed office door people passed by laughing and talking. *Am I the only person feeling miserable this morning?* She finally straightened up and looked at the clock. Nearly fifteen minutes had passed. Aloud she scolded herself, "Get a grip, Joanna Quinn, there's work to be done." She drank the last of the coffee, grimaced to find it now barely lukewarm, and then tossed the empty cup into the wastebasket.

Then, remembering her earlier intention, she looked for the pamphlet. A few minutes searching turned it up and she placed it on top of her lunch tote.

Alita phoned to say the meeting she was in was going on longer than expected and that likely it would be after lunch before she got to the office. "I'll try to hold the fort on my own," Joanna said to her. Alita laughed at her end of the line saying she was sure that things would be just fine then.

The morning passed as quietly as Joanna had expected it would. With time on her hands once she'd done the filing, she'd decided to go through some of the resource materials on their shelves and throw out what was outdated. By noon she had half of it finished and still had the place to herself. Knowing Alita wouldn't mind on such a slow day for them, she went outside to eat her lunch, armed with the OCC pamphlet. The front of the building faced west so that there was still shade against the day's growing warmth. Joanna made herself comfortable on the low wall that bordered the steps, opened the pamphlet and began to read.

"Well, look who's playing hooky."

Joanna looked up into Alita's sunny smile. "Caught me red-handed, boss."

"That I did. Of course you know I'm teasing you." She settled herself next to Joanna. "I think we should both play hooky for at least ten more minutes and enjoy some of this lovely day. My does that feel good!" She had slipped off her sandals and was wiggling her toes with their bright pink polish. "Not only that, but I'm delighted to see the reading material you brought along with you." She reached over and tapped the pamphlet. "Dare I hope that means you're giving it some quite positive thought? You know I wasn't sure how to bring the subject up."

"Where should I begin? Well, here goes. When you first told me about it I couldn't see how I'd possibly manage it. I mean, I was terribly flattered that you thought I could do it, but it just seemed so far beyond my reach and, the God's honest truth, it pretty much does now too." The pamphlet caught her eye. She picked it up and took a deep breath. "But I'll tell you, Alita, I'm beginning to see that I need to think about making some changes in my life. I'm tired of, oh how should I put it, living on the edge all the time. No matter how I try to keep things balanced, just when it seems they are, then something comes along and messes it all up. A perfect example is that right after I had our budget figured out for this summer, I find out the landlord is going to raise the rent. Oh, I can scramble and fix it for the next few months, but then something else will likely come along. Just this morning, the Nova acted up on the way here and now maybe I'll have a repair bill to add to the rest. So the question I should probably be asking myself is how much longer can I manage this way?" She waved the pamphlet. "Maybe something like this is what I need. But it's hard to know for sure or where I'd begin to do something about it." She stopped, having run out of things to say and feeling a little embarrassed at carrying on so.

Alita nodded in that knowing way Joanna had seen her do when she'd listened to someone closely and was preparing to offer direction. "Mmhmm. Well now, let's take one thing at a time. You're right in seeing that getting this degree would open up possibilities for you, possibilities for a much better job and income. I know you're getting things settled between you and Larry, but that by itself won't guarantee your life will become stable and comfortable. Think about this: even with the work that this program would require, your chances for that stable life which you want, and which you deserve, I might add, are ten times better than staying where you are now."

Joanna considered her words. "Well Gwen certainly deserves that sort of life. But do you think I would be accepted for this? And even if I was, it's been a while since I was a student. Maybe I'm kidding myself that I could handle that kind of work,"

Alita poked Joanna's leg with her bare foot. "Nonsense, Joanna Quinn, you're a terrifically bright young woman. And getting accepted is practically guaranteed. You'll recall my telling you that my friend, Betsy, wanted me to recommend someone for the program. Well, I can think of no one I'd rather recommend than you."

Joanna couldn't help but blush. "That's awfully nice of you to say. And you said that before so I guess I should just accept your opinion."

Alita chuckled. "While it's my definite opinion, that 'opinion' rests on facts. So, what's stopping you, I believe, is not knowing how you'd arrange it all, a place to live, where Gwen would attend school, and things like that. Am I right?"

Her words went right to the heart of the problem. "Yes, that pretty well sums things up. Our lives have been pretty chaotic for the last two years and I've finally managed to get us past most of that. Deciding about the divorce was a big thing and now that's done. The thought of uprooting Gwen right away seems wrong. I'm not sure I should do that to her. Maybe in another year or two I could look into something like this."

"Mmhmm. I can understand how you'd want to avoid that. But, and think carefully about what I'm saying, if you keep providing only temporary fixes to your life, the problems most likely will return." She tapped the pamphlet again. "Choosing to go in this direction can lift you past all of that, maybe for good."

Joanna looked hard at the pamphlet, her eyes drawn to the words, 'Let O.C.C. be your key to success'. Aloud she said, " 'Temporary fixes'...You know, I never thought of it like that."

Alita placed a hand on Joanna's arm, her dark eyes warm and serious at the same time. "Let me ask you something, Joanna. Is it a question at all of how much the program interests you?"

Joanna needed no time to consider her answer. "No, not at all. It sounds wonderful."

"Good!" Her bright smile was instantaneous. "Then what we're going to do from this point is work on figuring out how to make it possible. And we'll start by my calling Betsy this afternoon. I want her to know you're interested and get you there to talk with her. She should be able to connect you with someone who can arrange for financial help and a lot of other things you might need." She handed the pamphlet to Joanna. "So what do you say? Shall we get the ball rolling?"

How many times had she seen Alita work the same magical inspiration on people who entered their office discouraged and then walked out fired up. Perhaps it was her turn for some of Alita's positive coaching. She felt a smile blossoming from somewhere inside and realized she couldn't stop it widening on her face." You know, I think what I needed was a push to take the first step. So, yes, let's get the ball rolling."

The words were out.

If anything, Alita's smile was wider than hers. "Oh my, Joanna, I can't tell you how thrilled I am to hear you say that! I feel like we're football players who just got the ball into the end zone and we should be doing some sort of victory dance. We'll just have to make a hug do instead." She embraced Joanna in a warm hug and then reached down for her sandals. "Now then, let's get back to the office and start something!"

"So, who's ready to go back to the house for some Perry's

ice cream?" Her father looked at Gwen across the restaurant table with his practiced Grandpa-grin.

"Me, Grandpa!"

"Think you still have room after that fish fry?" He winked at Joanna.

"Plenty!" She bounced up and down on the booth seat.

"Okay, you two," Joanna said, pushing Gwen's half-empty water glass to a safer spot. "Now behave yourselves." She grinned at her father. "Really, Dad, don't get her going until we get back to your place."

Gwen led them out of the restaurant holding her grandfather's hand and sat between them on the drive back to Madison Street.

He'd called the night before to suggest that she and Gwen drive over to Berlin to meet him for a fish fry. "Give us a chance to catch up on things," he'd offered as the reason. "My treat."

"I can't say no to that then, Dad," she'd laughed in response. "And your granddaughter's already caught wind of this, so we'll see you around six."

They spent a pleasant hour at the restaurant noisy with a Friday night crowd. Gwen was full of chatter while they ate. She had endless details to relate about her school's end of the year program that was in the works. Joanna enjoyed looking on at the animated conversation between Gwen and her grandfather. She studied her father's face, still struck by her new understanding of him. It was as if a once-solid wall had yielded an unexpected opening allowing at last the chance to see the unfamiliar landscape beyond. At one point he looked over at her, their eyes connecting, and for a long moment it was as if neither one could look away. His expression registered curiosity, perhaps puzzlement. Then he half-nodded and smiled at her before turning his attention back to Gwen.

Gwen wiped her chin with a napkin, daubing away the traces of Rocky Road Supreme. "Do I have time to go out to Mommy's swing before we go home?" she asked. The late evening sun shone golden through the screen door behind her, haloing her head and shoulders.

"Sure enough," Joanna said. "Just rinse your dish out first and leave it in the sink." Gwen did so promptly and dashed out, letting the door shut with a bang. Joanna started to call after her, "Gwen, please don't..."

"Oh, let her go," her father said with a chuckle.

"Well, Dad, she should know better than that," said Joanna, getting up from the table to take her own dish to the sink. "Done with yours?"

He passed his empty dish across the table. "We both know she does so we can forgive her now and then." He chuckled again. "God, I get such a kick out of her. I'm going to have to see if I can get over to see her school program. When did she say it was?"

"The eighteenth. I'll call and remind you." Through the window over the sink she could see Gwen was already launched into an energetic swing ride, her feet pointing skyward on each swooping arch. "Would you like me to wash these up for you?"

"No, come on and sit down. I haven't heard much about how things are going with you."

She rinsed the last dish again and shut off the tap, reviewing one more time what she hoped she could say. "You're right," she said, sitting back down. "That Gwen is such a chatterbox that it's sometimes hard to get a word in edgewise." She toyed with the wooden lazy Susan in the middle of the round oak table. It was a fixture as far back as she could remember, holding the pink, shell-shaped napkin holder, a souvenir from a trip to the Jersey shore and her grandmother's milk glass salt and pepper shakers. Her father still kept them meticulously clean as her mother had always done. Their silver tops gleamed with a recent polishing.

She looked up at him. "Well, Dad, I was glad to have the chance for us to come over tonight so I could share a couple things with you."

"Everything all right?" His expression showed concern.

She strove to sound matter of fact. "For the most part, yes. And with luck, things hopefully will soon be more than all right. Larry and I are going to go through with a divorce." Her father straightened up in his chair. She hoped he would let her finish without interrupting. "We have an appointment with a divorce-mediator in Syracuse this Wednesday and it's really a pretty simple thing to manage. He and I met last Sunday when he brought Gwen back from Auburn and we had a long talk. There wasn't really anything that we didn't agree on. Actually he's dating someone in Auburn who sounds like a nice person. I think..." She frowned and gave the lazy Susan a half spin. Still her father said nothing, though she felt his eyes on her. "No, I don't just think, I *know* Larry and I are ready to move on with our lives. There really isn't too much more to say except it feels really good to be getting it settled." She looked at him then, finding not the disapproval she'd feared, but an expression that reflected, if not acceptance, then understanding. There was a long pause.

"Well, I can't say that I'm surprised. And what about Gwen? She knows this?"

"She does. I told her on the way back from the picnic at Aunt Phyl and Uncle George's. I think she's a little sad but Larry and I both have agreed to work together on keeping things positive for her. There was a time when I didn't think he cared very much about how his actions affected her, but I'm glad to say I think I misjudged him."

He nodded, appearing to be giving careful thought to what she said. Then he shook his head. "Divorce is a pretty sad business."

Her shoulders tensed. "Yes, Dad it is, but..."

He waved a hand. "Now let me finish. I wasn't being critical, because I do know Larry wasn't much of a father or a husband to you in the past couple years, certainly not in the last few months. Believe me I was very angry at him when I found out what had really gone on. But that's neither here nor there now. What I am glad to hear you say is that he's come around on things that Gwen needs from him. How about child support?"

"We're still working on it and he's promised to do what he can. It isn't likely to be a lot, but I'm pretty confident he's going to come across with something. I'll just have to wait and see. Actually that sort of leads to the other news I have to tell. And I think you'll be happy for me when you hear it." She paused for dramatic effect. "Alita, my boss, wants to recommend me for a training program in office management at Onondaga Community College."

"Really? That's in Syracuse, right?"

"It is. Someone she knows contacted her looking for candidates and she approached me about it. I've found out that with my credits from SCC, it looks like I could do it all in maybe only three semesters if I was able to go fulltime. There are a lot of details to work out, but I've decided to at least go there and talk to this person about it."

"Well, I would think you should, Jo. It sounds terrific." There was real enthusiasm in his voice. "Would you be able to get some sort of student loans?"

"Yes, probably I would. And there may be part-time work I can get through the program too. I'll know a lot more after Wednesday. Alita set up an appointment for me to see this woman after Larry and I finish with the other business in the morning." She sighed. "It's a long shot, I know. There's so much to try and figure out, but I know I'd probably regret it if I didn't at least go and see what it's all about."

"You're right there," he said and gave her a warm smile. "Think of how much it would have meant to your mother."

Joanna caressed the top of the salt shaker with her fingers. "I have thought of that," she said softly.

"So what are some of the bigger problems for you in this?"

"Most of it is how to manage finding an affordable place for us where there'd be a good school, and whether the Nova will hold together for another year, stuff like that. Even though

Alita's been full of good ideas and it looks in some ways like it might work, then I turn around and see all the reasons it really won't."

"I wish I was in a better position to help, Jo. Let me think about it."

"Thanks, Dad. I knew you'd feel that way."

Gwen trotted into the kitchen. "I need a drink," she said, panting for dramatic emphasis. "Grandpa, would you come out and push me?"

"We've got to be going pretty soon, Gwen," Joanna said before her father could answer, trying to convey with a shake of her head not to continue their conversation.

"Just for a little while, please?" Water dripped from the glass she had overfilled.

Her father was on his feet. "Let's you and I go and get in a few minutes more swinging before the train has to leave, little lady." She dashed back outside. He paused at the door. "So Gwen doesn't know anything about this?"

"Not yet. I couldn't see telling her until I had more to go on. One thing at a time."

She gave them a few minutes together and then went out to them. A towering maple tree graced the corner of the backyard. The summer she was six her father had hung a swing for her from one of its large branches, and it had been there ever since. Though the original woven rope had been replaced by a garish yellow plastic sort meant to never wear out, the wooden seat was still the same one protected by now probably a dozen coats of paint. How many countless hours had she spent beneath the maple's sheltering branches, sometimes just sitting quietly, lost in her thoughts, or swinging madly, fierce with happiness or hurt. Regardless of what brought her there, it had always been a refuge she could count on.

"Higher, Grandpa!" Gwen insisted and giggled as he gave her another push. "Hi, Mommy!" she called, spotting Joanna. "I saw over the lilacs once already!" She was swinging with her back to the house, a position that allowed a quick peak over the lilac bushes to the houses on the next street if you got swinging high enough. Joanna had told her how on clear days you could see all the way to the hills west of Berlin. And in her child's imagination, beyond the blue line of the horizon lay her future, baffling and mysterious, but always delicious in its promise.

Twilight was deepening to dark when they walked out to the car, Gwen between them holding both of their hands. "I've really enjoyed this evening with my two favorite ladies," her father said, smiling at Joanna over Gwen's head. "Now I think I know all the latest there is to know."

Gwen looked up at him. "Do you think you can come to my program, Grandpa?"

"You bet. I'll be clapping louder than anyone else, you can count on that." He leaned down for a hug and kiss. "Now go ahead and get in while I say goodbye to your mother." He turned to Joanna. The fading light caught the silver in his hair and softened the lines on his face.

She reached out and touched his arm. "Thanks so much for treating us to the fish fry, Dad."

"My pleasure. We should have more evenings like this."

"I agree." They leaned together and hugged each other. "Guess we'd better be on our way," she said, stepping away with a smile and getting into the car.

He came and stood by her open window, leaning down to look in at Gwen. "I'll be seeing you on the eighteenth. Have fun at school this week."

"I will, Grandpa. Bye."

He looked at Joanna. "About Wednesday, you be sure to find out everything you can about that new possibility and then call and tell me about it. Would you?"

"I'll do that, you can be sure." She smiled up at him. "Thanks."

His eyes were now deeply shadowed. "Just one more thing. Keep in mind all the challenges you've faced already in your life, Joanna. There's no reason why you shouldn't handle this one just fine too." He reached in and gave her shoulder a pat.

She backed the car out of the driveway and honked the horn. Gwen leaned part way out the window waving for half a block. "Get that seat belt of yours on now, young lady."

Gwen did as she was told, twisting around one more time to look back. "I can see Grandpa still watching us, Mommy."

Joanna glanced up at the rear view mirror and smiled.

# ~ Twenty ~

Joanna emerged from the administration building and blinked in the strong light. It had been an incredible day. Squinting at her watch she saw it was nearly four-thirty. If she got going right now, she'd make it home by six or so. She stood at the top of the steps and looked around at the campus. Its location on the hills west of Syracuse gave it a commanding view of the city. "What a great place to go to school," she murmured, finding it easy to picture herself here. And based on the hour's talk she'd just had with Betsy LoManto, it was all pretty much up to her to say yes or no. A shiver of anticipation tingled along her shoulders. *Well, we'll see.*

She thought again of dropping in on Marie who was only a fifteen minute or so drive from OCC. She'd anticipated needing some moral support after seeing the lawyer with Larry. But as it had turned out, their meeting had actually gone smoothly. And then, once she'd gotten to OCC, it had faded into insignificance.

By the time she reached the parking lot she made up her mind to pay a visit to the Grahams. She just had to share some of this growing excitement with Mimi.

The look of delighted surprise on Marie's face when she answered the knock on the front door was practically worth the drive from Rockford Mills.

"Joanna, what a wonderful surprise!" Marie pulled her inside and hugged her as best she could with her pregnant belly. Her hair was pulled into pigtails that bounced when she moved. "What on earth are you doing here in the middle of the week?"

"Remember I told you that Larry and I were going to meet with a lawyer pretty soon?" she said, disentangling herself from Marie's embrace. "That was today."

"Aunt Jo!" Allison dashed in and hugged Joanna around the

waist. "Is Gwen with you?"

Before she could answer, Christopher appeared with the same greeting. Joanna explained as best she could why Gwen wasn't with her and then Marie shooed them back to what they'd been doing saying they could all visit at supper.

"You will be staying for supper, of course," she said, leading the way to the kitchen. "Be warned, I won't take 'no' for an answer. Especially since it's Mexican meatloaf night."

Joanna laughed. "Then I guess my answer's 'yes'. As long as I can make a quick phone call to Kim and Gwen and let them know I'll be home later than I said."

"Please do. I was almost ready to put supper in the oven and then I'll get us something cold to drink."

Kim answered the ring and tried to pump Joanna for details about her OCC interview. "I'll tell you more when I get home," Joanna said to her, wondering what Marie was hearing of this. "But yes, I think it went well. I'll leave it at that for now. See you guys by nine, and tell Gwen I expect her to be in bed when I get there. Uh huh...okay. And thanks again, Kim. Bye."

Two tall glasses of lemonade waited on the breakfast bar. Marie was rinsing out a mixing bowl at the sink. "Not that I wanted to eavesdrop, but I distinctly heard the initials 'O.C.C'. What's this about an interview? You've been up to something more than seeing the lawyer." She dried her hands and came to perch on the stool next to Joanna, leaning towards her. "Don't keep me in suspense a minute longer."

"Mimi, you're as bad as Gwen," said Joanna and then she giggled. "Come to think of it, except for that fat stomach of yours, you look like a little kid with your hair in pigtails and wearing those shorts and cute tee shirt." Marie's shirt had Baby printed on it in bright purple letters with a large arrow pointing down.

Marie laughed. "A pretty pregnant little kid, I am. But don't change the topic."

"All right then." Joanna couldn't stop grinning. "Well, where should I start? So much has happened in just a short time that it's hard to know where to begin." She told Marie how she'd first heard about the program and her reasons for being lukewarm about it despite Alita's urging her to consider it. "Then last Friday Dad invited Gwen and me to Berlin for a fish fry, and when I told him about it, he said I owed it to myself to check it out."

"He was absolutely right. Thank goodness you went ahead and did it. So what did you find out from them today?"

"Well..." Joanna drew in a breath, not sure if she should give in yet to the excitement that had been building since she left Betsy LoManto's office. Maybe telling all of it to Marie would be fanning the flames too soon. "Well, two things. One is that my acceptance is almost certainly guaranteed..." Marie whooped with delight. "And...well...it really looks exactly like what I want to do. I'm telling you, Mimi, it almost seems too good to be true."

Marie grabbed both her hands, her voice rising in an excited crescendo. "Oh, Joanna, that is just so wonderful! So did you tell them 'yes'?"

With an effort, Joanna reined in her own leaping thoughts. "If only it were that simple. There's so much to consider, things like whether or not I could afford to do this, and where on earth Gwen and I would live while I was going to school."

Marie made a face and tilted her head. "Joanna, what kind of a self-defeating attitude is that?"

"A realistic one, I would say."

The stove's timer went off. "That's my signal to start the rice. Boy, am I glad you showed up here with this news so I can add my two cents to your father's and Alita's." She grinned at Joanna over her shoulder while she filled a measuring cup with water. "You do remember in the old days how we knew the importance of putting our heads together when faced with big decisions like this."

"Yes, I sure do." She slumped against the counter, poking at the ice cubes in her glass with her spoon. She fished one out and began to crunch on it. With her mouth partly full of ice cube she mumbled, "Maybe that's why I decided to come here first before I drove home and got discouraged about everything."

"Well, good for you for listening to your inner voice of feminine intuition. Speaking of inner voice, mine's telling me to go pee. This baby's sitting on my bladder a lot today." She patted Joanna on the shoulder when she went by. "Now you just stay there and start thinking positive thoughts. I'll be back in a jiffy." On her way out the door she added, "And don't chew on ice cubes. They're bad for your teeth."

"Yes, mother," Joanna called after her, nearly spitting out the ice as she laughed.

Lonnie's arrival delayed further serious talk. The kitchen was quickly engulfed in mild pandemonium. Greetings were exchanged, supper preparations completed, the table set by Allison and Christopher, and the dog and cat were fed. During snatches of conversation, Marie managed to explain to Lonnie what had brought Joanna to Syracuse.

Once they'd all settled at the table, he picked up the thread of their conversation. "I agree with Marie that this sounds like something you should take advantage of, Jo. How long do you have to consider their offer?"

"They've given me two weeks to decide," Joanna told him. "What it will come down to, I think, is if I can figure out living arrangements for Gwen and me that make sense." She was helping Christopher butter his potato. "There you are, Chris. Frankly, it's come up so recently and all that I just haven't had time to look into things much yet. Leaving my job at Seneca Community would be hard, but I know realistically that staying there doesn't offer much of a future."

Allison spoke up. "Maybe you and Gwen could come and live with us, Aunt Jo. Couldn't they, Mom?"

"How I'd love to be able to say 'yes', Ally," Marie said to her, "but with the new baby coming, there's no room for two other people as much as we'd love them to be here."

"Allison, that is so sweet of you to think of that." Joanna

smiled warmly at her.

"Does OCC have any sort of student housing?" Lonnie asked.

"They do, but nothing's available until January at the earliest. They did give me a list of college approved apartments, but it's already a little late for the fall semester."

"Why not take our morning paper home with you and see what's in there," Marie offered. "And I've got a couple of friends at church who might have some ideas."

"Believe me, Jo, we'll do all we can to help you out with this," Lonnie said. He exchanged a smile with Marie.

Joanna smiled around the table at all of them, feeling lifted by their loving concern. "You can't imagine how good it makes me feel to know that."

The car's headlights picked up the sign. Four more miles to Rockford Mills. A copy of the Syracuse paper lay on the seat beside her. Marie sent her off with a firm hug telling her not to worry, that everything would work out. But now her sense of optimism was fading as the elation of the afternoon was overtaken by how tired she felt.

Kim had the door open before Joanna could put her hand on the knob. "Hey there, college girl. You're ten minutes late for curfew."

Joanna grinned back at her. "Hope you didn't tell on me, roomie."

Kim shook a cautionary finger at her. "You're safe this time, but you owe me. Gwen's all tucked in and waiting for you. Oh, your Aunt Phyllis called and said she'd call you back around 9:30."

"Really? I'll bet that cousin of mine's been on the phone tonight." Kim looked puzzled. "I'll fill you in after I go and say goodnight to Gwen. Honestly, Kim, you're not going to believe what's been going on. Put on some water for tea?"

Gwen wanted all the details about her mother's 'meetings'. About seeing the lawyer with Larry, Joanna assured her that everything was set for her to visit her father two weekends a month, just as they'd discussed. About her college interview, Joanna told her that it looked like there'd be two people in their family going to school in September. Gwen seemed happy with both reports.

Reaching over to turn out the light, Joanna smiled down at her. "You know, Gwen, I've got a good feeling things are starting to turn out just fine."

Gwen nodded her head up and down. "Mmhmm. You know what I think will be the most fun of all?"

"What's that?"

"That we both can do our homework together every night."

"We'll have lots of chances to work together, young lady." Joanna planted a last kiss on her forehead. "And you are so right, we certainly will have plenty of fun, Gwenny Penny."

Just as she got back to the kitchen the phone rang.

"Joanna? This is your Aunt Phyllis. So you're home safe and sound."

"Yes, I am, Aunt Phyl. Kim told me you'd be calling. I've got to guess you and Marie have been talking to each other tonight."

"That we have, my dear." Phyllis's enthusiasm spilled from the phone line. "Well, I've got to tell you I'm just so excited about your applying for the program in Syracuse."

Joanna smiled into the receiver. "That cousin of mine. I knew she couldn't keep it to herself for long. And, yes, I'm pretty close to making my decision."

"Good. Well, when Marie and I were talking she came up with a wonderful plan. And we both liked the sound of it so well that I went ahead and called your father too. I hope you don't mind my going ahead and telling him."

"No, I don't mind. I can just imagine you and Mimi putting your heads together on this already," Joanna laughed. Kim caught her eye and cocked a questioning eyebrow. Joanna held up a finger signaling patience.

"Well now, just hear me out, Joanna. I hope this isn't too

presumptuous of your relations, but the three of us, that's counting your Uncle George, your father and me, want to propose an idea to you. What would you think about Gwen's coming to stay in Berlin during the week so she could go to school here this fall? Your father pointed out he has plenty of room and your uncle and I are only a couple of blocks away. Gwen could have her pick of places. As Mimi said, it would be sort of like commuting for you. That way you wouldn't need a big apartment in Syracuse and you'd have all the comforts of home on the weekends."

Joanna gripped the phone chord. "Oh my! That's an amazing offer, Aunt Phyl. I..." She looked at Kim. "...well, at the very least I'd like to think it over. And then we should probably all sit down and talk about it. Honestly, I'm just so touched at the offer."

"Well, the first thing you need to do, if you don't mind some motherly advice from your aunt, is to get yourself signed up for this program. The rest will follow, Joanna. You just wait and see. It's all going to work out just fine."

Joanna found herself repeating these words to Kim a short while later, remembering how she had said the same thing earlier to Gwen. "Boy, I'd love to think my Aunt Phyllis is right in that prediction." She looked into her nearly empty mug idly wondering if tea leaves really could tell the future.

"I say it's much better to be an optimist. You've got such a terrific family," said Kim. "You know, Jo, you really need to let people help you out more than you do."

She was swirling the tea around in the mug's bottom, watching how it clung in dark stains to the sides. "You're right. I probably should," she mused, half to herself. She tried picturing the whole thing, with Gwen living in Berlin and herself away for days at a time in Syracuse. "This plan for me to commute to Syracuse during the week sounds like it could work. I mean, what an opportunity. Of course, I don't know what Gwen would do, about having to change schools and all. And I've moved us once already this year. I think she would be happy about living at her grandfather's, or at Phyllis's and George's, if that's what works out. Oh, I don't know, though. There'd be so much to figure out."

Kim shrugged her shoulders. "There would be no matter what you decide. Even staying here for that matter. So don't go talking yourself into anything negative ahead of time. I predict Gwen will love the idea of going to Berlin. The only thing new and exciting for her here was that someone with a cat was going to move in. And then you two were still going to be sharing a room."

Joanna gave that some thought. "You're probably right about Gwen." She swallowed the tea, grimacing at the bitter taste, but then she smiled. "Maybe she'll try talking her grandfather into letting her get a cat."

Kim laughed. "That I can picture."

For a long minute they sat without saying anything. Kim continued to grin suggestively at her. Joanna drew in a deep breath. "So do you think I can really do this?"

She waved at the ceiling. "The sky's the limit, Jo. You know that."

The phone's sharp ring made them both jump. Kim got up to answer it. "Oh, hello, Mr. Smales. No, it's not too late. Joanna and I were just sitting here in the kitchen talking. I'll get her for you." She handed the phone to Joanna and said in a whisper, "I'm heading for bed. See you in the morning." She gave Joanna a quick hug. "Sweet dreams."

"Thanks, Kim. Sleep tight." She tucked the phone against her shoulder, "Hi, Dad."

"Jo, I sure hope this wasn't too late to call."

"Nope. Like Kim told you, we were still up. It's been quite a day."

"So I've heard from Phyllis. First, I want to tell you how happy I was to hear that your interview went well at OCC. It sounds like congratulations are in order here."

Joanna could tell he was smiling as he said this. A happy warmth spread through her. "Oh, thanks, Dad. Yes, they seem to want me in the program."

"That's great. Just great. Well, we all want to help make this work for you so I've been on the phone with Phyllis and George and we've come up with a possible idea."

"Yes, I already know about this plotting going on for you guys to maybe kidnap Gwen and then probably spoil her to death while I'm away in Syracuse working hard at my college courses during the week." She chuckled.

"Oh, must be Phyllis has talked with you already. Well, what do you think about that then?" He hardly paused for her reply and went on earnestly, "There's all kinds of room here for her and for you on the weekends. She's a pretty big girl, after all, and Phyllis and George are practically right around the corner. I think we'd all make out just fine. And with Gwen here in Berlin you could be in Syracuse focusing on your studies without any interruption whatsoever during the week. I know you haven't had much chance to consider it, but I'm hoping something along this line can be worked out." For her father this was quite a speech.

"Well," she said, grinning into the phone, "I know one thing, at least. It sure sounds like the three of you wouldn't mind having Gwen around for a year or so."

"You've got that right," he said with enthusiasm.

She smiled. "Okay. Here's what I'll do then, Dad. I'll think this all through and talk things over with Gwen. Probably I'll get back to you folks tomorrow sometime. And, Dad, I want you to know how much I appreciate what you're offering. It would be a lot of extra work you'd be taking on, after all."

"Not at all, Jo. I think that old expression, 'A labor of love' says it about right."


Twenty minutes later Joanna quietly undressed for bed in their dimly lit bedroom, still warmed by her plain-spoken father's eloquent phrase. Baxter had fallen onto the floor and she stooped to pick him up, brushing a dust kitten off of one brown plush foot. She placed him between Gwen's sleeping form and the wall ensuring he'd be there in the morning. Then she stood for a moment studying her daughter's shadowed profile, listening to the quiet cadence of her breathing. A shiver of love passed through her and she laid her hand lightly on Gwen's blanketed arm for a moment before turning away.

Snug under her own covers, she lay looking up at the street light's familiar angled path across the ceiling. She thought back to that dark March night she had first looked up and studied it, listening to Gwen's breathing, struggling with fears of their uncertain future. It seemed a sort of miracle that they had come so far in just a couple months. Where exactly they'd be in another three months, she couldn't be sure. But the thought that Gwen would likely be happy and secure there made her smile as she closed her eyes and found sleep.

# ~ Twenty-One ~

"How about some more potato salad, anyone?" Kim asked, holding up the nearly empty bowl.

"I'm saving room for dessert," Joanna said, patting her stomach. "That is if I actually do have room."

"None for me, hon. Can I get anyone another burger or a dog?" Gary got up from the picnic table and headed towards the grill.

The sun had started to slide down behind the trees. Long, angular shadows stretched nearly to the pavilion where they were having what Kim had dubbed their "Farewell and Celebration Picnic". She had even written it in bright yellow letters on the chocolate cake she'd made for the occasion. In the morning they'd finish moving out the last boxes, and she and Gary would be on their way to Rochester. Gwen had only three more days of second grade. "And of course we also need to celebrate your acceptance at OCC," she said to Joanna when she announced her plan for the picnic. Gwen had been allowed to invite Julie and so the six of them now were sitting around the table. Yells and cheering drifted their way from the Little League game going on at the ball field.

"Les, your potato salad was just delicious." Joanna told him.

It had seemed only natural to invite Les, and he said he'd be there if he could get out of his Friday night work hours. By the time Gary had the charcoal ready to cook the meat, Les appeared carrying a cooler, still dressed in his work clothes, apologizing for being late.

"Glad to hear it. It's my mother's recipe." He was straddling the bench next to her enjoying his first after supper cigarette, carefully blowing the smoke away from the table. "At least I've always got something to bring when I get asked to picnics and such."

"Word is that you're a pretty good cook," Kim said, making eye contact with Joanna. "Some woman's going to be lucky when she gets you to march up the aisle."

"That's one of the many things I tried telling Sherrie she was losing out on the last time I saw her," Gary added, grinning at Les and then Joanna. They'd recently broken up for good, Kim had reported to her just a day or two ago. Joanna was glad the teasing ended there since he now asked, "So who's for a stroll around the park before we serve up this fine looking cake?" He looked expectantly in the direction of the girls who both jumped up eager to go. "Looks like I have two volunteers. Anyone else joining the fun?"

"You coming too, Mommy?" Gwen asked, brushing crumbs off her shirt. She'd worn the yellow Atlantic City tee shirt in honor of the occasion.

"Absolutely. Give us a minute to clean things up." She helped Kim cover the food and then they joined the rest who had gotten as far as the stream. Gary and Les were showing the girls how to skip stones on the water.

Les was leaning down demonstrating for Gwen the right way to hold her stone. She took careful aim and hurled the stone away. It skipped twice across the water before disappearing with a splash. She laughed in delight. "All right!" he cheered her, holding up his palm for her to slap him a high five.

Just maybe there would be more evenings to spend with this gentle man. Joanna smiled at the thought. There was a time, and not that long ago, when she wondered if she was doomed to attract only the Larry Quinns and Eric Millers of the world. But now there was reason to think otherwise.

She looked upstream towards the bridge recalling the afternoon not long after they'd arrived in the Mills when she'd stood there transfixed by the spring torrent. That day memories had stirred of the April night in that dark clearing off Stone Road. Now the water flowed quietly out from under the bridge offering a smooth surface for  the rock-skippers to try their skills.

"Mommy," Gwen called out to her, "Watch me throw this one." She looked over her shoulder to be sure Joanna was watching and then drew her arm back and flung the small stone. This time it flew in a smooth arch skipping five times before sinking out of sight. "Oh! Did you see that?"

"Nice one, Gwen," Joanna called to her.

"Way to go, Gwen," added Les. He looked over at Joanna with a knowing smile. "Looks like your Mom's ready for us to get going on our walk around the park." Gwen reached for his hand and they started towards her. Joanna watched them approach. Whatever hold those troubled memories once had over her was slipping away, like a stone being skipped across the water to disappear beneath the dark and glassy surface.

Gwen and Julie jogged off together down the path in the direction of the ball game. She and Les fell into step beside one another while Kim and Gary strolled behind hand in hand.

"That's a great kid you've got there, Joanna," he said, nodding in the direction of the girls.

"Oh, thanks. I enjoy her, I do. I'm glad you finally had the chance to meet her." The girls had paused to look back, making sure the adults were coming. Joanna waved and the two waved back before turning and starting on. "She can be trying at times, like any child can be, but I know I'm lucky how easy she's been so far in her seven years."

"So is she looking forward to the move?"

"Thank goodness, yes. Well, that is, all except for not being able to see Julie as much once we leave here. She was upset about that for a while, but I've promised we'll get them back and forth to see each other as often as possible. And Julie's parents agreed to that too, so we survived that crisis." There had been one evening the week before when Gwen had alternated between crying and pouting about it until Joanna had yelled at her to snap out of it. She'd consoled her by saying she'd talk to Julie's mother and had done so the next night, relieving some of Gwen's anxiety over the matter. "Actually she's liable to be spoiled some while we're there, not only by her grandfather who dotes on her, but by my Aunt Phyllis and Uncle George. They're probably already scheming about luring Gwen to their house as often as possible." She laughed at her own description, thinking how accurate it was.

"And what about you? Are you looking forward to being back home yourself for a while?"

She narrowed her eyes as if focusing on the girls who were now quite a long way ahead of them. He had no way of knowing what a sore point his question hit. At the end, the decision to return to Berlin earlier than planned had been a hard one to make. "It's going to take some adjustment being back at my parents, or I mean my father's. I've had my own place for nine years, after all. But it just didn't make sense to spend the money on living here in the Mills for only another six weeks. I can really use it towards my tuition this fall."

They reached a bend in the path. Julie and Gwen were near the ball field bleachers talking to some girls that Joanna recognized as kids from their school. She tried to wave them over but they didn't see her. "Guess I'll go snag them. If you three want to go on, please do. We'll catch up."

She started towards them, her thoughts circling again around the choice she'd made to move back to Berlin with all its implications. The long list of positives couldn't be denied, and it was all coming together so well. It seemed everyone was pleased, especially her father who Joanna knew couldn't be happier to have a chance to help out his daughter and granddaughter. But there was a drawback. She wasn't sure when she first realized that despite all she'd gain, the one thing she'd be losing was her privacy. The more she thought about it the larger the truth of it loomed.

Their trailer home at Green Glade seemed like a long time ago, and heaven knew she wouldn't want to be back there. While they'd lived with Kim, even though she and Gwen had had to share a bedroom, they were still on their own. Very soon that would all change. Most of their things would have to be stored while they were in Berlin. What would she have that was really hers? By September she hoped she would be better reconciled to all of this.

With the girls in tow, they started back to the path. Les was waiting for them. She smiled to see him there. "Race you back to Les!" Gwen flung the challenge to Julie and they took off as fast as they could go. Even at this distance she could see him smile when he saw what they were doing, and he raised his arms high to signal he was ready to flag the winner.

A half-hour later daylight was fading rapidly and the lights along the street had begun to come on. While the adults took things over to the cars, the girls lagged behind entranced by the fireflies appearing in the tall grass. Joanna couldn't bring herself to tear them away from the fireflies' flickering magic. "Three more minutes and we need you two up here," Joanna called out to them on her way to Les's car with his cooler.

She lingered there to say goodnight to him while he said his goodbyes to Gary and Kim. He smiled as he approached her. "Thanks for lugging my beat up old cooler for me."

"You're more than welcome."

He unlocked the passenger door and set it on the seat. "So you don't need my help with your stuff before next Saturday morning? You're sure about that?"

"I think I'm pretty well set, thanks. I'm so grateful that you have time to help us then." Just that evening he'd found out when they were moving. He'd immediately volunteered his time and the use of a friend's pickup for as many trips to Berlin as would be needed. She looked up at him. "You're sure your friend won't mind giving up his truck for the day?"

"Not at all. He owes me a favor."

"And I'll be owing you one too, for all of this," she said and found herself blushing at the way the words had come out.

He grinned mischievously, his even teeth flashed beneath his moustache. "Well, you can count on my taking you up on that, at least once. With Gary and Kim, and now you gone from

the Mills, I'm going to be rattling around not knowing what to
do with myself. But it's all of twenty miles from here to Berlin
so I hope you won't mind my coming by to say hello now and
then. You could consider it as a way to repay the favor."

"Then I think we have a deal, Les Dawes," she said,
touching his arm for a moment before turning away, happy
with the secret electricity that was tingling through her and
imagining he was feeling some of it too.

"That was the best picnic I've ever been to," Gwen
announced as they backed out of Julie's driveway.

"Oh boy, I guess we did have fun, didn't we?" Joanna said.
"You'll sleep well tonight."

"Can Kim still read me a story even if it's late when we get
back? She said she wanted to one more time." Gwen sounded a
little sad. Thank goodness they'd had the picnic to keep
everyone's thoughts off tomorrow.

"If you can stay awake for it, it's just fine with me."

"Oh, I can do that all right." Joanna heard her yawn. "And
when we're at Grandpa's house, he can read to me sometimes."

"He sure will. I'll just bet he's looking forward to that."

"You know, Mommy, I'm going to like living with
Grandpa, but I'm going to miss not seeing my friends a lot. Are
you going to miss Kim?"

"Yes, Gwen, I sure will. Sometimes things happen in your
life that make it hard to spend time together with your friends.
But just because we won't see each other as much, Kim and I
are always going to be the best of friends."

"Like me and Julie."

Joanna thought of the two little girls coming out of the park
together, leaning against each other, laughing, their eyes bright
with shared pleasure. She said softly, "Oh, yes, just like you
and Julie."

"You know what I think, Mommy?"

"What's that, Gwenny Penny?"

"Best friends are about the greatest thing there is in the world."

"How right you are, Gwen." She put on the directional and slowed for the turn off Main Street towards Lombardy. "Oh my, how right you are," she said again, marveling at the whole of this special evening.

Phyllis had insisted on their all staying for supper. Even Les was persuaded to stay. The last of their belongings was stored in her father's basement by five-thirty. Joanna couldn't remember when she'd been as tired from a day's work. When she sank into the chair in Phyllis's dining room, it felt wonderful to have nothing more to do than fill up her plate with her aunt's delicious pot roast.

Gwen was bubbling with enthusiasm over having a room of her own at her Grandpa's house and was doubly pleased that it was her mother's old room. While they ate she carried on a lively discussion with Phyllis about her plans for how she was going to arrange all her things. Though Joanna had worried she'd be sad about leaving Rockford Mills, the opposite had been true. The wrench of saying goodbye to Kim was offset by the excitement of moving to her grandpa's house. On one of their trips earlier in the week, Joanna had taken her around to look at her new school and she'd been happy with what she saw. A visit with Julie was already on the calendar for later in the summer, so that part of their transition had gone smoothly despite her initial concerns.

Across the table from her, Les and her father were engaged in conversation. They seemed to have found lots in common and talked easily with each other. Les excused himself before dessert, thanking Phyllis with his understated charm. Joanna started to get up to see him out to his truck, but he waved her away saying he'd be in touch soon. Joanna knew he meant it. As tired as she was, she was relieved to not have to deal with whatever emotions might intrude saying goodbye outside where there would have been just the two of them. Her father went out with him to the kitchen. She could hear him thanking Les for all his help and then the sound of the back door closing signaled his departure.

Her father returned and sat down, directing a smile her way. "That Les is a nice young man."

"He is, isn't he?"

"Oh, I certainly thought so too," Phyllis added with obvious warmth in her voice. "What a wonderful help he was today." Her smile looked knowing and Joanna guessed she likely was recalling Marie's teasing her about Les the day of the family picnic. "Now, who's ready for coffee and apple pie? Gwen, would you like to help me in the kitchen?"

It was nearing eight o'clock by the time they'd finished dessert. Joanna could see that Gwen was starting to droop. Though she offered to help with the clean up and dishes, Phyllis wouldn't hear of it. After hugs and kisses from Phyllis and George, her father scooped up Gwen, long legs and all, and carried her out to the car.

Phyllis came out on the front steps and gave Joanna an extra hug before stepping back. Moths whirred and bumbled around the porch light above them. Joanna brushed one away that skimmed her hair. "Aunt Phyllis, I can't thank you enough for helping us out. I know it won't be the last time I'll be saying this either."

"You're entirely welcome, Joanna. Having Gwen nearby for a while will be ample reward, you can trust that. And you too, of course." They both laughed. She placed a hand on Joanna's arm. "You do know how proud I am of you doing this, Joanna, of taking on all this. And I'm not the only one who thinks so."

"I do, Aunt Phyl," she said, giving her a quick kiss on the cheek. "Thank you for telling me though. With all of you behind me, how could I do anything but succeed?"

Gwen was nearly asleep by the time they pulled into the driveway. Her father had the beds already made up, so all that was needed was to help her on with her pajamas and tuck her

in. Joanna had said the guest room downstairs made the most
sense for her so that she could stay up late to do her school
work when she was home on weekends and not bother anyone.
But there was another reason that she kept to herself. Moving
back into her old room somehow seemed a step backward
when she was trying to achieve the opposite momentum. And
as it was, Gwen was thrilled by the decision.

Gwen murmured a last goodnight as Joanna crossed to the
door. She had turned on her side away from the light, Baxter in
the crook of her arm, her breathing already deepening as
Joanna stood for a moment listening. Then she pulled the door
nearly closed, leaving enough space for some light from the
hall to shine in.

Downstairs in the guest room she unpacked a suitcase,
arranging things in her maple dresser they'd moved in that day.
The bed was the one that had always been in the room.
Eventually she wanted all the furniture to be her own. She'd
even fit in her kitchen table to use as her desk, its leaves folded
down. Now it was piled with boxes, but she could visualize
how it would look with a study lamp and her books spread out.

She finished and sat down on the bed holding her pajamas.
It was very quiet. "Well, guess I'm really here now," she
whispered, looking around the room that would be hers for the
next year or maybe two. Once things were organized and put
away it probably would feel cozier. Right now there was little
of that, or maybe it was just that she was tired. Earlier in the
day when they'd first started moving things in from Les's
borrowed truck, she'd suddenly been on the verge of tears.
She'd hidden in the bathroom for a few minutes willing herself
to calm down. Then she'd splashed water on her face and
looked in the mirror to be sure her eyes didn't look red.
'Joanna Quinn,' she'd said to her reflection, working up a
feeble smile, 'you do know that things could be a whole lot
worse than this. Stop being a twit and focus on what this means
for your future.' Her manufactured insight had helped and
she'd gone back out ready to continue.

Recalling this seemed to help now as well, and with a sigh she stood up and went to say good night to her father.

As she thought she might, she found him sitting at the kitchen table reading the paper, an empty glass near at hand which had held his bedtime drink of milk. He looked at her over his glasses and smiled. "Well, hi there. I wasn't sure whether to come up and say goodnight to Gwen, but I guessed she would already be asleep, so I didn't."

"You're right. She barely could stay awake to get her pj's on. Tomorrow night I'm sure she'll expect you to help tuck her in, though." She pulled out a chair and sat down. "And I know she's hoping you'll be reading her stories some nights too."

"Well, good. I'll be glad to do that." He removed his glasses and started folding up the paper. "Would you like anything? Can I fix you a cup of tea?"

"No thanks, Dad. Aunt Phyllis did a good job of filling me up." She yawned and stretched her arms, surveying the kitchen with much the same thoughts as she'd had in her bedroom. "Everyone was so great about helping us out today."

He nodded, looking around the kitchen as she had done and then at her. "I know this isn't exactly where you want to be, Jo."

The directness of his words caught her off guard and she couldn't stop her cheeks from turning pink. "Please don't think that, Dad. I'm truly glad to be here."

"I know you are, Joanna. What I meant is that I think I understand how hard it probably is for you to give up having a place of your own and move back in with your father at the age of twenty-eight." He looked at his glasses, picked them up, and then set them down again. "I'll tell you what. If it will help, you can make any changes you like while you're here, say here in the kitchen or anywhere in the house."

She was touched that he saw through to this. "That's really nice of you to offer, Dad. I'll admit it may take me a little while to adjust, but I know it's going to be just fine. One thing I do know is that Gwen is perfectly thrilled to be here. If anything, I'm a little worried about how hard it might be for you to have an almost eight-year-old around more or less permanently. And even though we talked about it already, I'm still thinking it might be asking too much, especially once I start school in September and am away all week."

He smiled and shrugged his shoulders. "You already said it. I know it's going to be just fine." He leaned forward. "So neither one of us has to worry. Agreed?"

"Agreed."

"Good. That's settled." He stood and took the empty glass to the counter. "And besides, I've always got back-up from Phyllis and George in case I run into problems with this potentially wild granddaughter of mine." He chuckled. "Tell you what, if you have to worry about something, worry about what your family will think if you don't bring home straight A's from that school you're going to go to."

Her smile answered his. "I'll do my best in that department."

"I have no doubt of that." He ran a hand through his hair and sighed. "Believe me, Joanna, I'm really glad that at last there's a way for me to help you out."

His comment puzzled her. "But Dad, you've helped me out more than you'll know over the past few years."

"Well, I'm glad you think so. In some ways, probably I have. But not always when it was really needed. If only I had, how do people say it, been there for you when you really needed me, then maybe none of this would be necessary now. Your mother tried to..." He seemed lost for words and turned away for a moment as if to look out the window at the dark night.

Joanna couldn't believe what she was hearing. Was he trying to apologize for being so silent during her mother's illness? And yet what did he mean by 'maybe none of this would be necessary now'? "Dad," she began, "when Mom was sick it was a hard time for all of us." She stopped at that, not sure of what to say next.

He came back and sat at the table, looking down at his hands folded in front of him. He spoke quietly and as if he was finding his way along through his words. "Yes, it was. But I'm talking about what happened to you before that. Back right before you graduated when...when you were going out with that boy. For some reason lately I've been thinking about it again."

"Eric Miller." She could scarcely breathe. "Then you knew what happened."

He looked at her and nodded, his face tight with his distress. "I decided to let your mother handle it. She said she could, that you were already upset enough. She thought since I was a man that it would be too hard for you to...to talk to me about it. I didn't know what to do, so I just tried to stay clear and hoped it would help. But I felt bad not being able to do anything. Later I thought maybe that had been a mistake, that if I had done something, or said something that..." he paused with the effort of his words and looked away.

"That what?" She pressed him to continue. She had to know what he was thinking.

"I'm not sure how to say it. Maybe that you would have had an easier time after that. That maybe you would have stayed in college and not married Larry. Or at least not right when you did. It was like you didn't expect more for yourself. Forgive me for saying all this, Joanna, but that's what I once thought." He placed a hand to his forehead briefly as if wiping away the sorrowfulness of his thoughts and then looked at her once more. "But now, here we all are. And maybe now I can do something that will help. At least that's what I hope."

For a long minute she could only sit silently trying to piece together all the things she now knew. "Dad, I..." She searched her thoughts some more. "I always wondered what you knew... back then. It...it was a pretty tough time for me, but Mom did what she could and after awhile things were okay. So I don't want you to feel bad anymore about what you did or didn't do back then, okay?"

He nodded. "Okay."

"You know, there's something I've just started to realize. I think that maybe sometimes we spend too much time looking back and not enough time looking forward. What happened with Eric and losing Mom are awful things, but it would be wrong to keep dwelling on them. If you do, then you stop moving forward with your life." She breathed in and let it out with a sigh. "I've done that for too long. And as far as what I did, marrying Larry and all, well, I guess it looks like I'm going to survive that too." She smiled at her father. "You know what? More than that, I'm going to succeed. Now that Gwen and I are here, that's what you can help me do. Help me succeed."

"I'd be only too happy to, Jo," he said smiling, his eyes suddenly glistening. "You can count on me."

The closing credits started to roll. She clicked off the evening news and leaned back on the couch closing her eyes, letting the quiet of the house settle in around her. A week's time had slipped by leaving just five weeks until she started at OCC.

Gwen was spending her first overnight with Phyllis and George to the delight of all three. Plans were to help her set up her own special place in their guest room for what promised to be frequent visits.

Her father was away at his twice a month poker game, a ritual of longstanding. They'd eaten supper together, a sense of comfortable companionship between them. He'd offered to wash the dishes but she'd shooed him upstairs to change out of his work clothes and get ready to go.

"Have a good time, Dad," she'd said to him when he came back through the kitchen.

"I'll see what I can do about hanging onto my pay check," he'd said with a laugh, pausing by the door. "No need to wait up for me. It's bound to be around midnight."

"All right. See you in the morning then." She'd turned part way around from the dishes in the sink to find him smiling at her.

"You know, Joanna, it's good to have you here again. It's been a good week for me."

She returned his smile. "I'm glad to be here too, Dad." And then he'd gone on his way.

It had been a good week. A comfortable routine was already established. She had to be up a little after six to allow for the longer commute to Seneca Community but she didn't mind. She took pleasure in having breakfast alone in the kitchen, watching the morning light grow outside. Just before she left she woke Gwen and made sure her clothes were laid out for her. Her father saw to it she had breakfast and then dropped her off at the Mannington's on his way to the garage. Each day she'd said to her mother how she missed Kim but appeared happy with most everything else so far. Another week or two would tell for certain, but Joanna was cautiously optimistic the move to Berlin had been the right one.

She sat up and stretched. On the coffee table was a large envelope that held her short story. Scott had returned it to her that morning. The night Kim left she'd stayed up late after Gwen had gone to bed and finished writing it. The next day she'd dropped it in his mail slot with a triumphant note announcing its completion.

Now she pulled it out of the envelope and read through his comments again. On the final page he'd written, 'Bravo, Joanna, not only for completing your story, but for some very fine work on your first venture into short story writing. As your writing-cheerleader, I am honored to read it and delighted by the results. Now that you've finished this, it's time to start writing your next story!' He'd drawn two squiggly lines underneath the last phrase. She must have smiled for an hour after she'd read that.

Smiling again, she got up and took it into her room, setting it squarely in the middle of her study table that was now clear of boxes. She smoothed out the sheets, her eyes lingering on Scott's words. Aloud she said, "So I guess it's time for me to start writing a new story."

Then she wandered upstairs to check things in Gwen's room. The summer evening's mellow light brightened the faded yellow wallpaper with its tiny sprays of wild flowers. Gwen had been busy transforming the room. Her extensive collection of stuffed animals was on neat display. While they lived with Kim most of them had remained packed away. Now they were lined up on every available shelf and chair in the room. Baxter retained his place of honor in the exact middle of her pillow. Joanna picked him up and straightened his rumpled bow tie. "You've seen a lot of changes in your day, haven't you, Baxter? Well, let's hope we can all stay put for a while this time." She kissed the bear's furry muzzle and set him back against the pillow.

Passing the door of her father's room she paused and looked in. Her mother had always kept things meticulously neat in their bedroom, something her father did still. His bathrobe was tidily folded on the chair by the bed, his slippers lined up precisely next to each other beneath. On her mother's dresser was her gold leather jewelry box exactly where she always had had it, their wedding picture standing next to it. Her perfume bottles, the round box of pressed powder, her hairbrush and hand mirror were all gone, but if she closed her eyes, Joanna could picture them there just as they had been.

Downstairs she busied herself in the kitchen putting away the supper dishes. Then she stood looking out the screen door. Perhaps she should go for a walk. She pushed open the door and went to stand at the edge of the small back porch. The remains of the daffodils lay in splayed disarray, browning seed heads having replaced the once jaunty blooms. She found a pair of scissors in a kitchen drawer and spent several minutes snipping off the pods and pulling a few weeds that were growing up around them. While she worked, a plan formed in her head of what summer flowers she could put in. Her mother's favorites had been marigolds. Joanna remembered seeing some nice ones for sale at the grocery store.

Straightening up, she set the scissors on the steps and went to look at her father's small vegetable garden. He'd been busy evenings during the week digging in its winter cover of leaves and turning over the soil. Now it was raked smooth and waiting. Two flats of tomato plants rested on the porch ready to be transplanted tomorrow.

Joanna crossed the lawn to the swing and sat down on the worn wooden seat facing the house, the lilacs at her back. Its present coat of black paint was peeling in a few places revealing the red of Gwen's preceding color choice. She looked up to where the yellow nylon ropes were knotted around a branch, its bark protected by two pieces of an old tire. She tried to remember how many years it had been since her father had taken down the old brown ropes. Funny how you could miss something like that. But how she had loved the old rope's sturdy thickness worn to a silky texture from the grip of her fingers pulling herself in and out of countless swinging arches.

This evening the sky above the rooftop was shading into aquamarine as the sun sank towards the horizon. Its orange rays glanced off the bedroom windows. The leaves of the maple stirred in an unseen breeze. A few houses down someone was running a lawnmower. She held her breath. Time seemed to catch and shift. If she sat quietly enough she could slip into her ten-year-old self, having just now escaped from the house to the swing's quiet retreat beneath the maple's sheltering limbs.

With the toe of her sneaker she moved herself gently back and forth for a time. Then she stopped and studied the ground beneath her feet, peering at the path worn smooth from Gwen's swinging. She leaned down and slipped off her shoes, setting her bare feet firmly on the powdery dirt. She smiled, finding the day's warmth still lingering there in the soil. Then, as if at some signal, she pushed herself up and off, lifting her feet from the ground, smiling again at the whispered rush of air brushing past.

A remembered rhythm returned to her arms and legs and she leaned back against the ropes, pulling more strongly, looking up into the intertwined branches and new summer leaves. She gasped, startled by their instantly familiar pattern. Silently she swung back and forth, now the child, now the woman. Unexpected tears welled up until she had to slow and stop. She leaned forward against the ropes and dug her toes again into the warm dirt, letting the tears work their gentle release.

She found a tissue in her pocket and daubed her cheeks. Inhaling deeply, she held her breath for a moment and then let it all go. She looked far up into the maple where the last of the sun lit the very top leaves. When it rose in the morning she would be one day closer to her newly chosen life.

She stood up from the swing and went around to sit facing the lilacs, their leafy barrier hiding the hills and the still beckoning promise that lay beyond them. Then she smiled and pushed herself up and away.

ISBN 1553692764

9 781553 692768